DEVIL'S
GAME

DEVIL'S GAME

A Novel

Charles A. Reap, Jr.

iUniverse, Inc.
New York Lincoln Shanghai

DEVIL'S GAME
A Novel

iUniverse books may be ordered through booksellers or by contacting:

iUniverse
2021 Pine Lake Road, Suite 100
Lincoln, NE 68512
www.iuniverse.com
1-800-Authors (1-800-288-4677)

ISBN-13: 978-0-595-39210-0 (pbk)
ISBN-13: 978-0-595-83601-7 (ebk)
ISBN-10: 0-595-39210-5 (pbk)
ISBN-10: 0-595-83601-1 (ebk)

Printed in the United States of America

DEDICATED TO:

My loving wife, Betty,
because without her support
and inspiration, this book
would never have been written.

CHAPTER ONE

GEORGE EXHALED A DEEP sigh of relief as he finally reached his freeway exit. Sweat was pouring down his back, and his hands ached from squeezing his steering wheel. *Now at last,* he thought, *maybe I can get away from that ugly fool. The stupid jerk and his big blue sport utility vehicle scared the life out of me. All that damn extra-close tailgating was bad enough, but when he drew along side me, and without his hands on his steering wheel, I was certain that it would be the end for me.* It had been scary as hell.

George glanced in his rearview mirror, happily noting that the SUV did not follow him up the freeway ramp. As he came to the top and was about to turn toward his office, he heard a huge crashing sound from somewhere behind him. He glanced back down on the highway, and saw a blinding explosion. The blue SUV had sideswiped a gasoline tank truck.

"Oh my God!" George blurted loudly. The tanker had jackknifed, flipped onto its side and ruptured, with several thousand gallons of gasoline flowing out and instantly igniting. Huge waves of flames rapidly swept across the highway. Plumes of thick black smoke began billowing upward, blossoming into a darkened mushroom cloud.

George pulled his car over to the side of the ramp and stopped. His mouth agape, he exited his car so he could look down on the sight more clearly. He immediately felt the blistering heat from the fire and heard its deafening roar above the traffic. A score of the rapidly approaching cars swerved, sideswiping each other in their attempts to avoid the accident. He had a sudden visualization of carnival bumper cars. There was a tumultuous screeching of tires and crunching metal. Being unable to stop in time, numerous autos barreled into the wrecks and flames.

Oh no! George watched a terrified motorcyclist attempt to miss the accident, but skid directly into the boiling chaos. Abruptly, two of the rushing cars swerved to the grassy band beside the highway. There they tilted precariously and then rolled down into the hungry engulfing flames awaiting them in the ditch. This developing tragedy was unlike any George had ever seen before—on television news or even in the movies. It was real, evolving before his thunderstruck eyes.

Good Lord! It was unbelievable. Horrible. Indescribable. Even being a hundred feet away from the flames, he felt the increasing intensity of the heat on his exposed skin. He tried to shield his face with one of his hands. Multiple automobile gasoline tanks rupturing and exploding magnified the blazing horror.

Several more cars had now come up the off ramp and stopped. George was too entranced with the scene below to notice them. A woman got out of her car and walked over to him. She asked, "How did it happen? Did you see?" In his state of shock, George did not seem to hear her and did not respond. He could not stop watching the developing calamity down below him. Somewhere, he heard someone sobbing, but it hardly registered. The catastrophe was too startling.

No, no, no! George put his hand to his mouth in anguish. He saw two little girls on the pavement. The legs of one appeared to be unnaturally torqued up under her body. Obviously, the pitiful children had been thrown from one of the crashed vehicles. Being in the middle of the inferno, their clothes were afire. They were not moving, and he could clearly see the small arm of one child burning. He could only hope that they were dead before the ravenous flames reached their little bodies. In addition, much to his increasing revulsion, he could see several other burning victims, screaming and writhing in the terrible torment. Torrents of tears swept down his cheeks, as he sadly watched one pathetic man struggling to walk, his clothes burning off him as he moved. He seemed to be trying to go toward a burning loved one lying on the grass. After a moment the man, in obvious agony, collapsed, and simply lay there, burning, just two feet from his destination.

However, even worse for George was the horrible smell. The wind had increased from the inferno and the foul stench of death, boiling blood and flaming bodies became increasingly strong. The odor of charred flesh was soon overwhelming. The taste of bile grew until he collapsed and the contents of his stomach suddenly exploded over the street beside him. Rising from his hands and knees, he seated himself on the car seat to recover.

He heard more of the unfortunate victims screaming in anguish, and looked down at the carnage once again. There was that damn light blue SUV right in the middle of all that horror, flames all around it! George had no pity for that crazy devilish driver since he was obviously the one that caused it all.

Yet, he thought, *burning to death just had to be a particular horror.*

George stayed for several more minutes, just watching numbly. He glanced upward and saw that the smoke cloud had hit upper winds and had become somewhat shaped like an anvil, reminiscent of a thunderstorm. But, this revolting storm was continuing. Wiping his mouth with his handkerchief after he had once again thrown up, he found himself spellbound, unable to make himself leave the scene. He knew there was nothing that he could do, but yet, he felt a strong morbid inclination to watch. The taste of bile rose ominously in his throat repeatedly. Tears of sorrow continued to flow freely down his face. He could see a few cars finally slowing down in their efforts to avoid the disaster. Several freeway drivers got out of their cars to watch also, but nobody could get close enough to the fiery turmoil to offer any aid for the poor victims.

As George heard sirens in the distance, he decided he just had to proceed to the office. He was now running late, but he would have just about as good an excuse as one could have. Surely, his boss would understand as he explained to him about the disaster. *Should I even mention the SUV?* As he slowly drove away from the tragedy, he felt a powerful revulsion for the driver of that sport utility vehicle. His recall of what he had just witnessed kept a knot in his stomach, almost to the point of having to stop and vomit again. His hands were shaking so much that he could barely drive.

Ten minutes later, he pulled into his parking spot outside the Williams Building. Before exiting his car, however, he sat there, still dazed and unable to fathom what he had seen. His encounter with that damned weird SUV driver had unnerved him. He gradually became aware that he no longer had that peculiar foul taste or the ear tingling that had occurred when the SUV had come close to him. Maybe the shock of what he had witnessed a few minutes earlier, plus the nausea, had slammed his body into a more normal condition. He was glad to note that his physical sickness had diminished.

As he slowly walked into the building, he tried to organize his overloaded brain and concentrate on his upcoming workload. *How,* he thought morosely, *can I have a normal day after witnessing such a horrible disaster? Nevertheless, I am a professional,* he told himself. *I will just do my job like always.* However, several thoughts kept nagging George. *Had that damn blue SUV been after him? Was it sheer good luck that he was not involved in the terrible scene? Was there any rational sense to be made of the entire happening during my morning drive?*

As George got off the elevator, he stopped by the coffee pot and poured himself a cup…black. Then, nodding his hello to a couple of fellow employees, he went into his office and phoned his wife, Deborah.

"That's been all over the television this morning," she said. "You say you saw it happen? You weren't actually in the wreck yourself, were you? Tell me all about it."

He told her and his experience with the SUV and its driver. "It's the worst disaster I've ever seen."

"Oh. Deborah, my other line is ringing, so I have to hang up now. Talk to you more about it tonight."

He responded to the other message briefly. George then left his office and talked to several of his fellow employees in the snack room.

"You heard about that terrible wreck on the beltway this morning didn't you?" He sipped on his coffee. "Well, I happened to be there and saw the entire thing." They all listened attentively. He continued, "It was caused by a strange-looking hairless guy that was driving a great big light blue SUV. He had shiny bright red skin all over. And, catch this; he didn't even have his hands on his steering wheel. Not only that, I got an awful taste in my mouth and my ears started twitching shortly before he showed up. It was almost like a warning to me."

They listened intently until, rising to leave, one man said to George with a grin, "Yeah, right. A weird red fellow caused it. Okay. In addition, you had a bunch of strange sensations. Sure, George. That makes a lot of sense, doesn't it?" He smirked and said, "You think we're dummies around here?"

George poured himself another cup of coffee and sat down as the rest were leaving. Embarrassed, he yelled, "Well, it's really what happened, believe it or not!"

Another grinning worker said as he left the room, "Sure. Now, let's see if we have it correct. A bald, red-skinned guy in a big blue sport utility vehicle caused the wreck. And somehow, you had a bunch of weird symptoms that warned you that something bad was going to happen. Right? Unh-huh. Whatever you say, old buddy."

Damn! Now they think I must be nuts for telling them about that devilish-looking screwball, he thought.

*   *   *

George Albert Sheldon was a quiet, gentle soul who loved his job as a mechanical engineer. His boss had always found him to be meticulous, and very stable, yet unassuming. His friends spoke of him as "good old dependable George." A couple of his closer friends, as well as his wife, Deborah, teased him unmercifully about his enlarging waist however.

Thinking back, his day had begun in a reasonably normal fashion. Sort of. As he was driving away from his house that morning, though, he had felt that things were not quite right. It was nothing that he could put his finger on exactly, but everything seemed to be slightly out of kilter…kind of "out of sync." Somehow, he felt, his mind seemed to be telling him that something unexpected was going to happen today. It seemed somewhat peculiar to him. *Oh well, so be it,* he had decided.

While stopped at a neighborhood crossing, he watched as an elderly woman with a medium-sized dog of some unknown ancestry hurriedly walked by. The dog was straining at its leash, nearly pulling her down. It stopped exactly in front of George's car and simply stood there motionlessly. He could see that it was staring directly into his eyes. *What in the hell is wrong with that animal?* The woman tugged and pulled for a good thirty seconds, until the animal finally moved onto the curb. She glanced over at George apprehensively, and he absently nodded back at her. He beat his fingers impatiently on the steering wheel. He had a lot of work ahead of him today at the office. *Now that was weird,* he thought.

*   *   *

As he was nudging his car onto the busy eight-lane highway, he punched on NPR's "Morning Edition." He enjoyed the distraction of the radio. He despised these excursions to and from work five days a week. There was never any stress on the freeway. Of course not!

He often thought *I wish I had stood my ground with that argument with Debra about where we would live. We could have had a nice apartment in the city near my work. But no, she just had to have a nice house out in the boonies.*

After so many trips, he recognized many of his fellow travelers. *At least,* he thought, *their cars.* He had noticed several attractive woman drivers as he made his way during the usual nearly hour-long drive. *After last night's heavy rain, at least the weather's shaping up to be a nice day.*

An additional diversion on his drive was one particular farm he passed. Glancing over, he observed several dozen "Oreo cookie cows" grazing peacefully on the plentiful grass. Each was black all over except for a white strip of hair extending around the center circumference of its body. Due to his inherent curiosity, he had previously researched them, and learned that somebody had originally bred them in the district of Galloway in Scotland. Therefore, their developer named them Galloways. Since they appeared similar to Angus cows, he presumed they were just as tasty on a plate with a baked potato.

Suddenly, he switched his attention back to the highway. *Well there's that drop-dead gorgeous redhead that drives that dented and rusting green Datsun wagon.*

"Why, hey there, you sweet young thing!" He said loudly to nobody. "And how are you feeling this lovely morning?" George knew she could not hear him, so he could say whatever he wished. In addition, since his wife was not along with him, he knew that he could flirt with impunity.

Somehow, he often imagined, *you would think a beautiful gal like that would be in a Jaguar, Porsche or maybe some classy convertible.*

"Lady, you need a rich boy friend or husband." He began to smile at his conversation to himself. "Then, you could be driving a real dandy car."

Something that annoyed George was those infernal road hogs and tailgaters. Dangerous as hell if you were to ask him. Especially, on rainy or snowy days. They nearly always seemed to be driving sporty hotshot cars, typically bright red or yellow. *Those bastards will frequently zip past, and then cut over and slide right into your lane with barely enough room between your car and theirs.* He could readily understand the term "road rage."

"You damn idiots!" He would yell his head off at them. No matter. They couldn't hear him, so what did it matter what he said? Sometimes he would blow his horn, frequently receiving in turn, "the finger." Anyway, it made him feel better.

Suddenly George became aware of a peculiar taste. And, almost at the same time, the upper tips of both of his ears began to tingle strangely. He used his free right hand and rubbed his ears to no avail. *Hmm,* he thought, *odd. And, such a lousy, really lousy taste. Almost sickening.* Running his tongue around in his mouth, he could detect nothing out of the ordinary. He had diligently brushed his teeth prior to leaving home.

He looked up in the rearview mirror and stuck his tongue out. It did not seem to be coated or anything that would explain his foul taste. At that moment, George noticed that the gray-haired old woman driving in the maroon sedan behind him saw him stick out his tongue and apparently assumed that he was making a face at her. She immediately nudged her car into another lane.

Hey here, what the hell's happening back there? George was still peering in his rearview mirror when he saw an oncoming truck-like vehicle, painted a bright light blue color. The sun's reflecting rays gave it an almost eerie, unearthly appearance. *It is coming up the highway at a good clip too, faster than the other traffic.* He curiously realized that he had never seen a vehicle of any kind painted that particular shade of blue before. *My mother would have called such a color "baby blue."* He could not quite recognize the make, though. He mused that it looked slightly wider and taller than most small trucks he had ever seen. It somewhat reminded him of those trucks many companies use to haul freshly made bread to grocery stores. Only, it was not box shaped at all, but nicely rounded, streamlined. Moreover, he could see windows all along its side.

Suddenly George's observance of the vehicle was broken, as he quickly had to tap his brakes.

"Damn!" He exclaimed loudly. He had allowed his own car to get dangerously close to the car in front of him. He noticed with some chagrin that the driver was indeed giving him "the finger."

George understood, and accepted the ignominy.

Peering in his rearview mirror once again, and as it got closer to his own car, George finally decided: *Hey, that's not a truck, not even a van, but it looks like one of those sport utility vehicles—SUV's! Big monster, though.* George decided that it was, by far, the biggest SUV he had ever seen. *Maybe it is somebody's homemade vehicle. Sort of an SUV "muscle car." But light blue?* George smiled as he thought, *a vehicle like that would almost command being painted a high-gloss jet black with simulated wind-blown red, orange and yellow flames painted along each side.*

Continuing to glance in his mirror, George could see the thing was just almost forcing its way in and out of traffic as it was coming up through the lanes behind him. Kind of hard to figure why the damn driver felt he had to be so stinking pushy on a busy freeway like this. *Damn, that's dangerous, especially with such a big vehicle. After all, wasn't almost everyone going to work just like him? And, probably due there at about the same time?*

George spoke aloud anxiously. "Why is it that everybody can't just cool it and relax and get there on schedule? Why drive recklessly and risk an accident?" *With all this traffic, how in the hell can you go the speed limit, anyway?*

Besides, he thought with some self-justified vexation, *where were all the cops during a rush hour like this?* George rarely saw a patrol officer on this highway. *Except of course, after an accident. Maybe they just felt that they couldn't do much to control the traffic even if they were out there with the rest of the vehicles.* As he was thinking of this, his mind recalled several humorous incidents where he had seen a patrol car out in front of a big long line of cars. The cop would be tooling along at or maybe just under the speed limit, but nobody would dare pass him. Yet everybody wanted to. So then, there would be this huge backup of cars behind him—almost like a parade. *Bet that silly cop carried a big grin on his face at his power of making so many drivers conform.* George smiled inwardly, *and when the patrol officer would finally drive onto an off-ramp, that darn bunch of cars would simulate the beginning of a speedway race. You could almost hear the sound of tires screeching and smell the burning rubber as the drivers shifted their gears for more speed. Then soon, the aggressive hotshots would just be elbowing their way along to be the leaders. Too bad there was no prize cup waiting for them at the end of the race. And, hopefully, no coffin.*

George grinned widely as he thought; *wouldn't it be funny if there happened to be another cop maybe a mile up front just waiting to catch the speeders?*

George's idle daydreaming was abruptly interrupted.

Well, damned if that big light blue thing didn't pull up right smack behind me. And is just tailgating me. Real closely—no more than a yard back, too. The jerk.

"Hey, you idiot. Back off!" George went through the motion of showing the tailgating driver that he was adjusting his rearview mirror. In this way, George hoped, the damn driver would realize that he was too close and would ease away.

George immediately became aware of that same ear tingle he had noted earlier. It had become much more pronounced. *Strange. This is very bizarre.* He reached up with his right hand and rubbed his ear lightly, but that did not stop the sensation. And the queer, ungodly taste seemed more pronounced now. *Very odd, and dreadfully annoying. In addition, this taste is just awful. Awful!*

George kept expecting the person behind him to zip out and pass him like he had been doing back down the freeway. He soon realized, however, that although the driver of the big vehicle actually had several opportunities, he remained closely behind him. George was concerned that he might bump him from the rear, but it seemed that all the driver wanted to do was to tailgate him. It was very disconcerting.

George looked up into his rearview mirror and studied the driver, observing a very weird looking individual. The guy appeared to have a medium build but possessed a glowing, fiery red face.

Finally, after about four miles of tailgating closer than George preferred, the SUV driver pulled out from behind him. When he saw this happening, George breathed a quiet sigh of relief.

"Well at last!" George exclaimed loudly. However, instead of passing him, the driver simply pulled the SUV alongside George and stayed there.

Snatching hurried glances over at the SUV, George noticed something else unusual about the vehicle. *Well, how about that? Damned if that SUV even has light blue tires! Now there's a first!*

Other cars on the freeway were doing their usual, but now this fellow simply stayed right along at the same speed as George. George took his foot off the gas pedal to slow down slightly. The driver of the SUV also slowed. So George sped up until he was almost tailgating the automobile in front of him. The SUV remained alongside him.

Now why in the hell is he doing that? Is this some kind of bizarre joke? Am I on "Candid Camera?"

Oh my gosh! George glanced over at the driver and noted with alarm that the damned jerk did not have his hands on his steering wheel. Moreover, in heavy rush hour traffic too. It even looked like the red-faced guy was reading a book or something. *Just piling down the highway reading a book. Sheer idiocy!*

"Good God!" George exclaimed loudly in his speeding automobile. He saw the red-skinned man turn his head and look at him. He did not even take his eyes away from George and just gave him a big smile—an evil stare—that made George shudder. The guy showed many ugly yellow teeth, and appeared to have fangs. And he was, indeed, completely bald. *Doesn't look like one of these people that shave their heads; he is hairless. Doesn't even appear to have any eyebrows.* As George stole other quick glances over at the speeding vehicle beside him, he could easily see that the red tone of his skin covered his entire head and neck. His skin appeared to be very smooth and shiny, except for two odd protrusions on his forehead. Those things reminded George of emerging horns on a young male goat. But the man just would not stop grinning at George, and he still did not have his hands on his steering wheel. George recalled a painting of the devil that he had seen in an art museum. *This person looks a lot like that. Could it really be the devil?*

"Damn!" he exclaimed. This was serious stuff now. *Would not take much to have a bad accident. I have to put an end to this matter.* George decided that regulated office hours or not, he would not let this danger continue. He pulled onto the next "off" ramp, and stopped at the traffic light at the bottom of the slope. The "slow" light held him back for nearly a minute, giving George an opportunity to catch his breath and relax for a moment. *He will be gone by now.* Then when the light finally turned green, he drove straight across and back up onto the freeway again.

George naturally assumed that the SUV driver would be well ahead of him by this time. *That guy sure was an absolute nut case, screwing around like that in traffic. People can't see the devil, so it could not have been him. Could it?* George shuddered at the thought.

George gingerly reentered the traffic pattern and resumed his cruise toward the city. He turned the volume up slightly on his radio and listened to the NPR announcer tell about some problems the elephants were having on the African plains. Maybe he could relax a while now. He presumed that the SUV had moved on with the regular traffic flow.

Oh my gosh! As George glanced up at his rearview mirror, he saw that big blue SUV coming up behind him, just like before. While he had stopped at the traffic light, George had been able to see clearly up on the adjacent highway bridge. He had seen no light blue SUV. Therefore, it had to have proceeded on. *Hadn't it?* Certainly, the heavy traffic would just about prohibit any chance of the SUV stopping and waiting for him. *Wouldn't it?* What in hell was going on here? He muttered under his breath, "Well, maybe it was just a strange coincidence, and there was a second huge light blue SUV traveling on the highway this morning." *Nah! This just could not be!* However, it was the same red-skinned, baldheaded driver and once again, he worked himself and his big vehicle alongside and gave George that same malevolent and unnerving grin. George felt tightness in his stomach. Something was definitely wrong here today. But what? *This cannot be happening to me. I have done nothing to that crazy fellow.* His knuckles were white from squeezing tightly on the steering wheel. He kept his right foot on the accelerator pedal and his left one positioned just slightly above the brake pedal—just in case he needed to stop quickly.

He pondered *should I just slow down and let that fool speed on? However, after what happened when I took that off-ramp, I guess it wouldn't do much good. Besides, I am almost at my turnoff now. Maybe I can lose him then.*

*   *   *

That evening, Deborah had prepared one of his favorite meals. But George had little appetite as he told Deb more details about the sport utility vehicle and the highway incident. He mentioned the strange physical sensations he experienced as the SUV had come near him.

After picking at his food, George pushed his plate aside. "Sorry Deb. The food looks real good as usual, and I didn't eat any lunch, but I just can't get the images of the crash out of my mind."

"I saw most of it on Channel Four's "Breaking News" this morning," she said. "The noon news mentioned eighteen people died at the scene." She frowned and her lips tightened. "George, you know, three of them were just children. Poor things."

"Yeah, Deb," he responded almost angrily. "Damn it. Remember, I was there. I saw it all. I smelled it all. It was sickening."

She continued that there were additionally, fourteen survivors with varying degrees of injuries, mostly with second- and third-degree burns. Five of those were not expected to live.

She went on, "Including the tanker truck, there were twenty-nine vehicles and a motorcycle involved."

George pursed his lips. "I don't suppose they mentioned that SUV I told you about did they? I know that damned driver caused it all. I guess I'm lucky it didn't involve me."

Deb looked down as she slid her arm down into a magazine container beside her chair. Pulling up a *Good Housekeeping*, she casually said, "No, there was no mention of that. I'm just glad you weren't in the wreck." *I wonder what he meant when he talked about those peculiar symptoms that he said he had.*

"Okay, thanks. I guess I'll go to the study and do some work now. Gotta write some letters."

*   *   *

About two hours later, Deborah turned off the television and walked into their study. They added this room to their home just before moving in several years previously. It had large windows on two sides allowing expansive views of their flower garden. It also served as her sewing room and her husband's computer room. He had lined the wall above his desk with his numerous plaques and awards.

"George," spoke Deborah. There was no response. A little louder, and pushing against his shoulder with her hand, she repeated, "George."

Her husband recoiled as if shocked by an electric current.

"What? What the hell?"

"You looked like you were in a trance. What is the matter with you? You were just sitting there with your hands in your lap staring at those swimming fish on your computer screen. You looked like you were sound asleep, sitting straight up in your chair with your eyes wide open. Are you feeling okay?"

"Ugh," George mumbled. "Yeah. I guess I was sort of in a fog. The damn computer's set to go to 'saver' after thirty minutes of inactivity." He sadly looked up at her. "Deborah, I guess that means that I've been sitting here in a damn stupor for over half an hour. I just can't get today's horror out of my mind."

"Well," she said, placing her hand on his shoulder. "I know it was terrible, but thank goodness you weren't involved."

"Yeah, I guess you're right."

Deborah said, "Come on. Bedtime."

George looked at the screen and tapped the space bar, bringing his letter back. He looked up at her. "I had started a business letter and only got five lines written. Um-m."

He stared at the computer again, and then said slowly, "I wasn't really asleep. Somehow my senses went blank and left me just sitting here staring at the screen. It must be because I have been so preoccupied with that awful stuff on the freeway this morning. Barely got any work done at the office. I just could not concentrate. I've never seen anything like it." He pushed his chair back from the desk. "And I hope I never see anything like that again. Deb, I simply cannot get the catastrophe off my mind. Those monstrous flames and thick black smoke. In addition, all those burning people. Those pitiful children—so many hurt. And, their screaming was horrible to hear. Blood—oh so much. Their blood was even running in little streams all over the highway." He moved back to his computer once more, but kept looking up at his wife. "I feel so sorry for those poor souls. What a terrible thing to happen. Honey, it just tears at my heartstrings. And, as I told you, there was that awful stench of burning flesh. I am sure I will never get that smell out of my mind. All because of that red-skinned bastard in that big blue SUV that I told you about. What on earth could have been on his mind to drive like he did and cause such a terrible wreck?" He turned his head and peered down at his keyboard. "Oh my God, I wish it were all a terrible nightmare. Then maybe I would wake up. I wish I had not been there to see it. It just makes me sick."

Deborah tugged her husband out of his chair and hugged him tightly. "I know. I understand. All the same, turn off your computer and come on to bed. You need to get some sleep." As she was leaving the room, she thought, *red-skinned fellow. Yeah, sure. I don't believe that for a moment.*

The quiet calm of sleep was slow in overtaking George Albert Sheldon that night.

The next morning's newspaper had two color photographs of the scene. One of these was from ground level, the other obviously taken from a news helicopter.

George inspected these pictures, but could not spot any remains of the light blue SUV. *Now that is strange, very strange,* thought George. He knew, of course, that he had observed the damned vehicle right in the middle of that fiery tempest. *Yet, what happened to it? That big SUV, and the strange looking driver, just couldn't have survived such a terrible crash. Curious.*

CHAPTER TWO

A FEW WEEKS LATER George had all but forgotten about his run-in with the light blue SUV. One morning he sat down at the breakfast table and began to eat the pancakes that Deborah had made for them. She was up earlier than usual to attend an early morning meeting of volunteers at the nursing home across the street. Normally, George left for work before she arose.

"Hey Deb," George said as he pinched off a small piece of pancake, and turned it this way and that, looking at it intently on the end of his fork. "Did you change the recipe for these pancakes? They don't taste right to me this morning."

She turned her head and looked at him curiously. "No George. Same as always. Why"?

"They taste peculiar. You taste yours."

She took a bite from her plate. She moved it all around in her mouth with her tongue. "Good as always," she said with a skeptical smile on her not-yet-made-up face. "Here, let me taste yours." Pushing her own fork into a corner of his pancake, she slipped a piece of the food into her mouth. Opening and closing her lips as her tongue worked the piece, she decided conclusively that the cakes were just fine and said so. "What's wrong with your taste this morning?"

He replied with a sour expression on his face, "I don't know. Neither does this coffee. For some reason I have a strange taste in my mouth today. Seems like I've had something like it before sometime, but I can't remember when or where." He put down his fork and took a small sip of his coffee. Making a sour face, he rose and placed his dishes in the kitchen sink.

"Blah!" He rubbed his tongue in and out, scraping it along his upper teeth. "Nothing tastes good this morning. Guess I will head on to the office. You know Deb my ears are tingling too. Now isn't that curious?"

"If you say so. Anyway, I think my pancakes are just fine." She continued to nibble while she glanced through her latest copy of *Elle* magazine.

"Okay, I'm heading on in."

Before leaving the house, George stopped by their bathroom, brushed his teeth and did a brisk swishing of his mouth with a medicinal flavored mouthwash. However, as he was getting into his automobile, George realized that his foul taste was continuing unabated. In addition, both ear tips were still slightly twitching and tingling. He rubbed them vigorously, first one, then the other, but the feeling remained. Odd. He had a busy day scheduled at the office and was somewhat preoccupied. He knew that he had some difficult determinations to get together for a new client. Therefore, as he drove along he was soon nearly able to ignore the queer symptoms. He did not recall any relationship between these indicators and the sport utility vehicle that had appeared the last time he experienced them.

His drive along the freeway was uneventful, but as he moved along the side street toward his building, he suddenly saw it!

Well, for Heaven's sake! There it is, parked at the curb just a block from my office. The foreboding SUV sat just in front of the fenced-off site where a fifteen story office building was being constructed. One could not miss the SUV because of its huge size and blue color. Moreover, it had those same light blue tires. *Damn! The same one as before? It has to be the same one.* Astounded, George slowed as he edged by it. Coming adjacent to the vehicle, he glanced over into the vehicle, and there was that same slimy-looking red-skinned individual. The man looked up from the book he had been reading and stared at George, as if he had been expecting him to drive past. He flashed that same unearthly grin at George. *Just like before. Now I remember about this awful taste and ear tingling. It has suddenly gotten worse. At least this time the guy's not speeding down the freeway. This is bizarre.*

George's thoughts and recall of the previous disaster and now seeing the blue SUV again almost overwhelmed him, and he suddenly had to slam on brakes. He had almost rear-ended a smoke-snorting city bus. *Now that would really have made my day!*

Just as he was turning into his parking lot, he suddenly heard a loud thud and crunching sound. He jerked his head to his right and saw that the entire façade of the new building was collapsing. Parking his automobile quickly, he ran back to the edge of the street where he could observe the developing catastrophe more closely. As pieces of concrete continued to give way, several pieces fell on several unfortunate workers trying to escape.

A massive cloud of dust was already forming, and in mere seconds, it had filled the chasm between the sides of the adjacent skyscrapers with thick gray dust billowing outward.

"My God," uttered George to an associate, Bill. He was just leaving his own automobile. "Look at that!" Both men gaped in astonishment as they could see the bodies of several workers that had already fallen to their deaths, and two more, hanging on desperately to ripped out cables. Likewise, they could observe the crushed and bleeding bodies of at least two passersby. The entire disaster had taken less than a minute.

Bill uttered, "Where's your cell phone? We gotta call nine-one-one."

"Left the damn thing at home, charging," responded George, despairingly.

George and Bill spotted no moving human limbs protruding from the massive jumble of debris.

His friend said sadly, "The wooden fence and sidewalk covering didn't provide any protection at all for those pitiable people under it, did it?"

George answered as he looked around in astonishment, "Nope. Those poor workers. This is awful. It looks to me like somebody cranked out a bunch of wrong figures for that building. Some engineering firm's gonna get the life sued out of it."

Bill responded slowly as he continued to gape at the destruction, "You can bet your bottom dollar about that."

Soon, they heard the sounds of sirens rushing toward the scene of the disaster. Dust and smoke continued to billow outward, causing George and his friend to grab for their handkerchiefs to cover their mouths.

As they watched, George could not help but look for the SUV. *Surely, the huge pile of broken concrete and steel crushed it, because it was parked at the curb directly in front of the construction site.* He could not see it now. Since there was a huge pile of shattered concrete, cables, bent ductwork and rubble lying immediately in front of the structure, he determined that it must be buried. *Eventually emergency crews will uncover it and remove the crushed body of that awful red-skinned guy.* It was obvious to George that there had not been time for the SUV to drive away before the terrible accident occurred. The remains of a small black car burned under the rubble, with smoke rising and joining the dust cloud.

It was somewhat difficult for George and his colleagues to continue with their work during that day. There was continuing movement of the ambulances, police and then the cranes and big debris-carrying trucks down below them. George could occasionally hear the "whap-whap" of news helicopters flying just above the tall city buildings. Periodically he would peer out the window, curious to see if the SUV had been uncovered. *Not yet.* Although the ear tingling and foul taste were now gone, George decided not to mention them, nor his observation of the blue SUV to any of his fellow workers. It would serve no purpose, take too much explaining, and, he decided, perhaps sound rather absurd. He recalled the kidding he took from them when he described the first accident on the freeway.

During their lunch break, he and a colleague strolled down toward the accident. The police had now cordoned off the entire block, so any viewers of the tragedy could not get close. However, George and his coworker could still see a huge pile of tormented steel, concrete chunks, drywall and insulation. They, along with many other curious people, watched the multitude of emergency workers crawling over the mass. Some of the emergency people wearing bright orange coveralls and hard hats, now appearing dusted as if with flour, were using specially trained dogs to seek out additional victims. George could see the front of an unfortunate station wagon, the rear of which was smashed nearly flat by part of the heavy concrete and steel façade wall. Workers were desperately attempting to extricate two infants from this wreck as the apparent mother stood by weeping hysterically in the arms of a sympathetic Red Cross worker. It appeared obvious to George that the children could not have survived. Already nine bodies lay on the street covered with white sheets as ambulance attendants stood by waiting for any victims that they might have a chance at saving.

However, *where in the hell was the damned SUV?* It was there when George passed it that morning, and now it was not there. *What is going on?* The spot where he had seen it had been uncovered by now, and there was absolutely no sign of it. He looked around thoroughly, but could not locate its mangled blue mass. *Something is terribly wrong here.*

Deeply saddened at the deaths and injuries and very curious, George and his associate slowly walked through the gathered throng back to their office. George's stomach rumbled ominously. He swallowed repeatedly and bought himself a soda at the office drink machine. Mr. Williams would simply have to accept the fact that very few of his employees would be at their best during the remainder of the workday. Most thoughts were on the tragedy in the next block.

That evening as George and Deborah were discussing the incident, the television news showed pictures of the two giant cranes gingerly picking off pieces of concrete from the huge heap. The pictures were "coming to you live from our on-site reporter." Several bright portable lights were now positioned around the complex. George watched intently as the camera panned first from one area to another. *Where was the SUV? What had happened to it?* George had passed it just prior to the building collapse that very morning. In addition, he had even spotted it in his rearview mirror when he turned into his parking lot at the Williams Building.

The television showed the cranes finally clearing away the major pieces of rubble blocking the street and the front-end loaders approaching. George, seeing the level of the street once again, still could spot no SUV. The crushed remains of several other cars were there, but not that blue thing. He slid off his chair and closer to the television screen. *Now where was it? What in the hell's going on here* mulled George? *This is truly bizarre.*

George looked over at his wife and said, "Deb, there was a big light blue SUV parked in front of that building as I drove past this morning. It should be right in the middle of all that mess. Help me look for it."

"Okay, George," she responded with resignation. She reflected for a moment. "Say, didn't you mention something about a blue SUV being involved in that terrible tanker accident on the freeway a few weeks ago?"

"Yeah. And you know what? I think it was the same one."

Deborah looked over at him in bewilderment. "That doesn't make any sense."

"No," George replied dubiously, "I guess it doesn't, does it?"

Deb could not offer any reasonable conclusions to her husband. *He said it was there,* she thought. *Now it is not. Why do we not see it? We were watching live television and certainly would have spotted it as we did the other crushed automobiles. What is going on? Something very screwy is happening. Is George just playing me for a fool? If so, what is his stinking purpose? What has gotten into him lately anyway? He has been sulking a lot, and I have heard him muttering to himself. In addition, of all things, he has been complaining about my cooking. He used to brag about how good a cook I was. Not only that, he has been ignoring me more and more. I just do not like this one little bit. In fact, it makes me damn mad, his complaining about every little thing I do.*

George kept surfing the local channels that evening for more reports about the incident, while Deborah sat half-asleep in her plush green velvet easy chair. Bedtime arrived, but once again, the luxury of sleep was not for George this night. He tossed and he turned for hours on end. About three o'clock in the morning, he finally roused himself from his rumpled bed and took two aspirin in his hope that perhaps they may ease his sleeplessness. They did not. So, at five thirty George reached over and popped the switch on the clock so that the alarm would not go off and perhaps awaken Deb.

Damn. I wish could sleep like Deb does. I think that woman could sleep through a tornado in this bedroom, he thought. In fact, as he sat there groggily on the edge of his bed, he had a disgruntled feeling at the thought that somebody like her could sleep so well while he could not. Maybe it was not anger, but jealousy. Or envy? Whatever, it sure as hell didn't make it any easier on him. It was pretty rare when he was able to get to sleep quickly and remain soundly asleep all night long. Yet, he felt, *she seemed to show him no sympathy whatsoever when he had insomnia.*

George was sometimes tempted to ask his doctor for a prescription for some kind of sedative or sleeping pills to help him at night. But then, George was conservative, and he had heard about movie stars, rock and roll band members, and even some athletes that became "hooked" on such things. Although he would sure as hell like to have some kind of relief for his chronic insomnia, he was even more afraid of getting addicted to something. In addition, he was somewhat concerned that his doctor might start asking him probing questions about his life stresses, and possible marriage difficulties. George would not feel comfortable talking about such. Sure, he and Deb had had quite a few arguments and disagreements lately—actually, more than ever before in their marriage, but that was nobody else's business. More of concern, his doctor might want to refer him to a shrink, and he certainly did not want to do that. So, he made a conscious decision to continue as he was and complain to himself—and occasionally to his nonchalant, yet sleeping wife. *I sure do wish that she would show a little more concern about my nighttime difficulties, though.*

CHAPTER THREE

FIVE MONTHS HAD NOW passed since the terrible building collapse. George still had never become adjusted to the terrible trauma and loss of life that he had witnessed during the past year. Repairs were nearing completion, and, weather permitting, George and a few of his colleagues watched the reconstruction nearly every day during their noontime stroll down the street. Being mechanical engineers, they had a natural interest in construction techniques. They had no access to the specifications of the new building, but made numerous conjectures as to the possibilities that may have caused the disaster.

"What do you think, George?" said his colleague, Bill. "Figure they got the correct structural data this time?"

Beverly, one of his other friends standing there watching, said emphatically, "They'd better have."

Scanning the construction continuing behind the scaffolding, George responded, "I read where the developers changed engineering firms. That shouldn't have surprised anybody."

Work back at the office was so engrossing that George had finally forgotten about the two SUV incidents. Well, perhaps not forgotten, but at least the episodes had drifted to the lower depths of his mind.

*   *   *

"Where do you want to go on our vacation this year?" asked Deborah one evening. She and George were sitting on their front porch in white wicker rocking chairs. When the outside temperature was nice, this was one of their favorite pastimes after they had washed and put away the supper dishes. Quiet time, sort of—if you could excuse the noise made by the cars and trucks driving by the street in front of their house.

In years past, they had watched as occasional couples casually strolled along the sidewalk in the evenings. Even the Sheldons had done so themselves. Now, it seemed like nobody walked anywhere anymore. One appeared to feel the need to drive, even if the destination was a mere block away. And of course, George and Deborah had gotten into that same habit. It just seemed more convenient to hop in the car and scoot down the street than to walk it.

The joggers that passed, George felt, naturally turned up their haughty noses at the drivers. *The damn showoff runners! They think they are so healthy, jogging and running like that! They will probably die someday too—just like the rest of us,* thought George with a smile. One of his favorite sayings was that he seriously doubted if any people were going to get out of this world alive. He liked to throw that declaration around at parties and other social gatherings. It usually got a few chuckles out of his victims. Maybe they did that out of sheer social politeness, but after all, George was after a good response no matter how he got it. He had tried to get on the "exercise kick" several years ago, but it just seemed to him to be too much trouble.

He finally answered, "I don't know." He had been watching and listening to a big Harley-Davidson motorcycle roar past. He noted in the graying twilight that the Harley driver was wearing a dress suit and tie. Now that seemed to George to be almost a sacrilege—a big, roaring Harley "hog" and a dress suit. *Hmm.* He turned his head back to his wife.

After a few moments George responded, "Any place in particular that you've been thinking about? We both enjoyed the mountains last year."

"You know, George," Deborah said, looking over at him. "I'd kind of like trying one of those cruise ships down in the Caribbean. We have never done that and the commercials we've seen make 'em look pretty nice. Could be a lot of fun, I think."

"Yeah, they do make 'em look good, don't they? Sounds okay to me. Where do you think you'd like to go?" George flicked a buzzing mosquito away from his nose. "I mean, as I understand it, you can get on different ships that go to different places, depending on how long you want to be gone."

An apparent family of four passed by on bicycles, hurriedly, with dark coming on.

Deborah said, "Oh, I'm not sure. If it is okay with you then I will just check it out with a travel agency tomorrow morning. Let's see, your vacation starts next month on the third doesn't it?" She returned a wave at a neighbor slowly driving by. "Want to go away for a week, or one of those ten-day trips?"

"Whatever," replied George absently; meaning, he had no serious opinion. He did not really care where they went or for how long. Just go on a vacation with enough time left after the trip to recover and recuperate from all the excessive eating, playing and walking they typically did on their vacations. George was thinking about the fact that so often after vacations, he had to go back to work in order to get some rest. He always felt that that was sort of amusing, yet typical of human nature. He thought to himself, *maybe a vacation trip will bring Deb and me closer. We haven't been getting along together too well lately. Deb's been seeming pretty snotty with me. Even her cooking seems to have gone bad lately. I have had a lot on my mind, and she has paying very little attention to me. Almost like she did not care how I felt.*

The next day Deborah made all the necessary reservations and three weeks later, the Sheldons boarded a plane for the flight to Miami.

George was just as excited as his wife was as they briefly paused for the mandatory "gala" photograph when walking across the boarding passageway onto the ship.

Deborah and the travel agent had booked a luxurious suite with a private verandah. *In this way,* Deb had thought, *they could spend their days at sea outside on their balcony where they could easily view whatever islands the ship was passing. They could read or even sunbathe without having to contend with a couple of thousand other passengers. Room service could easily provide for their slightest whims.* Deb was sure her husband would like this and perhaps, she hoped, even pull him out of his recent funk. *He seems to have been ignoring me lately and is way too snappy with his remarks to me. I do not deserve any of his recent rudeness and I am sick to death of it.*

Although several months had now passed since the last incident with the SUV, Deborah had noted all too often that her husband had not really been himself recently.

"George," she complained one evening. "You don't act like you love me any more. Am I right? Is there someone else?" Deborah had hesitated asking such for several days. There simply did not seem to be a good time, so she decided to plunge ahead and proceed with her questioning.

"What?" George laid his newspaper aside. "Where'd you come up with that dumb idea? One of your friends try to put a bee in your bonnet?"

"No. It's just that you've been so standoffish lately."

Angrily, he rose and stormed out of the room. "Nothing's changed except on your side. I've got feelings, too, you know. Besides, I've got a lot on my mind, and I'm pretty busy at work. So, just let it ride. Okay?" He closed the bathroom door behind him.

Deborah was in a quandary. *He sometimes acts as if lost in a fog. He is continually preoccupied. He has been somewhat forgetful and has certainly lost his sense of humor. I am having more and more difficulty in getting George to go out.* She glanced out toward the darkened garden. *He has even begun to neglect his hobby.*

George had won many awards for his hobby of elaborate garden layouts. Being a person plagued with frequent bouts of sporadic insomnia, he had developed the habit of working and reworking the positioning of various plants in his garden during his nighttime periods of wakefulness. However, lately, as he lay in bed, instead of pondering about his hobby, his thoughts inevitably went to the dreaded SUV. His mind replayed over and over the atrocious scenes of blood, horror and death he had witnessed. Also his worries of "Why me?" never seemed to lessen.

Maybe, just maybe, she hoped, her husband would be restored to the steady and secure man that she had married some twenty years earlier.

After settling themselves in their room and while awaiting the delivery of their baggage by the ship's porters, George and Deb parked themselves in the comfortable chairs on their verandah. There they gazed at the varied activities on the heavily oil-stained dock some fifty feet below them. It was warm, almost hot there in Miami, with numerous clouds merrily tumbling across the sky like small children in a grassy meadow. They watched additional passengers crossing the elevated gangway, less than one hundred feet away, boarding. Deborah "inspected" the various outfits that the women were wearing. She noted happily that her travel ensemble compared quite favorably with those she was observing. George, however, turned his attention more to the ship's hands unloading several large tractor-trailers that were backed up to the cavernous inside of the great ocean liner.

George reached over and lightly nudged Deborah's arm. "Here comes our dinner," he chuckled as he saw several huge sides of beef being moved on board down below. "I've always heard that these cruise ships serve just about the best food around anywhere."

"They'd better," said his wife, as she inspected her freshly polished nails. "We had to pay through the nose for this trip."

"Well," responded George, "let's not even think about the money. We are on vacation; it is already paid for and I just know that we are going to have a blast. I have been looking forward to this vacation because I've been needing it particularly bad. I want to forget about that damnable SUV."

Deb thought to herself, *what with your recent preoccupation about it, you are not telling me anything I did not know.*

As the afternoon progressed, they began to find their way around the gigantic floating palace. On the top deck surrounding the two swimming pools, a gala embarkation party had begun. Waiters, bar tenders, and various other activities personnel were kept busy. Attendants were passing out cardboard horns, hats and streamers for the passengers to cast about when the ship was ready to sail. The increasingly noisy multitude consumed free rum/fruit drinks. Suddenly George stopped his revelry and grabbed a railing. He touched Deb on the arm and said, "Uh-oh, Deb, something's not right. My damn ears have started stinging again."

Deb regarded him curiously, reaching over and laying her hand on his arm. "Oh George," she said with a tone of parental dismissal. "Just get over it. I think you ought to quit worrying about that stuff. Besides, it's probably the excitement of our trip. Maybe it came from the airplane's changing altitude and air pressures."

"Hmm. Maybe, but I'm not so sure." He was somewhat taken aback at this disrupting turn of events. "And besides I just noticed that that damn horrible taste in my mouth has come back." George looked down at the drink he was holding. "It's worse than a pig sty smells. I mean, it's absolutely awful." Then he held it up to the sunlight and peered through the amber liquid. "Maybe they mixed up the wrong stuff in my drink. I ordered a rum punch, but this stuff sure doesn't taste like any I've ever had before. Nasty."

Deborah, determined to have an enjoyable cruise, decided to ignore these peculiar whims of her husband. She said, "Oh, come on George, lighten up."

Just at that moment, the horn on the ship's flamboyantly streamlined smokestack blew noisily as the ship slowly began edging away from the quay. The numerous multicolored pennants hanging from fore to aft lines were fluttering noisily in the breeze.

The cruise director and his staff began encouraging all the passengers to begin throwing their streamers back and forth. The six exuberant band members manning the steel drums and keyboards began a lively Caribbean tune, and started singing loudly, encouraging the happy vacationers to join in with their own voices. Several of the crowd, now becoming even more spirited from their alcoholic drinks, tried to do so, while other couples danced joyously.

As it began its forward motion, slowly passing three other liners still berthed, George, Deborah and the many other passengers waved at no one in particular on the docks, cheered, and threw more of their multicolored steamers around and on each other. George fought to ignore his symptoms. A rock and roll band began to offer competition to the steel drum band at the other end of the open deck. All the passengers seemed to be very excited about the upcoming voyage as the ship moved very slowly toward the inlet and the Atlantic Ocean. Yet, in spite of it all, George could not ignore his unsettling feeling that something was just not right.

"Oh my God!" said George abruptly. His free hand went to his mouth, and he dropped his drink to the teak deck, the plastic glass spilling and rolling off the deck.

Deb stopped throwing her streamers and looked down at the spilled punch, and then at him. Annoyed, she asked, "Now what is it this time? What's wrong with you?" She laid her hand on his tense arm.

He was pale. "Look! On the other side of those docked ships we're passing. See?" He became more agitated as he pointed toward the dock. "There, between the 'Moonbeam' and the 'Caribbean Express.' Between them. On the dock beside the entry building. Can't you see it?"

"See what George?" She was exasperated. "What on earth are you looking at? What's got you so upset now?" Deb peered curiously toward where her husband was now pointing as their ship continued to slip slowly past the still-moored liners.

"It's there!" he cried. "Down there!"

Several nearby passengers stared over at George, curious as to the cause of the commotion.

Deborah looked incredulously at him and said, "What's there? What is it?"

"It's that SUV! The blue one! The one with the devil driving!"

Deborah tried in vain to see it. *Dammit. Now George is going off on another one of those screwy tangents.* The two turned sideways slightly as an alert attendant brought George another glass of punch.

"Now look, George, I don't see anything unusual. I do see two white vans. Is that what you saw?"

"No! Damn you. I said I spotted that same blue SUV that has been causing me all the problems. Didn't you see it at all?"

Debra sighed. "Oh, come on, George, honey. Lighten up, for goodness sake. This is our vacation." She thought to herself, *what on earth am I going to do about this? I hope he doesn't ruin our vacation. I'm not sure I can stand much more of this mess—or him.*

"Well, it's too late now," he replied in a resigned voice. "You can't see it now because we've already moved beyond it. Nevertheless, I swear I saw it! Dammit! The devil's SUV! Blue tires and everything!" George was becoming frantic. *What the hell?*

"Oh dammit George. Get over it." She breathed a tired sigh, and then tugged on his shirt. "Come on. We've got to go down to our cabin, get on our life vests and wait for the safety check." Distressed, she thought, *Oh God, don't let his craziness ruin our trip.*

*   *   *

For the next five days, George and Deborah had themselves a reasonably nice vacation trip. Certainly, it was one to tell their friends and coworkers about when they got back home. They toured four exotic Eastern Caribbean islands, ate sumptuously, partied, gambled, ate more, hiked up and down steep hills and through primitive rain forests, swam, ate, slept, read. Due to Deb's cautious foresight, and liberal applications of sunscreen, neither Sheldon acquired a severe sunburn. They took more than one hundred photos.

Nevertheless, in spite of all the excitement, George could not extricate himself from his feelings of anxiety about having spotted the SUV. He saw it—he knew he did. He was aware that he was not particularly good company for his wife. He could not explain it, but he continued to have those curious sensations of the ear tingling and rotten taste. Due to Deborah's frequent urgings, he tried in vain to push it all to the back of his mind. He too, wanted to enjoy the cruise. Nevertheless, he knew damn well that something was wrong. He just could not explain it.

Late afternoon of the next-to-last day of the cruise, as the liner was heading back toward its homeport, the partying on the big ship was forced inside. Thick gray, blossoming clouds, haze, a heavy wind and a driving rainstorm had altered the planned upper deck activities. Consequently, the throng had worked its way to the gaming tables of the big boat's two casinos. The huge two-tiered showroom was also filled to standing room only. The ship's activities director was leading his team in their attempts to elevate the passengers' spirits.

George and Deborah had drolly noticed that numerous brown paper bags had miraculously appeared along the various handrails of the carpeted hallways. However, chewing on their self-administered seasick pills, neither felt much queasiness at all. Both, however, noticed various passengers abruptly dash toward the bags or toilets. The ship's stabilizers had reduced the awkward sea motions to a minimum, but the storm outside was almost overpowering.

Bong! Bong! Bong! Bong! These sounds were suddenly heard echoing throughout the ship.

"Your attention please. May I have your attention?" The captain clipped his words.

Everyone stopped speaking. The bands and orchestras ceased. A huge crash was heard outside as a brilliant flash of lightning exploded like a howitzer near the ship.

The captain continued. "My chief radio operator has informed me that we have received an emergency 'Mayday' call from a nearby ship. For this reason, I am diverting from our planned course and we will offer any assistance and aid to the parties that we can. I am sure you all will understand."

Subdued conversations began as numerous individuals moved to the portholes and doors to peer outside into the driving rainstorm.

Two hours later, still in the heavy rains and mist, George and Deborah's ship arrived at the location of the accident. They stood on their room's covered balcony, enduring an occasional gust of wind that drove sheets of warm rain over them. They were aghast at the view of the horror across and down below them. There had been a terrible shipwreck. One of the cruise liners that their own ship had passed back in Miami, "The Moonbeam," had been hit broadside by a smaller rusty tramp steamer. The fog, mist and rain had inexplicably confused the vision of the two ships. Even with modern radar, presumably on both ships, the impossible had happened.

As their ship arrived on the scene, the Sheldons could see the old cargo vessel, its bow now remaining jammed within the great liner. They watched as it gradually began to break apart and founder. After about half an hour, the remaining rear part of the freighter finally settled beneath the ten-foot high storm-tossed waves. A dozen bedraggled seamen jumped off the doomed steamer and attempted to swim through the erratic waters to anything found floating. Several were seen to sink slowly beneath the surface, having given up their difficult struggles. The waters were covered with flotsam and jetsam, foul-smelling diesel oil, and screaming people. Their pathetic and hysterical sounds were terrifying to hear. George put his hands over his ears in a vain effort to shut out the piercing shrieks of the victims.

Deborah clutched her arm around George's waist, tugging herself tightly against him. "Oh George," she uttered, "Look!" Bodies were bandied about by the waves like shuttlecocks.

Shrugging his shoulders, George responded quietly with a resigned voice, "I knew something awful would happen. I just knew it. Remember, I saw that damned blue SUV on the dock back in Miami. Moreover, I told you I had those same symptoms. You didn't believe me, did you? I guess I could have predicted something like this. That damned SUV had been parked right beside the 'Moonglow' back at the dock."

Deborah released her hold on his waist and drew away from him. Tears of anguish streamed down her cheeks, mixing with the occasional rain that blew in on her. She bit her lower lip, saying nothing, but thinking, *how can he say such a thing? Certainly, he could not have anticipated this disaster. What is happening to George? To us?*

Suddenly, there was a piercing, tearing sound as the crushed bow of the steamer wrenched itself away from the liner and slowly sank into the sea.

Four bright orange lifeboats from the damaged liner had been lowered and the crewmembers were valiantly attempting to rescue survivors as they thrashed about in the foul waters. Few were wearing life jackets. George and Deborah noted their own ship's hands quickly lowering their lifeboats in order to help.

As torrents of tears continued to stream down her face, she tugged on his shirt and said, "Oh my God. Look, George. You can see right into the interior of the 'Moonbeam.'" George looked as she directed, seeing an oil painting hanging on the wall of what had apparently been the Moonbeam's library. There, a bleeding man was frantically assisting a fallen woman and her infant.

"That other smaller ship just ran into the side of that liner, and tore its side right out. You can even see the different decks and, look; you can actually see those poor unfortunate people running back and forth over there. It has got to be terrible for them." Gazing once again down onto the storm-tossed waves, they sadly watched as an older couple, soaked with oil, held each other closely and sank beneath the surface of the waters.

George gripped the varnished teak guardrail with white knuckles. He peered down at an increasing number of bodies floating in the scrambled mass of debris. He turned away gagging. He wanted to see no more.

Reentering his room he stopped, and turned toward his wife. "Hey. You know what? That damn taste and the ear tingling is gone."

Deb paused, and then decided not to respond. She felt heartsick at the terrible trauma they were witnessing and did not feel the need to concern herself with her husband's self-centered and petty foolishness. Instead, she thought, *I am getting awfully tired of this newly developed idiosyncrasy of his. After all, who could care about his selfish little peculiarities when such a terrible accident had happened? Has he no empathy whatsoever? I have just about had it with this stuff of his. I really do not know how much more of it I can stand.*

*   *   *

The remainder of the cruise was expectedly subdued. Over eight hundred survivors from the "Moonbeam" were brought onto their ship, issued blankets and directed to public areas. A U. S. Navy destroyer and a passing supertanker picked up the recovered bodies and the remainder of the victims. That evening CNN reported that, including the workers on the tramp steamer, eighty-five souls were lost that dreadful gray afternoon.

CHAPTER FOUR

"GEORGE, COME INTO MY office please," sounded the intercom speaker beside him. George looked up from studying the papers on his cluttered desk. *Okay, so this will have to wait.*

Entering the office, he sat down in a leather wingback chair facing his boss's desk.

"Yeah Mr. Williams? What can I do for you? I was just in the middle of working on that Harrelson mess." He looked at Williams' desk. George had never spoken to his boss about it, but had often wondered why the old man continued to stick to that beat up gray metal desk. He knew he got it from a navy salvage yard about twenty years ago. It was the original traditional gray, but now was heavily marked with brown and black marks from the toes of highly polished shoes bumping against it. One side had a huge dent. Certainly, since the business was thriving, his employer could easily afford a more modern, attractive desk that would go better with the contemporary design of the entire building. However, Williams liked it, so it stayed. Perhaps he had some sentimental attachment to it, but neither George nor any of his fellow employees had ever been able to glean any concrete information about it. Polished mahogany desks, side tables and leather-bound chairs graced their own offices.

Something else that sort of bothered George was the fact that Mr. Williams had some poorly built and ill-fitting dentures. They looked artificial and frequently would slip slightly when Williams was talking. Surely the old man could afford a new and better set, but, just like the office desk, he hung on to them.

One could often hear the old man clicking his dentures together as he worked on a difficult task.

Williams laid his partially smoked cigar onto the nearly overflowing bronze-colored glass ashtray. Since the ashtray contained numerous chips along its edges, it was obvious that it had fallen off this desk many times. Yet, like the old desk, Williams retained it. Although Williams was constantly seen with his cigar—lit or unlit—he disallowed smoking of any sort by any of his employees. No one, but no one had ever been able to get the boss to alter his views. At tense moments in the company, there could frequently be seen a cloud of blue-gray smoke emanating from Williams' office.

He unthinkingly put his right forefinger to his lips momentarily, and then said, "George, I want you to head over to Newland, Tennessee. We have a chance at a contract with the Arnold Company there and I figure that you can bring it off. The guy you're to meet with is named Smith. He's the CEO."

"Well…yeah. Sure. Okay, Mr. Williams." replied George slowly, with a mild frown on his face. "I've certainly heard about the Arnold Company. They do a good job from what I understand. But, where in the hell is Newland? Near what?"

"Out in the middle of Tennessee someplace. I have already had Joyce book you on a flight. She has your round trip tickets out at her desk. Sorry, but there are no first class tickets for you, because you can only get there by commuter hops. Your flight will be on Mainline Airlines. I think she said your flight leaves tomorrow morning about nine. She also booked you into a motel of some sort over there. You can get all the information from her. Okay?"

George did not really care to make this trip. He had already made plans with Deborah for hitting a restaurant and movie tomorrow night. There was a film showing that had gotten excellent reviews. They figured the ticket lines for admission would have dissipated by now. In truth, he was not interested in seeing the film, but Deb had seemed determined to see it. However, when the boss says, "go," you go. At least in George's code of ethics. He secretly held a slight hope that some day Williams just might ask him to take over the company. Then he would be set for life—if he lived long enough.

"Okay, Mr. Williams. Whatever you want. I'll do the best I can." George immediately began to think of what papers he might need to take with him and where they were in his file cabinet. *I'll probably need my trusty laptop computer, too. Well, maybe Joyce could gather it all together for me. After all, that is what secretaries are for, isn't it? Even if she is not actually assigned to me personally.*

*   *   *

"See you tomorrow, late morning," George said smiling. "The flight gets back here at eleven. Barring any bad weather, we should be just about on time. Of course I'll call if there's any problem." He reached down and picked up his laptop and carry-on. "I suppose it could possibly take more than one day, but I hope not. Mr. Williams said he really wanted me to get this contract."

Deborah said, "You don't suppose he'll give you a big bonus if you should land the account do you?" She held her hair as the wind from the plane's propellers blew against the two of them.

"Don't hold your breath about that. Gotta go now," yelled George over the noise. "What with the engines already started, it's obvious that they're ready to have me on board." He leaned over and gave her a quick kiss on the forehead. "Bye. Back tomorrow. Remember, I gave you the arrival time. It is at home on the refrigerator, just in case you should forget. See you when we land."

Just in case I should forget, thought Deborah irritably. *What is wrong with him lately anyway? Now why would the jerk insult my intelligence like that? Just because he seems to be lost in a fog so much lately, he acts as if he thinks I am too. Since he keeps bringing up that crazy blue SUV idea of his, I am beginning to wonder about his sanity. Maybe I can get him to see our doctor when he gets back.*

George wheeled and made his way through the wind and up the few steps to the open door of the plane.

The two-hour flight proved to be uneventful. Glancing out the plane's window from time to time, between the cottony clouds, George was able to see the beautiful Blue Ridge Mountains down below, with their majestic wooded slopes and blue-gray haze. Passing over a highway threading its way between the ridges, he observed a few cars, crawling along like ants on a trail. George settled himself into his seat and accepted a soft drink from the cabin attendant. She was a plump, dark-headed woman who looked as if she might have been with the airlines for over twenty years. Not this particular one, though, because George was aware that Mainline Airlines had only been in operation for six years. He was happy that she had left him alone after delivering his soda. He wanted some "quiet time" to contemplate his upcoming meeting. Mr. Williams put a lot of faith in George's ability to sell a business contract to new accounts. George had proven to him many times over the years that he was his most trusted employee. In fact, more frequently than Williams would care to admit, George had actually struck a far better deal with clients than he would have done himself. George knew when and where to cut expenses, and had shown that he had the business acuity to push his ideas through to the clients. George's quiet, mild-mannered personality somehow made the potential customers overestimate their ability to persuade him to go along with their personal preferences and selfish recommendations. They would complete their presentations to him, and typically, would sit back and gloat that they had bamboozled this naive simpleton. George would come right back at them with his own proposals. These would cleverly incorporate many points of their presentation, but with much more advanced and efficient figures and results. Thus, characteristically, the customer was left with nothing more to say, except, somewhat chagrined sometimes, "You know, I believe you're absolutely right. We'll go with it." George also always made certain that the customers felt as if they originated the new proposals. Because of this, Williams Company clients passed on glowing references to their friends and colleagues.

On the other hand, Mr. Williams was much more conservative and hesitant to offer a marginal contract. However, time after time, George had come through with excellence, so Williams had almost totally relinquished the new business part of his company to his best employee, George Albert Sheldon.

✳   ✳   ✳

Arriving at the small regional airport in Newland, he glanced around and noted that besides the small terminal, there were two large hangers and possibly thirty or forty small planes tied down around the tarmac. The small control tower was obviously kept quite busy directing the many private flights to and away from of the airport. There were two larger planes—obviously belonging to local industries—parked near one of the hangers.

George made his way through the unpretentious, nearly vacant terminal to one of the two taxicabs that were standing at the curb. He directed the driver to transport him directly to the Arnold Company out on Industrial Drive. The ride took less than twenty minutes, giving George only a minimum amount of time to scan the terrain. From what he could see off in the distance, Newland was a relatively small city built on lovely rolling hills. On its way to Industrial Drive, the taxicab passed by a shimmering silver lake and through a couple of miles of lush green forest. These acres of timberland slightly reminded George of his and Deborah's delightful vacation in the Bavarian "Black Forest" several years previously. He lowered the window of the cab to breathe in some of the pleasant woodland aroma, but only smelled fumes from the taxi's rusted tailpipe.

After the cab arrived at his destination, George walked up the white gravel walk to enter the aged brick building, unsure as to what he might find inside. To his trained eye, the exterior did not appear to be a very well kept facility. Small bits of mortar were noticeably missing, and the ancient bricks were showing a great deal of weathering. He did note with pleasure, however, that there was an abundance of well-tended grass and shrubbery surrounding the one-story building. Off to his right was a fountain shooting water high in the air. The sun's rays were hitting small droplets of spray and exhibiting a kaleidoscope of rainbow colors.

As he entered, he was intrigued to notice that the Arnold Company had totally redecorated the interior of the facility. Apparently, George decided, there was a big community-wide development project in the town of Newland to keep the ante-bellum buildings as close as possible to their original external characteristics. Obviously, the owners could renovate the interiors to whatever level they deemed pleasing. Since this building was adjacent to several others of similar age, George assumed that all were following the same objective. It reminded him of similar civic rehabilitation projects that he had seen in a number of other cities.

As he stood before the glass and stainless steel desk, all-weather coat and bags in hand, he announced to the attractive, slender brunette that he had an appointment with Mr. Smith. She nodded and smiled at him politely. Wearing a headset telephone, she reached over and pushed a button. Then she spoke quietly into the tiny boom microphone.

After a few seconds she said, "Mr. Smith will see you shortly. Why don't you just have a seat over there on the couch?"

Acknowledging his coat and bags, she said, "If you wish to leave your bags here by my desk, I'll be quite happy to keep an eye on them for you."

"Thank you."

He kept his briefcase, turned and moved to a leather-bound settee where he could observe the elegant skylight and live plants adorning the lobby. After a short wait, the brightly polished ornamental steel doors opened and a pleasant-appearing lady of about fifty came out. She walked over to where he was sitting, her comfortable medium-height heels clicking lightly on the marble floor.

She said, "Mr. Sheldon? I'm Mrs. Earlich, Mr. Smith's personal secretary."

She held out her hand to shake with him, and was carefully eyeing him as she was speaking, wondering what sort of man this might be to occupy her busy employer's time. Mrs. Earlich had worked for Mr. Smith for thirty years, and proudly and selfishly guarded his time.

"Please come with me, and I'll introduce you to Mr. Smith. You are early for your appointment, but he is available right now. Since he has another appointment scheduled one hour following yours, you might find yourself fortunate to have a few extra minutes for your discussion." In reality, she knew there was no one scheduled after George, but wanted to make it work out so that if Mr. Smith wanted to get rid of the visitor, he could easily do so. On the other hand, should he find the proposal interesting, he could readily push the button on his intercom and "notify" Mrs. Earlich to cancel his next appointment. This was a system that she had suggested to him many years before and it had been working successfully since that time.

"Well, hello, Mr. Sheldon," said Smith. He was an extremely overweight man of about seventy with stark white hair. He used his hand to offer George a seat in front of his cluttered desk. Rolls of fat overflowed his heavily starched white dress shirt that was unbuttoned at the collar. He had loosened his solid blue silk tie, and had rolled his shirtsleeves up to his elbows. *This is a busy, no-nonsense fellow,* thought George.

He said brightly, "Coffee?"

"No, but thank you. You have a very nice place here," said George. "I noticed Newland has a restoration project going on here."

Smith leaned back in his chair, smiled broadly and said, "Yep. That we do. I happen to have been President of the Chamber of Commerce when we decided to do all this." He grandly swept his hand around the room. "We had a little difficulty with a couple of companies, but I was able to win them over."

Nodding affirmatively, George responded, "I see it has paid off."

Abruptly Smith moved his chair forward and propped his elbows on his desk. He tented his fingers. "Now, Mr. Sheldon. Tell me what it is you have to offer. I've certainly known about your company for many years, and its good reputation for getting the job done quickly and efficiently." He paused for a moment, as he once again pushed his black leather-bound chair back from his desk. He put one foot up on the edge of the wooden trashcan beside him. "I've never met Mr. Williams, but have heard he's a good man to do business with."

George accepted these words of not-so-subtle praise and moved immediately on to his presentation. He had already removed his sheath of papers from his briefcase during his wait in the lobby. He had experienced many similar situations during his tenure at the Williams Company. As a result, he was fully prepared for whatever type of reception he might receive.

The presentation proceeded well, and since Smith seemed to be quite interested in what George had to offer, he did indeed push his intercom button and inform Mrs. Earlich to "cancel the remaining appointments" for the afternoon. Although George had suspicions that this whole setup was a ruse, he accepted it with the notion that his presentation was being considered positively. He felt good and continued his pitch to Smith with confidence. Yes, this was working. Mr. Williams was going to be very pleased. Surely, there would be a big bonus for this contract!

Later that evening, in his motel room, George fine-tuned his figures to meet a few thoughts that Smith had to offer during the presentation. Then he used the motel's fax machine, and sent them to Smith's office, where they would be waiting for him first thing the next morning. He also faxed a copy of the contract to Williams, who would then deal directly with Smith in the actual contractual agreement negotiated by George.

*   *   *

George's plane was scheduled to depart Newland Airport at five minutes after nine, so after a light breakfast of dry toast and coffee in the crowded motel restaurant, George grabbed a cab back to the airfield.

The ear tingling! The foul taste! Oh damnation, thought George as he sat in the well-worn and dirty back seat of the taxicab. *It has started again! Oh my God! What in hell is going to happen now? Am I in danger this time? Is my plane going to crash? What will Deborah do if I get killed? The way she's been acting lately, maybe she won't mind at all.*

George became very preoccupied with his disturbing symptoms, and fidgeted impatiently in the noisy terminal waiting room for the boarding call for his flight. He looked around the high-ceilinged room at other passengers, spotting nothing or no one out of the ordinary. He kept looking out the floor-to-ceiling window at what he presumed to be his plane, as it was being refueled and a pilot was going through the preflight checks. All appeared normal and routine to George. Yet, his distressing sensations continued—even growing stronger. A young man wearing a tan jacket and brown trousers, sitting next to him in the waiting room tried to start up a casual conversation, but George was so afraid that the foul taste in his mouth would convey a comparable nasty breath odor, he quickly excused himself. He bought a pack of gum in the terminal's snack shop in his effort to sweeten his mouth. George did not think it had any effect at all. When he returned, he took another seat apart from any other passengers.

Finally, the boarding announcement came and George and the other eight passengers strolled out onto the tarmac to board the waiting plane. George noted that Mainline Airlines had large numbers painted on the vertical stabilizer. His plane was number 612.

George began to think; *maybe I should not even take this plane. Maybe it is destined to crash. I am not ready to die. However, maybe it is not concerning the SUV. Maybe that damn thing is somewhere else today. However, why am I having these same symptoms? Is that really the devil I keep seeing? If so, why is he causing all these catastrophes near me? Why am I not involved in any of them? Oh well, maybe it will be all right. Besides, this is the only plane heading back toward home today. I would have to wait until tomorrow to return and I don't want to do that. Maybe it'll be all right.*

Climbing in, he took his assigned seat, was settling in for the flight, when he casually glanced out the window.

The blue SUV was parked adjacent to the other commuter plane across the tarmac. That plane's number happened to be 666. George was horribly taken aback as he sat there peering through the small window beside his seat. He suddenly broke out into a heavy sweat. *I must do something! Something terrible is bound to happen. Maybe with that other plane? What should I do?* He wondered how he could get someone to realize that some kind of tragedy might occur soon.

George unbuckled his seat belt, rose, and loudly called back to the cabin attendant. She was helping another passenger push her suitcase into the overhead bin.

"Miss!" called George. "I have to speak to you—right now!"

"Just a minute sir," she replied casually, as she continued to push against the bulky baggage. "I'll be right with you. Now please take your seat." She seemed to George to be a little on edge. *Perhaps she has had a fight with her boyfriend, and now she wants to take it out on the rest of us,* thought George. *Nevertheless, I need to speak to her now, so she can possibly get somebody notified of the probable impending doom.*

"Miss, it is imperative that I see you right now!" spoke up George, slightly raising his voice. He walked over to the elderly woman's bag and gave it a hard shove into the bin.

"There. Now that's done for you," he said firmly. "Now Miss, I have to tell you something, and you've got to take some action right away."

The attendant did not smile, or even thank him for his help with the bag, but ushered George back to the tiny galley area. She pulled the curtain closed and turned toward him.

She said in a hushed, but impatient, voice, "Now sir, what's this all about? I have duties with other passengers, you know."

CHAPTER FIVE

T HANKS TO A SLIGHT tailwind, George's plane landed only ten minutes behind schedule. He was very glad to be back home. His ear tingling and bizarre taste had cleared up, so he was feeling somewhat better about his experience than before the plane's departure. The cabin attendant did not acknowledge him as he exited the plane, and the door to the cockpit remained closed. As he was exiting the terminal, he spotted Deb and waved to her. She greeted him with a big hug, and they walked to their car.

"Hey honey, glad you're back," said Deborah with a broad smile. "I hope the meeting went well. Oh, instead of heading straight home, there is a big sale at Sutton's Department Store over at the Southside Mall. How about if we hit there first and maybe grab a bite in the food court? Okay?"

"Sure, if you want to," responded her husband casually. "The trip didn't tire me out much."

So, Deb spent about three-quarters of an hour shopping for a new fall coat, while George hung around waiting for her. He found an open bench with a back near the center of the mall, and, with several other men that George assumed were husbands, relaxed. He picked up an old newspaper lying on the bench, glanced at it, and quickly realized that he had previously read or heard about all the news in it. He located the crossword puzzle and saw with bored disappointment that somebody had already completed it. As he glimpsed at it, he quickly realized that not one, but several people had apparently worked on it. At least that was his determination, noting the use of several different types of handwriting and pencil leads. George also saw that some egotistical soul, assuming he or she would make no errors, had even used an ink pen for a few words. He laid the paper aside, crossed his arms and began watching the numerous passersby. He got no particular thrills from surveying a parade of the masses, yet there was nothing else for him to do at the moment.

He spoke to a man sitting next to him, "I'm glad the piped-in music has been turned off."

His immaculately dressed bench neighbor responded, "Yeah, me too. That repetitious music would drive me nuts."

George said, "I'd hate to have to work in a mall and listen to it all day long."

"Me too," said the man. "Oh, here comes my wife." Rising, he said to George, "Take care, fellow."

George crossed his arms again and sat back listening to the sounds of footsteps and rustling tote bags. He enjoyed hearing the happy voices of small children ambling around.

Shortly Deborah approached, wearing a bright smile and carrying three garments enclosed in plastic bags.

"Sorry I was so long, but I just had to try on several dresses that were marked way down," she said gaily. "Want to see what I bought?"

George rose, took the clothing bags from Deborah and said, "Nope. Not right now. I'll see them when we get home. Hungry yet?"

Her happy attitude was suddenly deflated like a burst balloon, as her husband declined to acknowledge her new purchases. *Well, after all. Here I am, ready to show off my new bargains, and he shows no interest in me. He is not even interested in how much money I saved.* After a brief moment, she expelled a slight sigh and said, "Yeah, okay. Let's walk around to the food court. Feel like Chinese?"

As they were casually strolling down the mall toward the grouped eating establishments, the two of them happened to pass by a home entertainment store.

Glancing in at the full wall of operating television sets, Deb grabbed him by his arm and exclaimed, "Oh George, there's been a plane crash. C'mon, let's go in and hear what they're saying." She tugged at his shirtsleeve and the two entered the store and walked up to the bank of sets. As soon as George saw the screens on the multitude of TV's, he turned a pasty white, and broke into a cold sweat.

Oh, God! No! He watched as the camera panned on the smoking crash scene of devastation. He could see the large lettering "666" on the remaining identifiable piece of tail section the ornamental red and green logo of Mainline Airlines. Also shown on the multiple monitors were rescue workers, firefighters and massive amounts of charred debris. Standard white sheets covered two bodies. George felt physically weak and sick to his stomach. *Oh my God!* He grabbed Deborah's arm tightly, almost to a point of pinching her flesh. "Deb, I saw that very plane over in Newland. I spotted the devil's blue SUV beside it and warned them." His knees felt weak, and he wanted to sit down somewhere. He used his arm to brace against a counter. He sighed deeply. "I had those symptoms again, just before we were ready to take off." He started to leave the store, pulling, almost dragging her behind him. "It's happened again." *Oh good Lord, what am I supposed to do? How can I stop that bastard devil from causing these things to happen? Is he ever going to harm or kill me? What have I done to deserve this?*

"Come on, Deb, let's get out of here. I don't want to worry about this now. Besides, I'm not hungry now. Let's just go on home."

He felt very drained. Deborah, somewhat perplexed and annoyed, followed him to their car and drove the two of them home. George laid his head back against his headrest and closed his eyes. His hands were clenched tightly. *Dammit,* thought his wife, *here I was, all set for some good Chinese food and this nutty husband of mine and his cockamamie story has to screw it all up. I am sure getting damned tired of all his baloney. Wonder if he's getting a brain tumor? He seems so sure that it is the devil that is causing all this to happen around him. I guess we are lucky he has not been directly involved in any of these tragedies. Gotta get him to a doctor. He is not well.*

The Sheldons arrived home following a twenty-minute drive in complete silence. George, still very upset, unpacked his overnight case, and then sat down beside Deb at the dinette table while she began sipping on a bowl of soup. He said that he was still not hungry.

"Deb," George began slowly, hesitatingly, "As I told you before, I saw that plane across the tarmac this morning over at Newland. I mean the one that went down. Really." Deb turned her head toward him quizzically. Did she suspect what was coming? "And I saw that same damn blue SUV parked beside that plane before we took off." His voice cracked when he spoke. "I wasn't even sure it was not meant to be our plane. I told the cabin attendant and pilot about it, but neither paid attention to me. I warned them!"

George took Deb by her hand and squeezed it. "They must not have believed me. Dammit to hell! I told them something bad was probably going to happen. I told them! I don't know what else I could have done. Now lots of people are dead. What else could I have done?"

His wife unclasped her hand and continued with her soup. Then she said, "You say you think this happened because of the SUV? Or, as you say, your seeing the devil? Now honey, look at it this way: nobody else has ever seen that SUV, have they? At least, nobody has admitted seeing it. Just you, right?"

Sadly, he glanced over at his wife. "Yeah, that's the way it is."

Deb took another spoonful of her homemade vegetable soup, put down her spoon, and said, "I don't understand what's happening to you, but I'm afraid that you must have something going on that neither of us can understand. I think these things must certainly have simply been a curious series of coincidences. Bad ones and it is strange, but still simple flukes. How else could you explain it?"

"Yeah, but…"

Deborah turned to face her husband directly. She took both his hands in hers. "Honey, I love you dearly. You know that. I want you to see Dr. Harrison first thing tomorrow. Maybe you have something happening in your brain. I hope not, but all the same…" Her voice died away slowly as she drifted into thoughts.

George's face suddenly became flushed with the red heat of anger. He pulled his hands away from his wife and vigorously slammed his right hand down on the table, causing a small amount of Deb's soup to splash out of her cup. His own wife was not accepting his story.

"Damn it. You are my wife and even you won't believe me! I saw it, honest I did. You gotta believe it." He then brusquely pushed his chair back from the table. Walking angrily into the living room, he said, loud enough for Deb to hear, "Well there's nothing at all wrong with me. I'd know it if there was." He sat down in his favorite easy chair, picked up the television remote, popped on a station, and said loudly, "Well you can all just go to hell!"

Deborah sadly brought her soup bowl to her lips, drained it, and used a paper napkin to wipe off the table. Then she slipped her chair back and placed the empty bowl into the sink. She stood there and stared vacantly out the window. *There simply must be some way that I can get George to go to the doctor tomorrow,* pondered Deborah. *I simply cannot let this mess go on. No. I will not let it go on. I just cannot take it anymore. I am afraid George is losing his mind. Does he have some kind of brain tumor? However, what would happen to me if they put poor George into an institution? He is too young for Alzheimer's—at least I think he is.* Deborah rinsed the dirty dishes and slipped them into the dishwasher. Worried, but reluctant to speak to her husband again about it at the moment, she moved into her sewing room. She would busy herself with menial chores around the home for a while. In this way, she would not have such an opportunity to worry about George's continuing idiosyncrasy. All the same, she still could not stop agonizing about him.

Meanwhile, George continued to sit sullenly before the television screen without either watching or listening. He had turned the sound up slightly higher than normal, so as to buffer any further words from Deb. He tried and tried to determine just what and why this was happening to him. His self-doubt was beginning to get to him, and George became increasingly despondent. Three times now he had become aware of the strange physical symptoms of foul taste and ear tingling. And three times the light blue SUV had made an appearance. There had been three major disasters. Were they related? As a highly trained engineer, he had learned to work with logic. *There must be some connection. There simply has to be. But what does it have to do with me? What on earth have I ever done to have that devil-looking guy and his big blue SUV doing this to me? Can it really be the devil himself? Since everybody knows you can't see the devil, why is it that I can? And, if I can, why can't anybody else see him? And now Deborah is acting as if she thinks I am making it all up. She will not even talk with me about it at all. It's worrying me sick and I have no idea what I can do about it. Maybe it is, after all, just a series of coincidences. Maybe I have suddenly become psychic. On the other hand, maybe I have always been this way and just didn't know it. What else can it be? Maybe that could explain some of this mess.* George knew that he had never before shown any signs of clairvoyance, and he had never heard of anyone in his family with such abilities.

I wonder if I should check with the people over in Durham, he thought. *Now what was the name of that place? Used to be connected with Duke University. Oh yes, "The Institute of Parapsychology," I believe. Maybe they can help me figure out what the hell is going on. On the other hand, maybe I've just gotten hold of some kind of virus that is causing this stuff. I don't know what the hell kind it might be though—I have never read about anything like that in the papers. Sure do wish Deb would be a little more understanding though. She ought to realize that I am telling the truth and that I can't help it. I wish some other people could see the SUV though. That'd help explain things. Why in hell can't they? That's what's got me so bugged. People might start thinking that I really am crazy. Maybe I had better not mention the SUV to anybody. If my own wife of over twenty years will not believe me, you can damn well bet nobody else will. However, maybe those parapsychology folks will believe me. From what I've heard about them, they will at least want to investigate me. Yeah, that is what I will do. I will call them over there in Durham tomorrow. However, I sure as hell will not tell Deb about it ahead of time. She would get on that damn 'see your doctor' kick again.*

Therefore, with Deb sewing, and George reading a novel he found that he had bought several months previously, the evening passed quietly and uneventfully.

Both Sheldons welcomed bedtime. Then, George assumed, there would be less likelihood of further discussion, and no more arguments such as they had had lately. Once again, like too many nights lately, sleep and its restful solitude was slow in coming for George that night.

Deborah, on the other hand, worried about the way her husband had changed and how it affected her and their marriage. *Just where and why did George come up with this ridiculous idea that the devil has taken hold of his life? He has declared repeatedly to her that it was true, yet can offer her no evidence. Granted, he was near those horrific accidents, but to suggest that he actually, somehow, had a part in them is utterly nutty. Things like that do not happen in real life...only in the movies or in books.*

CHAPTER SIX

THREE DAYS LATER GEORGE visited the Parapsychology Clinic, in Durham, North Carolina. George told the doctors and assistants details about everything that had happened to him. And, at last, he found someone who actually took a serious interest in him and his incidents. In fact, several additional psychologists, including an eminent psychiatrist from Duke University, came in to question George. The institute ran numerous tests on him, including two separate lie detector tests.

The doctors and technicians there observed that while George appeared to have no evidence or signs of clairvoyance or extraordinary psychic powers, he did show numerous signs of extreme anxiety and anger. They declared that they found George a reasonably normal individual, but had somehow created some "self-induced" stressful circumstances. They told him that his was a very interesting and unusual case, and asked him to relay any additional incidents to them for their study. Although the institute's doctors regrettably had no explanations for him, they did recommend that he check in with his personal physician for a complete and thorough physical examination when he returned home. *Damn,* thought George that evening as he drove back home from Durham and the parapsychology clinic. *They said the same thing that Deb did. "Go to my doctor!"*

"Well, to hell with all of them," uttered George aloud to himself. "I'm normal and I know it. I'll just get on with my life, and forget about the damned devil and his screwy SUV." His lingering self-doubt was somewhat assuaged now.

At that moment, George swerved out of the way of an opossum that had wandered onto the road. He was glad that he had seen it in time to miss it. He did not enjoy seeing death. Of course, bugs on his windshield didn't count.

"Hey George," said Deborah when he arrived home. She moved about the kitchen preparing their dinner. "You're a little bit late tonight. Have a tough day?"

Drawing in a deep breath, George replied, "Well, let me tell you about it." Then, as she placed a pot roast onto the table, he admitted to Deborah where he had spent the day and all about the battery of interviews and testing that he was put through at the clinic. He intentionally chose not to mention to his wife that the doctors there had also suggested, as she had, that he see his personal physician. Any more nagging from Deb he felt he could do without. Wiping her hands on a towel, she moved to the kitchen table, placed a basket of fresh baked rolls on it, pulled out a chair and sat down in front of George. As he continued to relate the incidents of his day, she accepted all he had to say with resignation. She thought to herself, *At least, George is finally taking some responsibility for his own problem.* After he finished his discussion, he was happy that Deb did not suggest again a trip to his doctor and George inwardly breathed a sigh of relief.

The following day George made his normal trek along the freeway to work. It was cloudy and rainy. He had many catch-up papers to handle due to his having been absent the previous day. This helped occupy his mind, rather than permitting a continual replaying of the events involving the devil. He found it difficult to concentrate, however. Later, sitting at his desk, already sipping his afternoon cup of coffee, his senses began to wander.

Somehow, he wished he could talk to someone about it. Someone nonjudgmental. Someone to use as a sounding board. Someone to help him determine how to escape this personal nightmare. Perhaps they could help him measure in his own mind what was happening to him. Maybe that is what bartenders did, as they listened to people's troubles. However, he had nobody to talk to—nobody that he would feel comfortable with anyway. Normally, concerning mundane problems, Deb was easy to talk to and could offer him suggestions that would help him work things out in his own mind. Nevertheless, this was a situation where Deb had quickly shown that she did not believe that he actually saw the devil or even a large blue SUV. She intimated that she did not think that it existed at all. At least, in reality. George correctly presumed from her responses that she felt that it must exist only in his mind. In addition, she simply did not know how to deal with such a perceived mind game. She was no help for him this time. George was determined not to see a shrink about it. *Only weak and crazy people went to shrinks. I did not really "visit" shrinks when I was over there at the Parapsychology Clinic. They came to me.* That made it okay in his frame of reference. Moreover, he knew he was neither weak nor crazy. *Dammit, I know what I saw, even if nobody else did.*

Suddenly, George's reverie was abruptly interrupted.

"George," sounded the office intercom on his desk. "Come in here for a moment please." It was the voice of Mr. Williams. George rose from his neatly arranged desk, glanced out his picture window, noting that it was still raining, and casually strolled into William's office.

"Sit down George," said Williams. George realized immediately that his employer seemed rather in a stern mood. *Maybe it is the rain.*

"George," said Williams, as he leaned his chair back. "Your work has been pretty sloppy lately. This is not like you. What is wrong? Got a problem?"

George perched on the edge of a straight back chair. *I cannot admit the truth to him. It would make me look like a fool.*

"Well, to tell the truth, Mr. Williams, I've been bugged with a personal problem at home." He shifted in his chair, and peered over to his left and out the large window. *Still raining heavily.* "Doesn't apply to Deb and me exactly, but I'd just rather not talk about it. Okay, Mr. Williams?"

"George, I've known you and Deborah for some twenty years, and I know that you two have one of the most stable marriages around. At least I have assumed so. Certainly, you are aware of all the messed up marriages and divorces with my other employees around here. I don't foresee that you and your wife would ever reach that point."

Mr. Williams leaned forward, opened his top desk drawer and pulled out a partially smoked cigar. Picking up the lighter from his desk, he lit it. The room was silent, as George waited curiously for William's next words. George felt as though he should say something, but nothing practical came to mind at that point. So, he simply waited as the silence of the room slowly began to envelop him. He absently watched the trails of rain racing each other down the window like the tracks of professional skiers racing down a steep slope of new powder. *What is coming next?* Finally, after several attempts to get the end lit to his satisfaction, Williams tipped the ashes off carefully on the edge of his ashtray, and then once again leaned back in his chair. The smoldering cigar sent a film of gray smoke signals steadily toward the ceiling.

"George, I respect you and your dedication to your work here. You certainly are aware of that, but now I have to tell you that you simply have to straighten things up. I shouldn't even have to mention it, but it's been pretty obvious that you haven't had your mind on your work lately."

Williams picked up his cigar, pulled on it, and tilting his head back, blew out a perfect light gray smoke ring. Then he looked carefully at the end as if he were concerned that he had somehow damaged a mass of the ashes. He admired his own ability to blow smoke rings. He had practiced and practiced it for many years. Each perfect one seemed to make him feel good.

Then he looked straight back at George, saying, "The bottom line is, George, that if you find you can't get yourself back on the straight and narrow, I'll have to see about making some changes around here."

George exhaled heavily and leaned back in the chair, concerned about what he had just heard.

Williams continued, "Do you understand what I'm saying to you, George? Any questions?"

George stood, replying quietly and somewhat sheepishly, "Yes sir, Mr. Williams. I understand. I admit that I may have been a little slack lately, but with these problems on my mind, it has just been a real nightmare. Listen, Mr. Williams. I'll do better, I promise you."

Williams said with finality, "See that you do, George. See that you do." He leaned over his ashtray and lightly eased a few ashes from the tip of his cigar. "And close the door behind you."

Whew, thought George. *First time Williams has ever raked me over the coals. I knew I had been a little off lately, but I sure as hell did not realize it had been that obvious.* He stopped by the water cooler, took a long sip, and then returned to his office. Well, he could not really argue with Mr. Williams. He would simply have to get back to concentrating on his work and watch his P's and Q's. *However, how in hell do I forget about the SUV?*

Fortuitously, his future was not to be known…

*   *   *

Ring! Ring! Ring!

"Now who on earth can that be at this time of the morning?" Deborah muttered aloud to herself. She placed the remaining clean plates from the dishwasher onto the cupboard shelf. She had not heard any car in their driveway and was not expecting anyone to come calling. And, rarely did anyone come to see them without first telephoning. *I will bet it is one of those fool salespeople,* she thought. *And here I am dressed in this old ragged housecoat, too. I will be so embarrassed, especially if it should be one of our friends.*

Deborah opened the front door only as far as the night-latch chain would allow, and stuck her head into the opening.

"Yes, what is it?" she said somewhat nervously, as she observed the two men standing there. Quickly glancing at the driveway beyond them, she saw a dark blue nondescript four-door sedan, carrying a U. S. Government license plate on the front. She observed that each of these men were dressed in dark suits and muted ties, and had neatly trimmed haircuts. One person appeared to be about forty, heavy set, bordering on fat, and the other, slender, in his early twenties with blond hair and a neatly trimmed mustache.

She said to herself, *Oh damn. Now the government is after George.*

The older one spoke, "Good morning. Mrs. Sheldon?"

Deborah answered with curiosity in her voice, "Yes?"

"We're from the National Transportation Safety Board," continued the older man. He flashed his official badge at her. "Is Mr. George Sheldon here?"

"No. Why do you want to speak to him?" Deborah felt as though she already knew the dreaded answer to her question. After what George had told her about the plane incident, she was not at all surprised.

"But he does live here, Madam?"

They call me a madam? So, it has come down to this, she thought. "Well, yes," replied Deborah hesitantly. "I'll have to ask you again. Why do you wish to speak to him?" She was not normally this obstinate, but felt for some reason that she wanted to make it hard on these two people. They did not look dangerous to her, but she was certain they would put George through a troublesome interview. At least she wanted to spare him that if possible. He had been acting so crazy lately that she didn't want anything else to add to his mixed-up worries. She realized that she didn't quite fathom, in fact, didn't really believe, all that her husband had told her, but it was between him and her, probably nobody else's business.

The older man glanced at his partner, smiled and then replied to Deborah's inquiry. "Mrs. Sheldon, it is our understanding that your husband made a few comments about the Mainline airplane that crashed last week. Perhaps he saw something that might help us in our investigation as to the cause of the accident. Now, can you tell us when he might be home so that we can have a few minutes with him? I presume he is now at work, and we'd really rather not disturb him there."

Satisfied with his response, and feeling as though she could do nothing more to help George at this time, she suddenly realized that she was nervously fiddling with the engagement and wedding rings on her finger. She unthinkingly glanced at the wedding ring. A very quick thought suddenly rushed through her mind, *why did I ever marry George in the first place? I could have married that handsome William Jeffries. His dad was rich, and we would be living on easy street now. Instead, I got George and now look at the trouble we're having. I just can't stand this.*

Deborah forced her thoughts back to the present and said, "I expect he'll be home this evening. Sometime after eight o'clock."

"Do you mind if we return at that time, Mrs. Sheldon? It's quite important."

Deborah sighed reluctantly and replied, "I'll tell him you came by." With that, she abruptly closed the door, as the two men turned and walked down the ivy-lined slate sidewalk to their car.

That evening when George arrived home, Deborah told him about the two men and what they had to say. George shrugged his shoulders with resignation. *So be it. I guess I should have expected this.*

At exactly eight o'clock that evening, the doorbell rang. Deb was putting away the dinner dishes and George was sitting in his favorite chair reading the newspaper.

"I'll get it," yelled George to his wife, assuming that it would be the two men to see him. He opened the door, and before either man could utter a word, said with resignation, "You fellows must be from the NTSB. My wife told me you would return. Come on in."

They followed him through the living room and into his study, where he offered them chairs. He sat down in the comfortable work chair from his desk, and left the two men to seat themselves in straight-back solid wooden chairs. George did not want the two men to get too comfortable and spend an excessive amount of time during this impending interview.

During the next hour, George explained as best he could, or dared, how he happened to create the commotion on the commuter flight. He was reluctant to mention the SUV, presuming it unbelievable. He fumbled through his "feeling" about the doomed flight, explaining that he really had no idea why he felt that way.

The investigators took careful notes of his conversation, and inquired as to his whereabouts the day before and the morning of the flight. They made a list of all his close friends, and their local addresses. They recorded all the organizations with which George had been affiliated during the past five years. They learned that he had never had flying lessons. He told them that he knew no one at that airport. He also pointed out that he had never before met anyone at the Arnold Company in Newland. He had no connections with Mainline Airlines. No, he knew of no one that would have wanted to cause the plane to crash. When read a list of the names of the victims, George denied knowing any of them.

"I told the pilot to warn the other plane," George said plaintively.

"Yes. We are aware of that Mr. Sheldon. And, for your information, he was promptly fired as soon as Mainline learned of it. The rules specifically require for all airport employees noting *anything* or *anybody* acting out of the ordinary, to report it immediately. We don't want another 'nine-eleven' do we?"

George sat quietly. He reflected, a*t least I tried. It is not my fault that nobody could see the damned SUV. I certainly saw it plainly enough.*

Finally, the lead investigator looked over at his younger partner, who had been squirming in his hard chair for several minutes. Then he turned back to George and said to him, "Well, I think that will be all for now, Mr. Sheldon. We will be back in touch if we have any further questions. Thank you for your time."

George ushered them to the door, closed it behind them, then turned abruptly and walked to the kitchen. There he opened a cabinet, took out a glass and a half-filled bottle of bourbon. Deborah, saying nothing, watched with some surprise and concern, knowing that her husband rarely drank any form of alcohol. The Sheldons kept several bottles of various types of alcoholic beverages in their home for serving drinks to any guests who might request such. However, she still said nothing. After pouring himself a half-glass of the caramel-colored liquid, he downed it quickly, and gave a big shudder. Then he sat down at the table beside her and told her about the evening's discussion.

"I told 'em all about the incident except for the blue SUV," he said.

Deborah responded, "Why didn't you mention that? You told me you saw it."

"They wouldn't have believed me any more than you do. And besides, they probably would have kept on asking me even more questions about it." George rose, moving once again to the cupboard and poured himself another shot of bourbon.

After returning to the table, he sipped on the whiskey as he continued, "I just don't know what the hell's going on. I simply don't know what to do about it."

George had self-analyzed himself many times during the past months and replayed each episode. *Yes, I have seen the SUV each time. In addition, I usually see that damnable devil sitting inside. I have had those annoying ear and taste symptoms each time before I spot the SUV. Moreover, after whenever the particular type of catastrophe has happened, the weird symptoms disappear.* He had absolutely no explanations for any of it. None of it made any sense to him at all. *Nevertheless, it did happen! Dammit! It did!*

George continued to wonder why this entire situation had happened to him. *What have I done to bring this entire emotional trauma down on me? It is horribly distracting, and I cannot get used to all the blood, suffering and screams of pain. The next time it happens, I'm going to confront that bastard and settle this whole thing then and there.*

Deborah listened to her husband's repeat of the evening's conversation with only mild interest. She was inwardly afraid that George's inadvertent involvement with the plane crash might lead the investigators to bring some type of charges against him. She thought, *I'm surprised they didn't arrest him at the airport for talking like that. And then, if they had, what would become of me? If he winds up in prison, how will I live? I have never held a job and have no skills that would help me get some kind of position. After all, he must be the only witness that anticipated the plane crash. Now the government officials are after him. Does he know something that he is not telling anybody or me? Is he in collusion with some bad people? Is he getting money that I don't know about from some gang or terrorists or somebody? On the other hand, is he just going crazy? What else could it be? Oh, I hate this, and I am beginning to hate that husband of mine for getting us into this damn fix in the first place.*

However, no further action came from the NTSB investigators; at least not directed toward George. Months later, their report would declare "pilot error," since no evidence of physical damage or sabotage to the plane or its engines were ever found.

✳   ✳   ✳

George and Deborah went along their standard mostly dull, but mutually accepted way. Their lives gradually returned to their normal as the myriad of a marriage's minute details occupied them. Usually, their increasing number of disagreements remained in the "mild" stage.

George puttered in his greenhouse and garden most weekends and on an occasional evening.

Deborah also puttered in their garden some, tended to her household chores and went to her biweekly bridge club meetings. She volunteered across the street at the nursing home every Thursday. If asked about her husband, she inevitably replied, "Oh, he's just fine, thank you." However, she continued to worry about his emotional upheaval and increasingly heavy drinking.

She decided not to probe her husband about his encounters with the SUV, and George was finally able to push most of his anxieties about it into the dark recesses of his active mind. His work habits improved slightly, and he and Deborah spent their evenings together in quiet harmony. On a few sporadic occasions, they visited friends' small gatherings, and at other times took in movies or traveling Broadway shows. Nevertheless, in each's mind the blazing question continued to linger: What about the mysterious SUV? Satan? This remained unsettled and unspoken by both, as neither had any desire to disturb their quiet controlled bliss. George often searched for the SUV on his daily drive to and from work. However, since it made no recent appearances, and he did not find himself with either the ear or taste sensations, he soon more or less forgot and settled into his regular routine.

CHAPTER SEVEN

ONE DAY EIGHT MONTHS later, George would not follow his normal route home from work.

Just as he was about to leave home one morning, Deborah said to him, "George honey, how about running out to the Discount Fabric Center for me this evening after work. Okay? I realize that it's a little out of your way, but it'll save me a lot of time."

"Yeah, well okay." George replied, standing in the open front doorway. "Where is that?"

"Over on the West side of town. It's on Spring Street. It should not take you very long. It's not very far out of your way."

"Way out there? What's there that you need? I mean, you don't expect me to pick something out for you, do you?"

"No, of course not. Wait a second and I'll give you a slip of paper with all the numbers on it." George suddenly realized *she is speaking to me as if I am a child or one of the senile patients across the street. That's belittling and I don't like her attitude.* "All you have to do is hand it to the clerk, and she'll take care of the rest. It's for a piece of cloth I need in order to finish a housedress that I'm making. Shouldn't cost over a few dollars."

Knowing that he needed to drive not "a little," but considerably out of the way on his trip home, he had left the office earlier than usual. Leaving early was rarely a serious problem. Although his employer was a stickler for arriving on time, at eight o'clock, Mr. Williams himself usually left his office about four o'clock. Thus, if their particular tasks were completed, the executive staff felt quite free to leave soon after that.

While he was waiting for a stoplight to switch from red to green, George suddenly noticed it! *Oh my God! It's back again! The damn ear tickling and bad taste is back. No! No! Now what? Dammit! Oh dammit to hell! Won't this ever stop?* He felt his face flush and he broke out in a cold sweat. His fingers squeezed the steering wheel as he felt a sudden tenseness in his stomach muscles. *Where is it? Where is the SUV? It has to be around here somewhere. What's going to happen now? Oh God, no! Why does this have to happen to me? What will happen now?* He briefly squeezed his eyes tightly, hoping in vain that somehow, that would stop his symptoms.

George looked frantically out the car window to his right, left, and kept checking his rearview mirror. He could see nothing out of the ordinary. Yet, the awful signs remained with him. He was very apprehensive. He just knew now that something horrible was going to happen—and probably very soon. *But, what would it be? Should I call the police? The fire department? What could I say to them? In addition, what can I do, except to continue my drive until I reach the fabric shop?*

His alarming warning signs began to become more intense. He worried if he would become sick to his stomach. He felt a trickle of sweat run down the back of his neck. This was becoming maddening to him. He pulled a tissue from the box that Deborah kept in the car and mopped his wet brow. Again, slowing his speed George kept his head swiveling back and forth in his effort to locate the dreaded light blue SUV. He drove on, one block after another, with no sign of it. His tingling and foul taste continued to grow stronger. *When will I find it? How much longer will I have? Oh God! Why is this happening to me? What can I do?*

His drive had now taken him into the far outskirts of the city, where big industrial complexes were located. *Now why in the world had Deb come all this way just for a piece of cloth? You would think she could have found some much closer to home. Stupid bitch. What a dumb thing*, George thought. *If I didn't have to drive all the way out here, maybe I could have avoided the damn SUV.*

Suddenly, as George was passing a large oil refinery with a huge oil storage tank farm, he spotted the SUV. It was beside one of the cracking towers of the refinery. *Good Lord! It will be a total catastrophe if that thing blows up.* As George looked around, he realized that an old mobile home park was just across the street from the plant.

"Oh my God!" exclaimed George to no one. His fingers squeezed the steering wheel to the point of pain. "I've got to try to stop it."

Frightened about the potentials, George hurriedly drove into the entrance to the refinery. He stopped at the chain-link fence gate. The attending guard put down his coffee cup and slid open the glass window of the guardhouse. "Wha'cha want?" said the guard, frustrated by having his TV viewing disturbed. George hastily spoke back to the balding guard. He appeared to George to be nearing seventy, and was grossly overweight. "I need to see the plant manager right away. It's very important."

"Can't do that. He ain't here no more," replied the guard casually. "Left the plant about an hour ago." The guard started to slide the window closed.

George was taken aback. *Why would an important company like this one hire a slovenly idiot like this old geezer to be a guard?* George knew he simply must warn someone of the impending peril. It was going to happen. He just did not have any indication when. He was becoming distraught in his worry. Angry and frustrated with the guard, George reached out his left hand from his car, and stopped the window from closing completely.

He said rapidly, "Well, who's in charge then?"

The guard, not being impressed with George's obvious distress, picked up his mug and took a long sip of his coffee. Then he looked over at a clipboard lying beside him, and turned back to George. He acted as if he was seriously bothered by being forced to shift his attention away from his small black-and-white television show. George could see that the guard had been watching an old rerun from the *Andy Griffith Show.*

"Billy Turnbull's supposed to be here right now. He's the assistant plant manager. Wanna talk to him? What's your name for my record?"

"My name is George Sheldon and yes, absolutely. I need to speak with him right away. It's urgent. Come on, now. Please hurry," said George, becoming more and more distressed. His ear and taste symptoms were increasing to near distraction.

The slovenly guard slowly took a pencil, touched its tip to his tongue, and began to write on his clipboard.

"George Sheldon," he said slowly. "Is that spelled with a 't' or a 'd'?"

"It's Sheldon, damn you. S-h-e-l-d-o-n. Now for Christ's sake, hurry up and let me in. It's very urgent!" George's exasperation was causing him to become even more upset. *How much more time do I have?* His warning sensations were now stronger and becoming worse than ever.

He had no way of knowing when the incident might occur—only that it would. *I sure as hell don't want to be around here when it blows.*

"Where can I find this guy? Can I get in to see him now?" George anxiously peered through the fence gate, and could still spot the SUV.

The guard moved with what appeared to be the speed of a sleepy snail on a frosty day. *Hurry, damn you, hurry!* After what seemed to be an eternity to George, the guard finally looked closely at him, then turned to his left and pushed a switch. The gate slowly began to open.

"Where can I find him?" asked George, his patience now running out. "Where's his office? Show me where to go. C'mon, hurry!"

"Well," he slowly said, "you go straight on in and when you get to that first trailer, turn left and it's the next one beside it. The black one."

George barely heard the guard's last words. He drove faster than he knew he should, with his tires skidding and throwing fragments of oily gravel, but he was becoming more and more frenzied by the minute. *How much time do I have left? I've gotta tell 'em and then get myself out of here.*

Sliding the car to a halt on the gravel drive, he quickly flipped off the ignition, and dashed up the four wooden steps and into the trailer.

"Where can I find Turnbull? Quickly!" George said rapidly to the young secretary, sitting behind a computer. Her printer was noisily spewing out documents.

She turned to him and said, "Sir, I'm afraid I didn't hear what you said. This printer makes so much noise, I can hardly think. I have asked and asked them to replace it, but they just don't ever get around to it. You'd think a company this big could afford to get me a new one, wouldn't you? Here, I have been with this company for three years and you'd think they would care a little about how I feel. Now wouldn't you, huh mister?"

Once again, George felt his face turn crimson, and he became very vexed. *What can I do to make this girl realize that I'm in a hurry?*

"I said I need to talk to Turnbull—right away. Quickly. It's very urgent."

"Oh? Well let me see where he is. I think he went over to one of the other buildings a few minutes ago," replied the young lady casually. She raised her hand and studied her polished nails.

Oh my God! Can't anyone around here pay attention to me when I say something's urgent?

"Miss," spoke George, his patience wearing thin, "It's imperative that you locate him immediately! It may well be a matter of life and death. I am serious. Now find him—fast!"

She peered at him curiously for several seconds, but finally leaned over an intercom speaker, pushed a button, and called, "Billy, you over there?"

A voice crackled over her receiver, "Yeah, 'course I'm here. What do you want? Dammit, I just finished telling you I'd be back in a few minutes."

The secretary spoke back into the speaker again; "There's a mister..." She stopped, looked up at George and said to him, "What did you say your name was?"

"Sheldon, George Sheldon," uttered George in his distress. "Tell him he doesn't know me, but I have to talk to him right now, and it's very urgent."

"Billy, he says his name is George Sheldon and he needs to talk to you right away. Can you come back here or shall I send him over there?"

George felt like grabbing the speaker off her desk. *Could nobody at this plant pay attention to him? Time might be running out!*

"Hey, let's see. I'm almost finished here. Tell him to have a seat in my office, and I'll be back over there in a few minutes," crackled the intercom.

George was becoming increasingly frantic. His patience had run out. He had lives to save. He quickly moved around the desk, pushed the button and spoke rapidly and harshly into the intercom. "Listen, Turnbull, what I've got to say can affect your life, and everybody around here. Now get your ass over here right now. You hear me good?"

"Well goddam, fellow," replied Turnbull quizzically. "I don't know you, but don't get your balls in an uproar. Okay. I'll stop what I'm doing, but you'd better be damn sure it's really important. Out."

George paced around the small office. He suddenly realized that he was hyper-ventilating—almost to the point of dizziness. Finally, he heard the front door slam and a gruff, heavyset man of about forty stomped in, his unshaven, reddened face filled with rage. He was clothed in a tan jumpsuit partially covered with oil stains. He did not remove his streaked silver hard hat. George read the name "Turnbull" printed on the front of the helmet in bright Day-Glo orange. The man pulled a dirty rag from his rear pocket and began to wipe grease from his hands. He stared angrily at George.

"I'm Turnbull. Now what the hell's this all about?" He did not offer George a handshake.

George took a deep breath as he and Turnbull stood facing each other.

"Sorry to bother you, but I have to tell you that I think your plant's going to have a major accident soon."

Billy Turnbull stared at George with disbelief.

"What in the hell are you trying to pull, mister? And just who the hell do you think you are to come in here and say something like that?" Turnbull moved somewhat closer to George in a menacing fashion. He had balled up his fists, and his red face was exuding sweat droplets.

George stepped back slightly, and continued, "I can't tell you what will happen or even when, because I don't know. But I can only tell you that you need to shut the place down and get everybody out as soon as you can." He could not help but notice that Turnbull was furious at being disturbed, as well as hearing such an absurd story.

"Aw now, come clean mister," said Turnbull. "What in the hell are you talking about? Are you threatening me? You some kind of terrorist or something? Well I ain't buying it. Now just you get the hell off my property or I call the cops. You hear me good?" He grabbed George's elbow and roughly shoved him out through the front room to the steps. "Now get the hell away from here, you hear?"

Flabbergasted, George uttered, "But, you really do need to clear the plant! I promise you this is not a personal threat, but just a warning that something is definitely going to happen here—probably this afternoon or tonight. Please pay attention to me."

He grabbed George by the front of his shirt, and lifted him up onto his toes with his force, his face torqued in anger.

"I told you, mister, and I'm gonna say it one last time. Get the hell away from here and don't you ever let me see your face around here again. Now git!"

Seeing it was all to no avail, and he could not possibly convince the man of the dangers he faced, George got into his car anxious and perplexed. *What to do? What can I do?* As he was starting his car, he turned his head and searched for the blue SUV. *There! It's still there!* His physical symptoms were continuing—stronger than ever. George was at his wit's end! What could he possibly do? How could he carry on now? His ear was continuing to tingle. He had the usual evil taste in his mouth. Yes, he had all the usual symptoms that he had before when the other disasters occurred. He knew something terrible was bound to happen there at the refinery, and yet he felt powerless to prevent it. He simply did not know how. The burden of his anxiety was almost overwhelming.

He started to drive away from the trailer, but then stopped abruptly. Exiting his car, he ran across the large yard to the blue vehicle. It was just sitting there, motor humming quietly, with the evil red-skinned driver inside, staring at him. He grinned at George just as he had done previously. George was going to confront the evil man. He motioned with his hand for the side window to be lowered. Nothing. The individual inside just sat there with the corners of his mouth raised, exposing his yellow teeth. George tried the door handle and found it locked. He slapped on the window with his fist, then the top of the SUV. Still nothing. The driver looked around, and then turned his face back toward George.

"Satan," George screamed, "Get out of there and talk to me! Come on, you son of a bitch—get out!"

The red-skinned individual smiled, but did not start to exit his SUV.

George saw two refinery workers nearby. "Hey, you guys," he hollered, "Come here and help me."

The two men stopped and peered curiously at George. One spoke to the other, and then they walked on.

Increasingly angry and frustrated, George looked around, found a large rock and banged it forcibly against the window glass. It did not show any change. He crashed the stone against the top of the vehicle's hood time after time. It did not even scratch the eerie light blue paint. Seeing it all to no avail, George stepped away from the SUV and threw the stone at the vehicle's window as hard as he could. It made no sound as it fell harmlessly to the ground. Terribly frustrated and angry, George yelled loudly at the driver, "You evil devil bastard! I hope you burn in hell!"

George finally left the refinery grounds in a storm of exasperation. *I tried to get that son-of-a-bitch out of his car where I could at least talk to him. Nothing I tried worked. How can I stop him? I simply don't know what to do.* He turned his car in the direction of the trailer park just down the street. Maybe someone there would listen to his pleas. Although he did not see anyone out and about, he judged that there might still be a few people in their trailers. *Perhaps I can find someone in there that will listen to me, and maybe evacuate,* he thought. *If I can't stop the devil from doing his atrocious deeds, maybe at least I can save some lives.*

Turning onto the park grounds, he parked beside a single automobile in the small parking lot. He rapidly walked into the main building where he read a sign: OFFICE. Entering quickly, he found a secretary casually leaning on a counter. She was smoking an unfiltered cigarette and working a crossword puzzle. An obviously old stereo was playing at full volume across the small room. She turned when he appeared and asked if she could help him.

"I need to speak to the manager here right away," spoke George. He spoke at the top of his voice over the music. "It is very important, and urgent."

"Huh? Why just a moment," said the secretary. She was a middle-aged full-figured woman, with her once-brown salt-and-pepper hair pulled back into a tight bun. She walked across the room and twisted the music down to a whisper. Turning back to George, she frowned and said, "Does this concern one of our residents?" She flicked her ashes on the worn painted floor. "Are you from the police?"

"No!" George suddenly realized that he was almost yelling. He lowered his voice somewhat. "Now will you go ahead and get the manager out here. Please. It's very urgent."

She said, "He just went down to the store a coupla minutes ago. He oughta be back pretty soon. Wanna sit down and wait for him?"

George could not help but wonder how much time he had left before the tragedy struck. He glanced down at his watch, but then realized that that would not give him any clues as to when the refinery might blow...or whatever would happen. *Is my time almost gone?* He had no way to tell. His hands were shaking. The other previous situations with the SUV had exhibited warning times from almost instantaneous to days. *What would it be this time?* How long had the blue SUV been at the refinery before George spotted it? *Oh Lord, what else can happen now? She doesn't know when he'll get back. I need to get this place evacuated. Oh, I'm so sick of this ungodly mess. Well, if her boss isn't here, maybe I should tell her.*

However, after less than half a minute, a freckled-faced man of about thirty came in a side door. He had bright red hair in crew cut style with sideburns. He was carrying a six-pack of sodas. Looking at his visitor, he offered a friendly smile.

"Good afternoon," he said to George pleasantly. He glanced at the secretary. "Can I help you? Do you want to rent a home here?" He extended his hand toward George. "Actually, we have one on the market now. Interested in buying?"

George moved forward, shook the man's hand, and as discretely as he could manage in his agitated state, said, "I don't have time to explain it all to you now, but you'd best evacuate the entire place right away."

The secretary, casually leaning against the office door, straightened up, opening her eyes as big as saucers in surprise.

The young man frowned deeply. He glanced around in startling disbelief. "What on earth are you talking about, sir?"

"Now listen carefully. I have certain knowledge that the refinery across the street is going to have a major accident and probably blow up very soon."

The manager's face paled, and his expression of concern spoke volumes. He braced himself with one hand on his neat desk. Clearly, he was immediately concerned and listened intently to what this stranger was saying.

George continued, "How many people are living here in the park? How long will it take to get everybody out and away from here?" He noticed the expression of distress come on the man's clean-shaven face. "Believe me," George continued, "this is very serious. I mean it. Something awful is going to happen. But I don't know how much time we have."

The young manager had only been on the job for little more than a year and so far, everything had gone quite well. Now, however, this was a very sober decision for him. Clearly, he was taken aback with what this anxious stranger had to say. He was aware that there were at a minimum, at least a dozen residents there now. This would mean a great deal of time would be necessary to contact everybody. If this was as urgent as this obviously frantic man was suggesting, there might not be enough time for a proper evacuation. He was all too aware that mobile homes do not fare too well in severe winds like tornadoes and hurricanes. An explosion across the street could be devastating.

On the other hand, could it be a false alarm? *Was this stranger standing before him some kind of fruitcake?* Yet, somehow, as he looked into George's agonized face, he perceived honesty. He believed his visitor, and felt that he had no time for questioning him or for contacting the police or fire department for any type of confirmation. He must act right now!

He moved past George and spoke rapidly to the secretary, "Marti, get out and tell everybody to get away from here as fast as they can." He stole a quick glance at George. "I'll go get Mrs. Aldridge into her wheelchair and outside. You get Hank Stone to stop by her trailer and pick her up."

"Mr. Stone?"

"Yeah. I just saw him pull into the park half an hour ago, so I know he's there. He'll do it. You heard this guy say that the refinery up the street may blow up soon!"

George found that he was left behind and ignored in the shuffle. He was at least delighted and comforted that someone was finally heeding his frantic pleas. The young manager actually seemed to believe him. *Thank God!* He did not know if any of the trailers would be damaged if the refinery blew, but, just in case, maybe some lives could be saved after all. He felt relieved as he rapidly walked back to his car. He could hear the secretary and manager calling to various trailers and knocking on doors. Shortly he saw numerous people, including a few youngsters, rapidly leaving the buildings. Several cars sped past him out of the lot. He breathed a deep sigh of relief, and realized that he was sweating heavily.

What George did not realize was that the young manager felt that although there was absolutely no proof of truth in George's warning, he could ill afford to take any chances with his wards. He could take the heat from his employer for a false alarm later, if necessary. The young redheaded man looked around for George after he had finished alerting everybody, but could not locate him.

As George was about to head his car down the street away from the mobile home park and refinery, he became aware of sirens in the distance. The secretary had apparently sent an alert to the fire department after all. *Well*, thought George, *that's good. When the refinery blows, the fire department and police will already be on the scene. Maybe that will keep damage at a minimum and save lives.* He felt a huge wave of relief sweep over him like a soft summer breeze. He began to breathe more easily. His hands were still trembling as he realized that his shirt was drenched with sweat.

George drove down the street as a police car and two fire trucks, blue and red lights flashing brightly approached him at high speed on their way toward the mobile home park. In his rearview mirror, he also spotted another fire truck coming toward the park from the opposite direction.

Just at that very moment, George was about to redirect his eyes toward the front of his car when he caught a glimpse of something that startled him. The hairs on the back of his neck prickled. He spotted two men running across the street, away from the refinery. One almost ran into the side of the passing fire truck, jumping back out of its way just in time. All at once, there was a sun-bright flash, a huge tower of flame and a tremendous explosion occurred! *Oh Lord, it has happened!* Almost instantly, George felt his car pushed by an invisible hand as the force of the explosion hit it. He had to fight to regain control. He peered once again in his mirror and saw that one of the fire trucks was now on its side in front of the now-flaming refinery.

George stopped his car, got out, and looked back at the inferno. Even at a distance of over half a mile, he could easily hear the "swoosh" of the multiple geysers of flames as they erupted from the various refinery towers. Several additional explosions occurred. He could not see anyone walking from the fire truck. He assumed that they were killed or critically injured from the flames and pressure of the explosion. Nor could he spot the two unidentified men he had seen running from the area just before it blew.

In a tormented eruption of anger and frustration, George looked up into the sky at the drifting black smoke. He raised his clenched fist. "Damn you! Damn you to hell, you damn evil devil and your SUV! Why are you killing all these innocent people around me? Why are you doing this? Why don't you just kill me and be done with it?" He fell on his knees and cried unashamedly.

Finally rising again, he noted with dismay that the thick grass surrounding the trailer park was now burning. He had correctly guessed that the growing flames from the refinery might race across the street with fury. All of this seemed to have taken no more than a minute. He looked at the office building and noted it was no longer resting on its foundation. Several of the trailers had been demolished. With some additional self-satisfaction, he could see that a few individuals were continuing to dash away from the park—safely. They congregated in small groups, and watched as the firefighters began to stretch out their hoses and pour water and foam onto the inferno. Shortly, he heard more sirens in the distance as additional fire equipment and police began to arrive. George also noted happily that ambulances also arrived and the paramedics were tending to some of the injured firefighters from the overturned truck.

George felt that he had seen entirely too much horror during the past two years. He slowly drove himself on toward his home—his inner torment beginning to dominate his thinking. He had forgotten about Deb's fabric.

When he arrived home, he found Deborah sitting in front of the television, watching live pictures of the refinery disaster.

She looked up and said, "Hey George. Sit down and watch this. There has been a terrible disaster at that oil refinery on the other side of town. Just look at these scenes. They say that at this time they do not know what happened at the refinery to make it blow up, but that a trailer park across the street was heavily damaged when the first explosion occurred. There have been several additional blasts, too. They say that several big chunks of metal were blown nearly a half mile away." She looked back at the screen and added, "Did you remember to get my cloth?"

George grimaced to himself. *The bitch doesn't even care about the people that were killed. Or even the fact that some folks lost their homes. All she wants is her damn cloth.* He laid his briefcase on the table beside the door, took off his overcoat, hung it carefully and methodically in the closet, and then sat down beside his wife to watch the scenes again. Deborah leaned over and gave him a perfunctory kiss on the cheek, and then turned back to her viewing. George said nothing, but just sat there, his mind in terrible turmoil.

Deborah nudged him in the side gently saying, "They say that some man ran into the trailer park's office warning them about the explosion even before it happened, and they evacuated most of the people living there. That probably saved a bunch of lives." Deb paused. She did not look at George, but kept her attention glued to the television screen. "They said they're looking for the man for questioning."

George said only, "Humph." Then he got up, picked up his briefcase and strolled into their study. After all, he had been there in person. He had no desire to watch any more of the tragedy, instead preferring to busy himself at his computer. He saw no need to discuss it with his wife. His mind was racing. *What, oh*

CHAPTER EIGHT

It WAS A COOL Saturday, cloudy, having rained just before daybreak. Deborah wanted George to drive them over to the next town, some thirty miles north of the city, to visit a fashionable antique mall. She wanted to find a small table to place under a mirror hanging in their hallway.

"You're perfectly capable of driving yourself. I've got a pretty good novel I'm reading," responded George. He did not feel like being a chauffeur for her today.

She said pleadingly, "Oh come on, and bring your book with you. You can sit in the car and read while I am looking. Then if I find something interesting, I can come out and get you to come in and okay it. That work with you?"

"Oh well," he resignedly. "I suppose."

The two were donning their all-weather coats when the doorbell rang. Opening his front door, George noted a squatty man of about sixty with thinning gray hair, wearing a beige trench coat. George could not help but notice that the man's coat badly needed pressing, and was missing two buttons. He reminded him of an old television show, where the protagonist, a police detective who always got his man, wore a similar trench coat as his "shtick." He could not immediately recall the name of the detective or the show. Besides, he had only watched the show a couple of times, finding it basically one plot, replayed with different locations.

George observed a police cruiser, blue lights flashing, being driven by a uniformed officer waiting in his driveway.

"Yeah?" George asked of the man standing on his front stoop. George suddenly had a bad feeling about this man.

"Mr. George Sheldon?" inquired the man, keeping his hands in the pockets of his trench coat.

George replied, almost knowing what this guy might want with him, "Yeah, that's me. What do you want? My wife and I were just on our way out."

"Sir, I am Detective Johnson, with the city police department, and I need a few words with you." He pulled out his wallet and showed his badge to George. "May I come in?"

Deborah walked into the living room, glanced out the window, and noted the flashing lights atop the black-and-white. Her anger topped that of her husband's as she began to think that they were being treated as if he had committed some heinous crime. She could just imagine all their neighbors peering out their windows, then gossiping about what must be going on over at the Sheldons. She was mortified that George's actions had brought this mess down on them. *What on earth has he done now? Damn his sorry hide! I'm embarrassed to death. This is absolutely awful. Damn him!*

George turned his head as he stood holding the door, and looked over at Deborah. He rolled his eyes upward, as she placed both her hands on her hips in a show of embarrassed disgust.

"Can't you come back another time?" asked George in his most polite manner. "We really need to be on our way."

Deborah added from the living room, "Yeah. We've got this trip all planned."

"Sir, ma'am, this is a matter of major importance." He did not bother to look at Deborah. "I just need to ask you a few short questions, and it shouldn't take very long." He took a couple of steps forward, as if he would not take "no" for an answer.

"Oh all right. Come on in," replied a resigned George Sheldon. "Deborah, this is Detective…Uh, what did you say your name was?" Deborah peered at the man as he entered without removing his noticeably soiled raincoat.

"Johnson," he replied, barely glancing at Deborah as he walked impertinently past her and into their living room. There he abruptly sat down on their couch and pulled a note pad out of his inner coat pocket. He fumbled in his shirt pocket for a moment, finally coming out with a green ballpoint pen. He looked at the tip of his pen as if to ascertain that its point was in the writing position.

"Mrs. Sheldon, as I just said to your husband here, I'm Detective Johnson. George quickly realized that the man had an obvious affectation of popping the pen point in and out, in and out. I am very sorry to intrude like this, but as I just told…," he turned and looked George squarely in the face. "George here, it should only take a very few minutes." He popped his pen. "Then you can be on your way." *Pop! Pop!*

With that said, he motioned for George sit in the adjacent chair beside the couch. *Damned rude,* thought George. *Making me to sit down in my own chair in my own house.* Nevertheless, George did sit down, while Deborah took off her coat and moved into the back of their home.

"Now sir," began Johnson. "I have information that you visited the Electra Refinery just a short time before it blew up last week. Is that correct?" *Pop! Pop!*

This question stunned George. How did this person know that?

"Well. Ugh, yes, I was there for a few minutes. Why? Is it important? I think I was lucky that I left before the explosion. Don't you think so too?" George hoped this answer would disarm the detective.

Johnson stared at him for a moment without exhibiting any emotion. "According to our information, you were signed in at the guard's booth at four seventeen that afternoon." *Pop! Pop! Pop!* "Does that sound about right to you?"

"I suppose so. I went in to speak to the manager, but he wasn't there, so I talked to another guy, whose name I don't remember."

Johnson jotted down a few items on his pad, then looked over at George again and said, "That would have been a William Turnbull. Is that correct?"

"Yeah, I guess that sounds about right. You know, that jerk threw me out. He was very rude to me."

"Mr. Turnbull was horribly burned in the explosion, and is not expected to live. However, in fact, just before they carried him away in the ambulance, he told one of the paramedics tending to him that some guy had just warned him that something bad was going to happen at the plant. Now, Mr. Sheldon, I ask you: are you that man?" *Pop! Pop!*

Damn, damn, damn, George thought to himself. *How in the hell did they find that out so soon? And, why in the hell has this been happening to me, anyway? What in the hell have I done to become the brunt of all this mess? All because of that devil and the damned light blue SUV.*

Reluctantly, George stammered, "Yes, Detective Johnson, I was there. I cannot tell you how I knew, but a feeling just came over me that something bad was about to happen at that refinery. I tried to get that guy Turnbull to evacuate everybody, but he just threw me out. Would not even listen to me. But, at least I tried." George took a deep breath. He listened to the incessant popping of the detective's ballpoint pen. *I don't think there's any point in mentioning that I tried to confront the devil.* He continued, "Then, I went over to the mobile home park, and had it cleared out. That saved a bunch of lives, don't you think?" George knew he was in some kind of trouble, but felt he had to do everything possible to help relieve his burden. *Pop! Pop!* Maybe mentioning his doing the park bit would help his case. George became very uncomfortable. What could the detective do to him? After all, George knew, he had done nothing wrong. On the contrary, he had actually tried to prevent any injuries. George had expected when he pulled into the refinery that he would not likely be able to stop some sort of an accident from happening, but at least he thought he might get the place evacuated before whatever was destined to happen occurred.

"Mr. Sheldon," the detective responded, continuing to pop his pen, "Let me get this straight. You say that you just had a 'feeling,' like a premonition maybe, that you'd better get everybody to evacuate the entire refinery plant. Is that your story?" Johnson had emphasized the word, "feeling" as if to say it was incredulous.

"Yes, that's about it."

"One of the burned survivors told us that they saw some guy standing out in the refinery yard ranting and raving and carrying on. He said the fellow acted very angry and acted as if he was talking to somebody. Yet there wasn't anybody there."

George sputtered, "That was probably me. I tried to get some help."

He glanced down at his pad, hesitated momentarily, and then looked back at George. "And you say you cannot explain why this feeling came over you. It just did. Is that correct?" Johnson asked this with a skeptical tone to his voice. *What kind of a story is this yokel trying to feed me, anyway? Does he think I'm an imbecile?*

George could easily note the expression of doubt on his visitor's face. But, what else could he say? He certainly could not talk about the SUV and his warning symptoms. When even his wife chose not to believe him, how could he expect anyone else to? George was very discouraged, and becoming more and more afraid of his future. The great unknown was alarming to him.

Johnson looked down at his pad again, and stopped popping his pen for a full minute. Silence enveloped the room like a tight glove. George heard a noisy motorcycle roar past his house on the street outside. He glanced through the open blinds out the front window and saw the patrol car's blue lights still flashing. He said nothing, and then just stared back at the detective.

Johnson had learned over the years that sometimes his silence could be unnerving to the subjects that he was interviewing. He remembered the so-called axiom from his long-ago high school days, "Nature abhors a vacuum," never exactly understanding what it really meant. In fact, many times he recalled that he had passed his physics class with a "D minus". Damned old Miss Hatley never did like him. She could just as well have given him a "C". Nevertheless, Johnson remembered, she always seemed to cater to the jocks, and he was forced to keep after-school jobs in order to help prop up his mother's meager income. Dad had walked away to parts unknown when young Jesse Johnson was four years old. At any rate, the detective had become an intense student of human nature as a novice police rookie, and his superiors had quickly observed his ability to get his suspects to confess. (The truth?) Johnson's technique typically worked well when following his own tried and true axiom, "Suspects abhor a silence." Johnson used his trick of "silence" often, and during an interrogation, he would simply stop speaking and stare at the detainee. This, he found often allowed the ensuing dead silence to besiege the suspect, much like a dark room can throw a small child into a panic. This usually created wonderful results. It rarely failed, because, hating the silence, or feeling awkward, the suspect would frequently speak up with something that Johnson could find useful. Perhaps it would even open up a new line of questioning. A buddy at the station had suggested the "pen-popping" contrivance to him as a precursor to the silence, to further disrupt his interviewee's thinking patterns.

But George switched his staring to the floor and remained silent, as did his tormentor.

After a moment, the detective, realizing that his ploy did not have the desired effect on George, said, "Sir, I have been informed that you also were also involved with that Mainline airplane crash that occurred a while back. Would you care to comment on that?" *Pop! Pop!*

This took George aback. He had not realized that anyone other than the NTSB was aware of his involvement with the crash. After all, these were two different agencies: The NTSB and the city police department. Could he be getting a reputation with the law enforcement people? How was it that the two agencies, one national, one local, were in touch with each other? *I have to tell him. There's no way any other answer will satisfy him. I don't want to, because it will make me look like a nut. However, what choice do I have?*

He said, "Okay, Mr. Johnson, here's the absolute truth: I have been warned about these things by seeing an oversized light blue sport utility vehicle in the vicinity of the potential accident. I think the driver is the actual devil."

"What?" interrupted the stunned detective? "You say you are warned by seeing a simple blue SUV?"

George paused, listened to Deborah rattling some dishes in the kitchen. He figured that she was probably fixing a snack. Then, he took a deep breath and continued, "Well, sort of. The SUV is real big—bigger than normal—and a very light blue. It even has light blue tires. I also get a strange tingling in the upper tips of my ears and a lousy taste in my mouth before whatever is going to happen, happens." He had an instantaneous thought about the possible incorrectness of his grammar, but figured this damn detective probably would not even notice it. George noted the strange interest in his interviewer's eyes, as the detective glanced away for a brief moment. "I have no explanation for any of this," continued George. "I just woke up one morning last year and it started happening."

The detective said nothing, but continued popping his pen. This time he was unconsciously doing it as he wondered where this conversation was now heading. He was curious as to what his colleagues back at the station would say about this one. He reached up and scratched a vague itch on the top of his head with the end of his pen, then casually glanced around the room. After some time he said to George, "Sir, that's a very interesting story, but frankly makes no sense to me. I'll tell you what: I want you to come down to the station with me and tell this story to some of my colleagues." The detective thought to himself, *I want the police shrink to hear this crazy tale.*

George stammered, "Come down to the station with you? Now?" He looked over towards the door of the kitchen, wondering if his wife had heard. "But we're scheduled to go out. I told you that. How about waiting until we get back from our trip, and then I'll swing on by the police station?" Somehow, George strongly suspected that Johnson would ignore this request.

"Sir, I want us to go to the station right now," the detective said with firmness. "Please get your coat back on and we'll take my car. Tell you wife you'll be back after awhile."

"Am I being arrested? Do I need to call my lawyer?"

"Oh, no sir, this is just for an informal group interview." Standing and handing George's coat to him, he continued, "Perhaps we can clarify this matter better at the station. Some of my associates may have some questions for you. I am not charging you with anything, but certainly, you must realize that some of your story contains some way-out responses. Okay, now let's get along."

George walked to the kitchen door, where he found Deborah rinsing out a coffee cup. He gathered that she was more or less aware, but said, loud enough for Johnson to hear, "Honey, I'm running down town to the police station with Detective Johnson for a little while. We will leave for our trip when I get back. Okay?"

Turning, and expressing a view of anguish, his wife uttered, "Well, hurry back." She wanted to say, "Being arrested are you? You damn fool. Now maybe you will get yourself straightened out. You are embarrassing me half to death with all these shenanigans. Seeing things, huh? Ear tingling? Foul taste? What a bunch of unbelievable junk." At the moment however, she held back on her desire to zap him with her feelings. *George Sheldon, I am beginning to believe you are really going nutty. Now they are arresting you! What in the hell will happen to us next? And, now you've gone to drinking heavily. I am just about at my wit's end with you, and don't know how much more of this I can stand. Now everybody will have seen a police car in our driveway with those blue lights flashing. A uniformed cop. Oh, the sheer embarrassment of it all.*

"Okay, honey, just call me if you get delayed," Deborah said to him stiffly, as she walked over to him and kissed him lightly on the cheek.

George donned his coat and grudgingly followed Johnson to his car. He presumed neighbors were watching. He just knew that that damned old busybody, Ralph Crasty, who lived in the nursing home directly across the street, would be peering out his window. *As a matter of fact*, thought George, glancing across the street as he opened the right rear door of the police cruiser, *I can see the curtains pulled back right now. That nosy old son of a bitch. It will not take five minutes for the entire population of that place to know all about this.* George strapped on his seat belt, and Johnson's driver backed out of the drive. To George's relief, the driver had finally turned off the flashing blue lights. He was also thankful that the driver did not turn on his siren.

At the police station, George was led into a windowless interrogation room, roughly fifteen feet square, offered coffee in a Styrofoam cup, no sugar or creamer available. "Sorry." There he sat in a straight-backed wooden chair as the detective excused himself. Two other similar chairs in the room surrounded an ancient beat-up wooden table. George looked directly in front of him at a large mirror attached to the wall. Having seen a number of police/detective television shows, George rightly assumed that there were probably viewers surreptitiously observing him from beyond his view. That made him feel self-conscious and uncomfortable. He felt the need to pick at his nose, but declined to do so. He was clothed in a dark blue jumpsuit and dirty sneakers. He somehow wished that he he'd had an opportunity to dress a bit more formally. He felt as though he would be able to make an appearance that was more dignified had he dressed up in a suit and tie. George began to wonder if he would need a quick trip to the toilet. He did not spot one on his way in, but as he sat there in the hard chair, he realized that he had begun to feel a slight pressure in his bladder. Having had two cups of coffee for breakfast only a couple of hours ago, and now a third one, he was reminded that caffeine-laced liquids had always traveled through his body with amazing rapidity.

His physician had once jokingly informed George that he suffered from "CI/COR Syndrome." Seeing George turn pale and nearly faint when he told him that, he promptly explained that it humorously stood for "Coffee In/Coffee Out—Rapidly." Only then, did George relax and understand the morbid humor offered by the doctor.

He figured he could wait for a little while longer. Besides, it might give him a needed break if the upcoming questioning got uncomfortably tough.

George had tried to question Detective Johnson on the drive to the station, but all he got was an abrupt, "We'll see. Now just sit back and enjoy your chauffeured ride." Then, Johnson grinned at his attempted humor.

After about an hour of impatient waiting, George finally saw the door open. In walked Detective Johnson along with two other individuals. One was a well-dressed African-American lady of about sixty, wearing, what he had heard Deborah call, a pinstriped navy blue "power suit." She appeared to be at least six feet tall. The other person was a man wearing a bright red turtleneck, navy blazer, well-creased gray slacks and Birkenstock sandals with no socks. This man appeared to be in his mid-thirties, with a heavy dark brown beard, penetrating gray eyes, and swept-back hair ending in a braided pigtail. He was carrying a metal folding chair. George learned from Johnson's formal introductions that the matronly lady was Lieutenant Cotton, another police detective. In fact, she was Johnson's supervisor. The other man was introduced as Dr. Mitchell, a local psychiatrist on call to help the police department from time to time. The interrogation began…

*   *   *

The police finally returned George to his home at eleven that evening. He was totally exhausted and frazzled. This time he was discretely delivered in a plain, non-marked police car. *Why in hell could they not have come this morning without the lights flashing?* He found Deborah already in bed, but as he entered the bedroom, she rolled over, flipped on the bedside lamp and asked him what happened.

"Good God, Deb," snapped a drained George, pulling off his sweat-stained jumpsuit. "I'm too tired to talk about it now. Wait'll morning and I'll tell you then. Okay?"

Not giving her an opportunity to answer, he walked into the bathroom and turned on the shower faucet. He noticed that the shower stall was still dripping with moisture and condensation, so his wife had not been in bed long. What he needed right now was certainly not another defensive conversation with Deborah. *Hell no, not right now.* He needed a good hot, stinging shower, followed by a stiff drink, then bed. Oh, how good that bed was going to feel! He was thoroughly exhausted—mentally, emotionally, and physically.

Deborah let her husband remain asleep the next morning, sensing that that would probably be good for him. *Maybe,* she thought, *just maybe, he had gotten a good lecture from the cops and would now settle down and straighten himself up.* She was so sick and tired of all his zany stuff, and very chagrined and angry about having the police show up at their house—particularly with blue lights flashing. She knew that their friends and neighbors had always considered them a very quiet and respectable couple. She decided that when he did awaken, she would cook his favorite Sunday morning breakfast consisting of a three-egg omelet with ham chunks and sharp cheddar cheese, two pieces of well-buttered toast, orange juice, and a couple cups of coffee. That should make him feel better. She smiled to herself.

About eleven, she heard George rambling around in the bedroom area. *Well, the damned lazy bum finally decided to get himself up out of bed,* Deb thought to herself. She had unconsciously let her increasing anger at her spouse override her original "wifely" plans to be good to him. *Well, if the jerk was going to sleep all day, he could just fix his own damn breakfast. I do not have time now because there are things that I want to do for myself.*

She left the kitchen and walked to the bedroom door, saying sullenly, "I left the frying pan out if you want to fry yourself some eggs." Then she turned abruptly and walked back down the hallway to her sewing room.

George, sat on the edge of his rumpled bed, looked up at her as she walked away, wondering who put the bee in her bonnet. *Boy, what a lousy attitude she has this morning.* He said to himself, *I sure don't like her much this way. And, she's been real snotty for some time now. Now what got her all that snuffy? My God, I had a distressing day at the police department, and what do I get? Crap, that's what. And, I still have this damn devil and SUV stuff bugging me. You would think a guy's wife would have a little sympathy for him. Damn her miserable hide. After all, she only had to sit comfortably around the house yesterday, while those bastard police were buttonholing me, especially by those stupid questions from that way-out nutty shrink.* George was becoming angrier by the second. His head hurt, his mouth tasted lousy, but not, thank goodness, like the SUV taste, and his thoughtless wife would not even give him the consideration of cooking his breakfast for him.

He stood, scratched his crotch, and then smoothed his hair back as he walked slowly to the sewing room where his wife had gone. The motion of his hand through his hair subconsciously reminded him that he was beginning to lose a little hair up top. George had been quite proud of his locks since in high school. In fact, the high school yearbook called George, "The most handsome guy in the class with the best chance to become a movie star."

Entering their den, he found his wife not sewing, but parked in her sewing machine chair, reading the Sunday morning newspaper.

"How about cooking my breakfast for me?" he asked sluggishly.

"Well, you damn lazy jerk," she quickly retorted in an angry voice. "I've got some things of my own to do, so just go fix it yourself. What am I, your personal slave?"

That took George aback. *What brought that out?* His thought processes were not functioning all that well, being hung over from the two stiff drinks of bourbon he downed before bed last night.

He was still reeling from yesterday's discourse with the police and that idiot psychiatrist. He was not certain which part he hated the most. The police had hounded and hounded him about the fact that he "knew" that certain disasters would take place before they actually happened. Then the psychiatrist acted as if he thought George was a total loser, and not worth his time.

✴   ✴   ✴

As he was frying himself some eggs, George recalled the interrogation with disgust…

"How could you have known about them in advance if you were not in on part of a conspiracy," the woman detective had queried. "Now, we know that there must be more of you in on this."

George had already told all three people in the interrogation room his complete and factual story. Yet, because of the declaration of the SUV, his story naturally sounded implausible to them. He knew that. But yet, he felt that his only chance for clearing himself would be for him to be completely honest.

"Mr. Sheldon," Detective Johnson had said, "You say there was nobody else in on these capers with you? You're sticking with that story, are you?"

Johnson pulled out a piece of bubble gum, carefully unfolded the wrapping paper, and inserted the pink tablet into his half-smiling mouth.

"Now listen to me, George…" Johnson stopped talking as he chewed the gum vigorously in his effort to get the mass properly softened. As he did this, he carefully refolded the wrapper into the exact creases that came with the gum. Then he gently placed the refolded wrapper on the edge of the table. He looked at it intently. No one else in the room spoke a word.

"We think," the detective continued, "that you and at least two others are involved in some sort of terrorist plot." Now he stopped again, raised his right hand and brought his open palm rapidly down on the wrapper. *Smack!* George jumped with surprise.

Then, brushing the flattened piece of purple and white paper onto the floor, Johnson continued, "What we figure is that you became disillusioned with your partners and that's why you started tattling on their plot. Am I right so far?" He smiled as he turned his head, gloating first toward the lady detective, then to the psychiatrist. He knew he had this jerk figured out by now. All he had to do was worm a confession out of him and then they'd go after George's accomplices. Simple case to solve. Terrorists. That is what it was all about.

He could just see his year-end bonus right now. Or perhaps a well-deserved promotion. He had always had his eye on that position held by the bitch Cotton. He had joined the force four years before her and just knew they should have promoted him to lieutenant over her. But, no. She was a female, and an African-American one at that. Politics, that was pure and simple what it was. Damned police department politics. He had seen her mistakes, watched them very carefully, expecting her to be demoted on several occasions. Detective Johnson especially figured she would catch it when she blew that child molestation case two years ago. The mother indeed! Anybody with half a grain of sense could easily have proved it was the stepfather. They released the guy and Johnson felt like he could have shot him for getting off Scot free to continue his vile actions. Johnson subconsciously felt as though he could have shot Cotton too, for fumbling the case so badly. Well, that was another story. This time Lieutenant Cotton would be able to watch a true expert detective in action. He was using all his little tried-and-true techniques to get the suspect nervous. Then, this fellow Sheldon will open up.

However, George had been truthful, that was all there was to it. He had even voluntarily submitted to a lie detector test. It showed that in all likelihood, George Albert Sheldon was truthful with his story. But that and nearly ten hours of grilling, and repeating his story over and over, Johnson still would not believe that he was innocent of anything. The detective simply had been on the force too long. His credo had evolved, contrary to standard police rules, that the suspect was guilty, period. Otherwise, they would not have brought him for interrogation. Right? It was as simple as that. All he had to do was break down the suspect until he got enough proof to put him or her in jail. He was proud of the fact that he had gained a large number of "confessions." It was not his fault that the district attorney's office did not get a conviction on many of them.

Finally, the three investigators left the room. The officers allowed George to visit the toilet at periodic intervals, always accompanied by a uniformed cop. This in itself was unnerving and somewhat embarrassing to George, but he found that he could do nothing about it. He would simply have to brave it out.

After being returned to the interrogation room, George was "allowed" to sit in solitary silence for nearly an hour. The lack of sound in the room became so deadly that George finally became acutely aware of the ticking of his watch. He tried to reassure himself that this was all part of a standard plot to get a real criminal to confess his crimes. He could just "feel" the people outside behind the mirror, watching his every move.

This time the psychiatrist entered the room alone. This made George feel somewhat better, because he thought he might find a more benevolent ear. Whether or not the two detectives were behind the big mirror was something about which George could only speculate. In truth, they had gone downstairs to grab a bite to eat at the delicatessen next door to the station.

"Well, Mr. Sheldon," began the shrink with a noncommittal smile. "Now that the others have left, why don't you and I just have a chat for a while? I have heard your story, how many times now? I'll bet anything that you're tired and pretty sick of repeating it, aren't you?"

George wondered what this guy would ask him. He was smart enough to realize that his true tale was not credible. But what else could he do? George looked at Dr. Mitchell. He was still displaying that *Mona Lisa* smile. George did not exactly hate people like that—those that conveyed uncalled-for smiles, but he did have a certain mistrust for them. They tended to project an image of "Ha! I'm a lot smarter than you, and I know something that you don't." This type of attitude may have been subconscious and unintended on the part of the person presenting it, but it still bothered George.

"Well, hell yes," responded George in a slightly raised voice. "Wouldn't it bother you?"

Dr. Mitchell again smiled, peered intently at George, and uttered quietly, "Why do you think it might bother me?"

Exasperated, very tired by now and angry at the entire procedure, George sighed, banged his fist on the table and said, "Come on doctor, let's cut out the bull. I have told you my story as accurately as I know how. I passed the lie detector test, didn't I? You have heard it, as you said, how many times? Now they want you to analyze me and tell them that I'm just a normal guy in on some kind of

malicious plot." George was somewhat surprised at his instant anger. He was usually a slow burn—never becoming extremely angry abruptly. He had always been
proud of his self-control. "Now let's get the two cops back in here and finish this
up, so I can go on back home." He looked pleadingly at the doctor.

"Is that all you have to say about it?"

"What else do you expect from me, anyway? A confession that a bunch of guys
and I are plotting all these terrorist attacks? And that we're gonna hold the city up
for a big ransom?" His anger was showing in his reddened face. "Well, I can't,
because it simply isn't so. As strange as it sounds, my story is exactly as I told it. I
have absolutely no idea why it's happening to me. I have even tried in vain to
approach that devil." Tears of exhaustion and frustration appeared in George's
eyes. "I don't know how else to say it. I do not understand any of it and I hate
that it is happening to me, but I cannot help it. It is making me sick. It is just the
crazy, simple truth. I swear it is." He laid his head down on the table in resignation. He had had it.

Abruptly, Dr. Mitchell, saying nothing, slid his chair back from the table, the
wooden legs scraping noisily against the worn vinyl tile floor. He rose and left the
room, again leaving George in his solitude. *Now what,* thought George. *I guess the
three of them are standing just behind that two-way mirror, plotting what to put me
through next.*

After a wait that seemed interminable to George, but in reality was only four
minutes, the door to the stark interrogation room once again opened, and Detective Johnson stepped partially into the room.

"Okay, Sheldon. We are finished with you for now. I'll have one of the uniforms take you back home." George noticed that Johnson was stern and grouchy.
Even across the small room, George could perceive that the detective's own anxieties had produced a considerable amount of body odor. However, George did
not give a damn about how the detective felt at this point. George knew he had
done no wrong, and the stinking detective just simply would not believe him.
"We'll call you when we want you back. Don't leave town without checking with
me first, understand?"

At this point, George was exhausted, angered and frustrated at what had happened in his life today. He was numb. He rose obediently, pulled his coat off the
back of the hard chair and followed Johnson out without saying a word.

Just as he was leaving the front door of the police station, he finally said to the
detective, "Hey Johnson. Why don't you people put out one of your 'All Points
Bulletins' for that big light blue SUV I've been telling you about?" They ignored
his request.

CHAPTER NINE

GEORGE AND DEBORAH CONTINUED to argue almost daily about his situation. She just could not or would not believe what George had told her about his physical symptoms and mental angst concerning the big SUV. However, he simply could not get the dreaded despicable devil completely off his mind. He could easily delete a contrary program from his computer by simply pushing a single button. If only he could do the same with his mind. He had begun to wonder every day whether this would be another of "those days" when he would feel the alarming sensations. It was exceedingly unnerving and driving him to absolute distraction. He tried to get Deborah to listen to his concerns and understand his difficulty, but she found herself simply unable to believe or relate to his anguish. In addition, George was becoming increasingly angry and distressed that his own wife would not believe him or even side with him; even a little bit. It was her job, he felt, to be on his side. After all, their marriage vows had said, "for better or worse." Now, here was some of the "worse," and she was not paying any obvious attention to her obligation to him at all. On the contrary, she acted as if she thought he was nutty. She would not have anything to do with him any more. She bitched continuously about his now-heavy drinking. Would not let him make love to her, dressed in the closet, would not even go out to the movies with him. In fact, she would barely speak to him, except when arguing and haranguing him about his attitude. She even made an appointment for him with his personal internist without first consulting with him. Treated him like a child. *How ridiculous! Damn that woman! She'd sure better straighten up, or else,* reflected George angrily.

Like most nights lately, George poured himself at least one tall glass of whiskey. Although he had not conscientiously noticed it, the amounts he imbibed were steadily increasing. It took more and more booze to take away the constant worry about his confrontations with the devil and the SUV. Often, he would fall asleep on the living room sofa, fully clothed.

He had tried discussing the blue vehicle incidents with several of his closest friends, and even they had laughed at his story. He could not forget his embarrassment when telling his story at to his fellow office workers that first day.

Deborah, on the other hand, wanted to believe her husband, but wondered seriously about his sanity. *Why is he suddenly like this? He has become moody and standoffish lately. Is this what is called a nervous breakdown?* In the beginning, she wanted to help him, but he sharply rebuffed her. This, in itself angered her. They just could not carry on a decent conversation any more. He had become cranky, and even disheveled. He had stopped taking care to be as clean-shaven as formerly, and was long overdue for a haircut. He did not bathe every day, and often skipped his tooth brushing for several days at a time. In addition, sadly, her husband was drinking more heavily than she had ever seen him do. As a result, he was becoming more and more obnoxious to her daily. She was having to wake him nearly every morning and struggle to get him to the office. In fact, more than once she had observed him sneaking a quick nip before he left for his morning drive to work. *He is going to have a wreck out on the freeway, and then be arrested for drunk driving,* she worried. *Worse yet, he may kill himself or somebody else.*

Nevertheless, no matter what she did, she could not seem to break through his self-imposed shell. She even tried once again to persuade her husband to visit his physician. *Maybe his doctor can give him some medicine that would help him.* Being aware that even if he might resent her efforts, she felt she had no choice. She simply could or would not go on living like this. Life was too short.

"George, you've simply got to go see a doctor. Don't you realize that?"

"Now, why don't you just go to hell? And, quit bugging me about it. I have worries and you don't act like you even care how I feel. Besides, there is not a damn thing any doctor can do to help me. So just shut up about it."

He had never before seriously raised his voice at her. He was just becoming impossible to live with. He had not even tended to their garden in weeks. In fact, her husband was no longer acting as she thought any husband should. He seemed to spend nearly all his time at home in front of his computer. He rarely typed anything much, just sat there in a sulk. Lately, he simply gazed blindly at his "swimming fish" screen saver. He all too often had an open bottle of whiskey on the table beside him. Deborah knew that he nearly always had brought work home from the office, and he had never before complained about that. Now, however, he grumbled not only about that obligation, but was actually ignoring the work. In other words, Deborah sadly observed that her husband was becoming a shiftless and irresponsible drunk. He no longer represented the man she had fallen in love with. She thought to herself, *if he's going to act that way, then to hell with him.*

During one of their increasingly frequent arguments, he drunkenly picked up a large telephone directory from a nearby end table and almost threw it at her. She had never before seen this side of him. His anger was becoming uncontrolled, and Deborah was becoming more and more afraid of what George might do—to her, as well as to himself. He had always been a caring, gentle man. Yet, in spite of all of her attempts, he would do nothing to help himself, rejecting out of hand any attempts she made to help him. She had had all she could take. She was just about finished with trying. She was at the end of her rope.

CHAPTER TEN

"SHELDON, COME INTO MY office," announced the black intercom on his office desk. George was blandly staring out of his office window while in the middle of eating a sugar-glazed doughnut and having his third cup of coffee. He was watching the wind-driven rain as it rattled noisily against the glass window-pane. Although it was only nine-fifteen in the morning and he had eaten a bowl of cold cereal for breakfast a couple of hours ago, he was hungry already. He seemed to need more snacks lately. In fact, he forced coffee down hoping to help mask the alcohol odors from his now-habitual nightly drinking. He also kept a packet of breath fresheners in his pocket. He figured he could handle the alcohol intake, though. *It is nobody's business, but mine.*

George was having a great deal of difficulty getting his contract figures to respond for him. He could not seem to get them to add up to the net profit level that he had anticipated. This seemed to be his norm lately. Previously, he had nearly been able to mentally put his numbers together in his head, having done it so often over the past twenty-some years. But now, he found it necessary to use his calculator more and more. Moreover, he was noticing that any work that he tried to do at home needed recalculating the next day at the office. *Maybe if that damn wife of mine would quit bugging me about my having a couple of drinks every night. Hell, I can handle it. I know when to stop and can do so whenever I wish.*

"Yeah, Mr. Williams," mumbled George with a mouthful of doughnut. "I'll be there in a minute. I just wanna finish up something here first."

The voice over the intercom immediately came back, loudly this time, "*Sheldon!* I said come here. And, I do mean right now. Drop whatever it is you're doing and get in here. NOW!"

Good Lord, what's the old sombitch want with me now? George put down the food and sloppily wiped his mouth on his shirtsleeve. While standing up halfway, he grabbed a quick sip of the tepid coffee. As he was placing the cup back on his desk, he accidentally tipped it over. Streams of the brown liquid flowed haphazardly onto his blotter and several copies of a contract on which he was working.

"Damn it," he uttered loudly, as he looked around for something with which to blot up the spill. Realizing that he had previously thrown the napkin that came with the doughnut into the trash, he stooped to retrieve it from the basket. At the same time, he inadvertently allowed the end of his yellow silk tie to rest in the spilled puddle of coffee. *This just isn't my day!*

At last, George entered Mr. William's office, looking somewhat the worse for wear. Williams could not help but notice the lingering bit of glaze from the doughnut on his cheek, and the tip of his tie wet and badly stained from the coffee. George's shirt collar was open, leaving his tie unprofessionally askew. It was obvious that he had worn his wrinkled shirt for several days in a row. He agitatedly sat down in the chair in front of his employer.

"What'd you want," he said with some antagonism in his voice. "I'm pretty busy with that picayune new contract for the damn Rodman and Sons Company."

Williams looked at George, noting his disheveled appearance. Having observed him like this during the past several weeks, he was distressed to note the transformation.

Williams' forehead showed deep grooves of anxiety. He glanced at his desk for a good eight seconds, then straight into George's face.

He said, "George, for your information, we have been servicing the Rodmans since I started this company. We are certainly not going to quit on them at this point." He nestled his chair closer to his desk. "You've been with this company a long time. You've been a most valued employee, and I think I've let you know how much I respected you and your service to me." He paused, glanced at the several manila folders on his desk, and then continued, "But recently all that has changed. You will remember, I spoke to you about this not too long ago." His unlit cigar dangled from the corner of his mouth. "For some reason you've let yourself go, and your work has badly suffered. I have had complaints from several longtime customers that the numbers you gave them were not at all in line with our previous service. In fact, I have had to go behind you and double-check your work lately. Did you know that? I find it hard to believe that you have not been aware of all this. Now just look at yourself today." He paused again to let that sink in, while repositioning the folders on his desk. "George, I've also had some complaints from your fellow employees about your smelling strongly of alcohol here at the office. Now what do you have to say for yourself?"

"Now what do you have to say for yourself," repeated George angrily, with a raised voice. "That's what my daddy used to say to me when I was a kid, and I did something that he didn't like." His cheeks flushed as he remembered the frequent admonishments as he was growing up. How he hated his dad at that point. "Mr. Williams," he finally said, "I told you before that I've got some personal problems that frankly aren't any of your damn business. I'm doing my job as best as I can, and that's all you should be concerned about."

Mr. Williams was quite surprised and hurt over George's obstreperous attitude. He had intended to give George another warning, but now he decided that it was all over.

"George, I'm sorry about any difficulties you might be having, but in fact, you're not really doing your job. I cannot and will not allow your sloppy work to continue. You'll ruin this company's reputation." Williams repeated, "I've warned you before." He pulled his unlit cigar out of his mouth and laid it down on the edge of his ashtray. Tenting his fingers, he remained silent for a moment, recalling the good work that George had done for him over the years. He then said with finality, "But now you have become a disgrace to my company. Therefore, as of right now, I'm letting you go." Williams paused again, taking a deep breath, to let his statement sink in like a stiletto. He picked up his cigar, and stuck it in the corner of his mouth. He stared at George for a few seconds. George, astonished, said nothing. Then Williams removed the cigar, and said to George, "You have one hour to clean out your desk and leave the building." He picked up the large glass lighter from his desk and lit the cigar stump. "Now get out of my office. We'll send you your final paycheck, and anything else that's due you."

George's face dropped. He was stunned. He had expected, perhaps, just another warning from Williams, but not this. Not being fired! After all these years! He could find nothing to say. He wanted to hurl something at Mr. Williams, but could locate nothing at the moment.

"Damn you Williams. Damn everybody. Damn my wife. Okay, I'll go, but let me tell you one thing. I've been the best damn, and I do mean *the* absolute best employee you ever had in this Godforsaken company. And, you know it. I gave you a hell of a lot of my time and effort." He took a deep breath. "And now you're firing me, you old bastard. You're sure as hell gonna miss me, I'll tell you that, you damn SOB." With that off his mind, George stood so rapidly that his chair fell over backwards. He turned and stormed out of William's office, loudly slamming the door behind him. Seeing several of his fellow employees looking curiously at him, he angrily raised his right hand, middle finger extended at each of them. His reddened face showed his extreme anger. He wondered which of the bastards had been talking to the boss behind his back.

He arrived home, two hours later, having detoured by a bar for several stiff drinks. Still consumed with his indignation and torment, George stormed into the house. Deborah was sitting on the living room couch watching an old black and white Western on the television.

She looked up at him startled, and said, "Well, what on earth are you doing home at this time of day? You sick or something? Do you have to go on another business trip someplace?"

Her husband looked at her with squinted eyes, "No, goddam it! As if you'd care about me or anything else. I was just fired. That son of a bitch Williams fired me. And after all this time."

"Fired?" repeated his wife looking up at him in utter disbelief. "You've been at Williams Company for over twenty years and now you've been let go? Humph. Well, I am not surprised. Just look at you now."

"Not surprised?" George snapped as he brushed past her toward the liquor cabinet. Red-faced, with shaky hands, he lifted a bottle of scotch to his lips, taking three long swigs. He told her of the incident in Williams' office. "Now, what in the hell am I going to do?"

Deborah stood, and faced George. "I guess since your day is messed up anyway, I'll just add to it. Maybe it won't hurt any worse." She glanced at his soiled tie as he took off his suit coat and threw it haphazardly over the edge of an easy chair.

She took a deep breath, clutched the arm of the couch and said in a resigned voice, "George, I'm through. I've had enough. I am divorcing you. I saw my lawyer yesterday and he is drawing up papers of separation. You cannot stay here tonight, so you will have to pack your things and find somewhere else to go. I've had it up to here with you, your drunkenness and your continuing craziness." She hesitated just long enough to suck in another deep breath. "George, whether or not you realize it, you've changed and are no longer the same man I married. You have destroyed my love and respect for you. Did you hear that? I no longer love you. And, it's obvious to me that you don't care for me or love me anymore. Otherwise, you'd have done something to help yourself. Therefore, that's that. I am sorry it had to come to this, especially now that you were fired today, but that's the way it is. You've got to get out."

George was stunned.

"But…" He drew back his hand as if he was going to slap her. *That wouldn't solve anything,* he said to himself resolutely. *My goddam day is already so screwed up that nothing else can possibly go wrong.* He lifted the bottle to his lips for another long draw on the dark amber liquid. Shuddering, he sat the bottle down with a thud. The inexplicable horrible episodes with the SUV and corresponding disasters were ruining his life. He felt like an insignificant ant on a leaf being carried away in a torrent. His life was out of control. He said nothing in reply, but just stared at her as he lowered his hand. Then he angrily rushed past her to the bedroom closet where he pulled out his largest suitcase. Grabbing some clothes out of the chest of drawers and closet, he stuffed these and his bathroom implements into it. Then he silently glared at her as he moved past her out of the house. Getting into his car, he rapidly backed out of the driveway, spinning the wheels and throwing up showers of gray gravel. He rolled down his window and held out his left hand, middle finger extended for all to see. He drove slowly down the street, away from his home of twenty years. *The bitch!*

CHAPTER ELEVEN

GEORGE, STILL INTOXICATED, ANGRILY drove out of the suburbs and into the city proper where he easily located an available mid-priced hotel. He parked his car in the hotel garage, walked into the ornate marble-floored lobby and reserved himself a single room. He had no idea how long he might be staying, but was well aware that his funds would not allow very many nights. After the bellhop ushered him to his room, George checked out the bed, and found it acceptable.

As he tipped the young twenty-something bellhop, he asked, "Say fellow. Is the bar open downstairs?"

Smiling, the young man replied, "Yes sir. It opened an hour ago. It's on your left after you get off the elevator."

Shortly George ventured back downstairs to the bar. He needed another stiff drink very badly. His ruined day needed some more tempering.

He entered the shadowed room, noting the highly polished teak bar, and nautical motif. The subdued blue lights created an illusion of being underwater. Instead of smelling like a smoke-filled beer hall, there seemed to be some sort of special aroma in the room. It reminded George of a salty sea. He immediately liked the ambiance. A piano soloist played across the room. It surprised George that the hotel provided such in early afternoon. Moving to a tiny glass-topped table near the piano, he sat down. As he looked around the room, he spotted only two couples, one at the bar, the other in a small banquette along the far wall. They were smiling and in animated conversations. George presumed that they were having some sort of afternoon rendezvous. *Humph*, thought George with a mild smirk on his face, *I only want a rendezvous with a good drink. First, that bastard Williams, and then Deb. Well, they can both just shove it!*

When the trim young waitress arrived at his table, he ordered a double Scotch on the rocks. That drink was soon followed by another, then another. As he sat there by himself, his tormented mind began to review the unpleasant happenings of the day. His anger gradually began to turn to drunken remorse.

Why is the goddam devil picking on me so much? It's not fair. I've just gotta figure out some way to get him off my back.

Several apparent executives entered the shadowed confines, glanced over at George and then settled at the bar. Finally, George ordered a full bottle of Scotch whiskey brought to his table. The price surprised him, but he was beyond caring at this point. George, with only peanuts to nibble on, became quite drunk. By this time, the late afternoon had arrived and the spacious room had begun filling up.

Noting that George had continued to pour in the alcohol, the bartender came over and politely said, "Sir, you've been here all afternoon. Maybe you would like to visit our restaurant. It's first class."

George stared vacantly into the distant shadows for perhaps a minute. His befuddled mind finally convinced him that perhaps he should get something in his stomach.

"Yeah. Guess so," he mumbled drunkenly. "I'll head there right now." However, on rising, he fell over the table. The glass top crashed loudly and splintered over the floor. George numbly stared at the thousands of shards of sparkling glass at his feet. The bartender held George by the arm and firmly eased him out of the lounge. As he was doing this, George fumbled his wallet out of his back pocket and handed it to the bartender.

"Here's ma wal't," he slowly mumbled. "You jus' get wha'ever you need, ma good man."

Getting the necessary bills, including a hefty, well-deserved tip from George's wallet, he stuck it back into George's shirt pocket. Then, the bartender firmly placed his staggering ward into a cushioned chair in the hotel lobby, afterward returning to the increasingly busy bar.

By the time the bartender returned, the attendant had already cleaned up the glass from the broken table, and had brought another from the storeroom. The pianist played on The establishment was all too accustomed to drunks and their shenanigans.

George flopped in the chair, his arms dangling over its sides, and he half slid out. He barely managed to catch himself just before his rump touched the lobby's polished marble floor. He'd just rest there a moment or two, and catch his breath.

*   *   *

George awoke with the sunshine beaming through the window directly into his eyes. *Ugh!* He stuck out his tongue and licked his dried lips. *My mouth tastes like the bottom of a chicken coop,* he said to himself. He licked the back of his hand and smelled it. *Smells like the rotten stuff, too.* His stomach rumbled ominously, and his head ached. *Where in hell am I?* He slowly turned over in his rumpled hotel bed. He became aghast as he found the nude body of a young blonde-haired woman asleep beside him. *Oh my God, what in the hell have I done now? Where'd she come from?*

As he sat up in bed, she stirred, rolled over toward him, and slowly opened one eye.

"Why, good morning, Georgie Boy!"

She continued to rest on her pillow, and sleepily and peered at him. She had a bright toothy smile.

"You feeling good this morning, sweetie?"

She gradually sat straight up in the bed and George became more aware of her nakedness. She showed no signs of embarrassment. George was not sure how she happened to arrive in his bed. In fact he had no recollections whatsoever of last night past entering the lounge. *What happened?*

He pulled up the badly rumpled sheet, and said, "And just who in the hell are you? I don't know you. How did you happen to get here?"

"Well hells bells, Georgie sweetie, don't you remember? You stopped me in the hotel lobby and brought me up here last night. You still don't remember?" She sat up on the side of the bed and flipped her ruffled hair away from her eyes. She stuck her lower lip out, pouting. "I'm so disappointed. Last night you told me some of the sweetest things. I thought you liked me."

George sat there, finally swinging his own legs over onto his side of the bed. He stared back across the bed at her.

"I'm afraid I have no memory of any of that. I'm sorry, but I think you'd better get yourself dressed and leave."

"Why honey," she said in a squeaky voice and with a frown on her face. "You told me that you'd take me out to a nice store today and buy me something. Now you tell me to get out. Well, I like that! Boy, what a two faced bastard you turned out to be."

The young lady arose, ran her thin fingers brusquely through her disarranged hair and walked unashamedly to an adjacent straight-backed chair. George could not help but notice the large gaudy tattoo of a bright red rose on her left buttock.

What in the hell is going to happen to me next?

George watched her donning her clothes. His head was aching severely. The sheet continued to partially cover him. He could only imagine what went on between the two of them. He felt physically terrible, was very hungry and thirsty and had a bad taste in his mouth.

Finally, she was dressed, went into the bathroom for a moment, where she quickly applied some lipstick, then came out and stared at him with a questioning look.

George pointed to the hallway door, and said a precise, "Go."

She opened the door, went out in a huff, slamming the door loudly behind her. At the noise of the door, George's head pounded. He glanced across the bed once more, noting the remaining lingering fragrance of her body across the sheets. It brought to him a vague memory of some fragrance in his past, but his mind at this moment simply could not bring it to the fore.

I have to find myself some place to live besides this hotel, he thought.

"I can't let anything like this happen again," George said aloud to no one but himself. He was very concerned about his apparent actions last night. He slowly arose from the bed, holding his throbbing head in both his hands, and walked unsteadily to the bathroom. He located his shaving kit, and, examining his image in the never-lying mirror, he saw a pasty drained face. He noted large bags under his bloodshot eyes, deepening jowls, and a grubby beard. He leaned forward and became aware of an increasing number of gray hairs in his beard. *Hmm, must have been a hell of a night,* he mused. He brushed his teeth, shaved, brushed his teeth a second time, and then took four aspirin tablets from his toilet bag and swallowed them rapidly. He then eased himself into the shower for a long, steamy session. Glancing down at his groin area, he was happy to see that all was intact.

Afterward he donned a pair of beige trousers, with a light blue long-sleeve dress shirt, open at the collar. He checked his wallet. He did not think she had taken any money. He then went down to the hotel restaurant where he helped himself to the sumptuous breakfast buffet. With the aspirin's soothing effect and his appetite satisfied, he began to feel almost like a normal human again. *Maybe I am going to live for another day or so after all.*

He left the restaurant, walked across the lobby, and bought a copy of the local newspaper. He knew he needed to locate a suitable apartment right away. Although he had what he thought would be ample cash in his wallet, plus two credit cards, he was aware that in her anger, that damn Deborah just might have tried to block their shared bank account. *She's even probably going try to stop me from using our credit cards.* He was not sure she could do the latter, but was afraid she might try.

After he returned to his sixth floor hotel room, he called room service for a pot of coffee. He then began perusing the classifieds for furnished apartments for rent. He circled several possibilities with his pen, and began calling them on the telephone for details. His primary concern was location. He felt that he wanted to be somewhere near the central part of the city, if at all possible. He anticipated seeking and finding a new engineering position somewhere in town as soon as he became settled in a new residence. He realized that he had a lot to do. Nevertheless, as his mind became clearer and the drink-induced cobwebs began to vanish, he kept remembering the pretty young lady that had slept with him. What happened between them? He had no memories whatsoever of their encounter, but in a way, wished that he did. He fantasized that it must have been a very interesting night. After all, she was a right pretty thing. George did recall that she exhibited a very nice body—slender, pale, clear skin, and a superior figure. He did not care much for her tattoo though.

CHAPTER TWELVE

GEORGE SET OUT AND investigated several apartments, eventually deciding on a furnished single bedroom efficiency near an old strip shopping center that contained a major grocery, pharmacy and a fast food restaurant. Signing a three-month lease, and making the down payment with cash from his wallet, he returned to the hotel room for his meager luggage.

Before leaving his room, he called Deborah. "Hey Deb, I've got a new place where I'm going to live." He told her the new address. "Now honey, are you absolutely sure you want to go through with this? Maybe we can work things out."

She did not respond. He went on to explain that his phone would not be turned on for three or so days. Then he would pass along his new number.

"I need to stop by and pick up the rest of my things."

"George, I do not want to see you—or talk to you." Deb told him curtly that she would be out of the house the next day after two o'clock.

"You can stop by then. Do not take anything that does not belong strictly to you. She also sternly reminded him that he should leave his house keys on the dressing table beside her bed.

He asked one more time, "Honey, are you absolutely sure that you want to go through with this damn separation and divorce?" He stopped talking for a moment. She said nothing. "Sweetie, I'll try real hard to get myself together." More silence on the phone.

Deborah finally said, "Just leave your keys where I told you, George," and abruptly hung up.

So, she really intends to make this final, he reflected sadly. Somewhere in the depths of his mind, he felt as though she might still love him and would not truly go through with the required yearlong separation and inevitable divorce. Should he try to fight it?

However, he did not want to think that far ahead at this point. Like Scarlet O'Hara in the movie, *Gone With The Wind*, he would think about that tomorrow. He was feeling saddened and forlorn. *Why had all this come about? What had made this happen to him?* He had never offended anybody, at least not intentionally. He had tried to follow the Golden Rule. George had always considered himself a pretty nice, honorable and respectable person. He had a fair number of friends; not that he was what might be called a "social animal," but enough so that he would certainly not be classified as a hermit. *Same with Deborah.* She had always gotten along well with other people. He was friendly with most of the people at work—or at least where he used to work, he reminded himself. That brought him to another point: he needed to find another job. But where? Doing what? He could not use the Williams Company as a reference due to his being fired, and he had not worked anywhere else since college. He was confident that he was one of the best engineering company representatives in the state, but how would he explain his job loss at Williams Company? What could he tell a prospective employer about where he had been for the past twenty years? If they should contact Mr. Williams, what would *he* say? He would have to spend some time thinking about that—tomorrow.

George left the hotel parking garage and drove toward his new apartment. On the way he stopped by his main bank's ATM. Inserting his card and P.I.N., he requested the maximum amount of cash. Momentarily, out it came. Similarly, at his alternate bank's ATM, he also gained the maximum funds allowable. He was very relieved that so far Deb had not cut off his ability to remove funds. With no job and only a limited number of dollars left in his wallet, he had been concerned about how long he could last without employment. But now, he felt he could survive a little longer without a job.

Next, he stopped by a food store and purchased some groceries. He had never done much cooking, but told himself it was not too late to learn. He tried to remember some of the fine meals Deb had prepared, and what she used and even what spices he might need. *Oh well, I'll just wing it,* he decided. He also passed by the wine rack and bought himself four bottles of his favorite red.

So, George retreated to his new apartment, unloaded his groceries, and poured himself a glass of wine. He sat down on his couch, placing the wine bottle on the coffee table in front of him. Having found no wine glasses in the kitchen cabinet, he used a standard water glass as his goblet. *Not very elegant,* he thought, *but it will suffice. I'll fix dinner in a little while.* First, he wanted to scan the paper for job possibilities. The wine was quite tasty, so he decided to have another, then yet one more. The ads in the paper somehow lost their importance as the evening wore on.

Much later, George found himself sitting on his couch, staring blankly at the opposite wall. He reflected about the SUV. *When would it strike again? Would it strike again at all?* Lately there had been no warnings, and he could not even arrive at any correlation of time between "attacks." It all seemed so random. There was the gas tanker crash, then the building collapse, the ship tragedy, the plane crash and lastly the refinery explosion. He had difficulty remembering if there had been any more. His brain was becoming more and more muddled by the wine, as he tried to determine what he could do about the incidents. He alone was aware of the connections between all these tragedies. Well, perhaps Deb was aware, as he had told her of each incident, but she did not believe him at all.

The police and NTSB had not been told of all of George's links with each of the tragedies. For all these people knew, there had only been two incidents. George had definitely been implicated in both of those, although he was clearly trying to prevent any injuries or deaths. He wondered if the police were going to interview Deborah. If so, she might tell them of the other episodes. That might get him into more interrogations, and after the awful strain of the last one, he did not care to be put through another. He knew in his own mind that there would no point in telling about his fruitless attempt to confront the devil. He could now understand why he'd read about innocent people confessing to crimes that they did not commit. He thought of the constant grilling by the police, repeating the questions, one after another, attempting to gather all bits of information available. Such repetitive behavior would confuse anyone—even the brightest of individuals, what with the increasing tiredness, then complete exhaustion. Yes, he could easily see why a confession, even if not true, could be forthcoming; anything to stop the relentless and exhausting questioning.

Finally, having consumed two entire bottles of wine, George forgot about his dinner and fell asleep on his bed, fully clothed.

*   *   *

"Damn it," said George as the sun's rays crept across his whiskered face the next morning, rudely awakening him. "I must have drunk a little too much wine last night." He realized that he was talking aloud to himself, but continued, "I don't even remember fixing supper."

He slowly ambled toward the bathroom, taking off his wrinkled shirt as he proceeded, and struggled to shave. He determined that he would have to buy some new razors, after barely managing to eliminate the facial growth with an old, dull blade. He was pleased to have only cut himself twice, but had some difficulty stopping the oozing from the small cuts. One would appear to have stopped, so he would carefully tease off the small piece of toilet tissue he had used as a blotter. That would start the bleeding all over again. This went on for the better part of an hour as George strained to stand in front of the mirror, not understanding that his recent near-addiction to aspirin led to a decreased tendency for blood clotting.

Okay, now for some breakfast. Moving into the small, compact kitchen, he opened a loaf of bread, stuck four pieces into the toaster oven and made himself a strong cup of instant coffee. His taste buds felt as though they belonged in a goat's mouth. He hoped the coffee would help straighten that out. He thought of the SUV taste, and was glad that at least this stale alcohol aftertaste was not as foul as that. Besides, he could partially control this bad taste, or at least change it. The SUV taste would linger and remain for the duration of the incident regardless of what he put into his mouth. He vacantly glanced up from his breakfast room chair, observing, but not really seeing, the cheap framed print of a sailing ship on the opposite wall. He thought fleetingly how nice it would be if he could only sail away from all his problems. George wished that he could put his concerns about the SUV behind him. He had quite enough to worry about, thank you very much!

After breakfast, finally feeling slightly more refreshed, he turned back to the newspaper, searching the "help wanted" ads. He found several that he felt might work for him, so he went out to a local convenience store, bought himself a beer, turning a ten dollar bill into change. He then began his telephoning response to these ads. He inquired about the engineering positions. George felt that the beer would sort of relax him a little so that he could sound more important over the phone. He also dug out his notebook of addresses and phone numbers and began to call old friends and business acquaintances for leads. No one would help him much more than requesting that he stop by the company or office with his résumé and fill out an application.

None of his personal calls showed any promise. In fact, when he was forced to explain to several of his friends that he was no longer working at the Williams

Company, George was reluctant to explain why. He finally told them that he and Mr. Williams had several differences of opinions and a resultant falling out.

He said to them, "I simply couldn't force myself to work for the Williams Company any longer." They offered their polite sympathy, but at the same time proffered no leads for possible positions for George to investigate.

During the time required for his telephoning, the sun rose to its peak, pouring down its piercing rays on George. His cotton sport shirt was now a wet sheet, sticking to him like a second skin. Following a series of numerous extended calls, he found himself running low on change, so he went into the air conditioned convenience store and bought himself a chilled six-pack of beer and obtained another hand-full of coins. Standing at the phone booth out in the blazing sun, George again quickly became drenched with sweat, his hair matted. By the time George had nearly completed his calling, he had again entered the cool store and purchased four more cold beers, rapidly gulping them down between calls. He had now become drunk, but after receiving so many rejections, he did not care.

He said loudly to no one in particular, "God damn it!" as he dropped his coins into the phone slot. "I'm pretty sick and tired of all these bastards telling me where to go. I'm gonna tell the next one that says no to just shove it…"

However, George could not find the money slot for his final call of the day. It seemed to be moving away from his fingers every time he tried to insert a coin. His legs were aching and his clothing dripping. Finally, in his drunken disgust, he simply laid his last quarter on the top of the telephone box and walked away. *I'll go home, cool off, and get some rest. That's what I'll do.* The damn jobs could just wait until tomorrow. He pulled an extended draw from his last beer, and angrily crushed the can with his hand. Then he tossed it into a clump of green ivy he was passing.

As he staggered back home toward his apartment, he passed a package store. *Booze. Yeah, tha's what I'll do. I'll buy me some good booze. He entered and ordered a fifth of vodka.* However, the clerk, a middle-aged African-American gentleman noted George's already inebriated state and declined to sell it to him.

He said, "Sorry, mister, but you look like you've already had enough for today. How about you just go on home and sleep it off."

"Wha?" George's face turned crimson, and the veins in his neck became extended. He pounded his fist on the counter and exclaimed, almost yelling, "Damn you. I said that I want a fifth of vodka and I want it now. You hear me good?"

The clerk stepped slightly back from the counter.

He said, "Now sir, don't get so upset. You might have a stroke right here and now. But, like I said, and I'm real sorry about it, but rules say that we cannot sell to a person, man or woman, who is already showing signs of intoxication." The clerk glanced down at the counter, then back to face George. "You show these signs, sir, so I cannot let you have any. Now mister, just go on home quietly, will you please?"

George moved closer to the counter and started to raise his fist at the clerk. But just at that moment, another clerk, this one quite burly, rounded the corner of a stack of bottles. George, even in his drunken state of mind, decided that perhaps he would just finish the wine he had left at home. He turned on his heels and started out of the store without saying another word. He just glared at the first attendant as he shoved against the glass door.

When he noted that it would not open that way, he turned to the serious-faced clerk and called out, "You damn SOBs even put the door in wrong. You'll get no more of my business. Bastards."

Finally realizing that he was wrong, he pulled on the handle, slipping down slightly, and staggered back out onto the sidewalk. He almost tripped over some poorly patched concrete. George bent over, picked up a fist-sized piece of broken pavement and threw it at the brick wall of the package store. He had been aiming at the glass door. Storming down the sidewalk, he maliciously overturned a full garbage can.

The worries were getting to George. He was only slightly aware that he was indulging in more alcohol than ever before in his life, but he just could not seem to control it at this point. He felt as though he needed it in order to face his now-sad existence. Not only was he out of work, and not only did he have to worry about Deb's lawyer's potential attacks, but the nagging worry about the SUV may have been the worst.

Somewhere, somehow, deep within his soul, George knew he was a good man. He had done no serious damage to anything or anyone in his entire life. However, was that red-skinned man with the gloves really the devil himself? He had made himself known, or at least shown himself to George on two different occasions. Surely, that must mean something. But, what? Was he really the devil? Or, just a poor sick unfortunate human? Did he know George from somewhere? Certainly not that George could place. Maybe he had run into him on one of his business trips for the Williams Company over the years. Did he have some unexplained ferocious anger at George? However, with a red-skinned face like that, George would surely have remembered him. Unless the man had had a terrible accident of some sort, perhaps being badly burned around the face, and possibly his hands, also. *Yes,* mulled George. *Maybe it was some accident and the fellow somehow thinks that I had something to do with it. I'll bet that's why he's out to get me.* But then he realized that he could not remember any news of an accident on any of his trips.

George decided that he would go to the public library the next day and study over back records and newspapers for terrible accidents in cities near the time when he might have been there. He would do that tomorrow. Right now, however, he felt like he needed a stiff drink. George had never been much of an alcohol drinker, but he determined that he had so much pressure on him right now, a little booze might just take away some of the strain. *Besides, it was his own life and who in the hell was around to tell him what to do or not to do? Nobody, that's who.* Following a "luxurious" dinner of overcooked scrambled eggs, undercooked bacon strips, and hard dry toast, he used the last two bottles of wine to drink himself into oblivion that evening. No more worries for George Sheldon. No siree! The following day the idea of visiting a library had simply disappeared from his consciousness.

That afternoon, after numerous additional phone calls, he finally arranged to have a couple of interviews with local companies. George had already decided that for any manager asking for references, he would simply lie to them and say that he had been overseas for the past twenty years. He hoped that former colleagues would not have spread the word about his firing. George determined that one of the drug-infested countries, in either Central America or northern South America would be less likely to be contacted for any kind of reference. Knowing very little about any of these areas, he went to the library, not remembering his previous plan to look for accidents.

George walked up to the busy attendant and rudely asked, "Where can I find some books on Central America or northern South America?"

The matronly attendant glanced up at him from her desk, and then looked back down at her work. She finished recording some notes, and stuck her pencil into her hair. Then she again looked up at him with haughtiness and asked, "Now what was it you wanted when you so rudely interrupted me?"

George stood there silently for a moment. *This bitch sure doesn't like to help a patron.* He then repeated his question.

"Sir, go over that way and look under…"

Even though he was still nursing a severe hangover, George researched for a couple of hours, finally determining what his résumé would carry. He would say that he had been living and working in Paraguay. There, he had been an engineering consultant for a small company that was working as a subcontractor for a huge new dam on the Parana River. Unfortunately, he would tell them, his employer had gone bankrupt and was no longer in existence. George had no contacts with the now-nonexistent company. Sorry.

Much to his chagrin, however, neither company that accepted George's application and interviewed him would hire him with no confirmation of previous employment, even at a beginning engineer's salary. Now what was he to do? He knew he would have to deal with the inevitable divorce and suspected that would probably cost him a bundle. Well, he guessed, it could not cost him too much, because he did not have anything. *I wonder if she has gotten my final pay from Williams.* Deb already had everything. He did not think that he had done anything wrong against Deb, so she should have no cause to try to take him to the cleaners. Probably they would settle on an equitable split of assets, with little if any alimony. That would give him a little something at least. He hoped.

Still, he had to find some sort of employment. He had been distressed as well as angered to learn that Deborah had finally shut off his access to their bank accounts. He also expected that his bankcards had already been disallowed, and that his earlier usage of the ATMs had simply beaten the logistics of the banks to the punch. He would try them again tomorrow, doubting if he would obtain anything from such actions. However, he figured, as long as he lived frugally, he could manage as he was for several months. He knew he would need an income eventually—the sooner the better, of course.

George walked down to the corner and bought newspapers from surrounding cities from the half-dozen boxes there. Maybe they would have some job opportunities for him. He had no desire to leave his hometown, but in a pinch, he would do whatever necessary. Upon entering his apartment again, he noticed that he had left a slightly used wine bottle out on the counter. Before browsing through the employment ads in the papers, he would just have a glass or two of wine and relax a little bit.

Several hours later, he awoke on his couch, with the room in disarray. Not only was his wine bottle empty, but, he also found six empty beer cans lying on the floor and coffee table in front of him. *Now when in hell did I buy that beer?*

"Didn't realize that I drank so much," he finally mumbled aloud to no one in particular, as he forced his mind to begin to focus. Struggling to stand, he slowly walked over to the refrigerator, head bowed with gray fog. He opened it and found nothing inside worth eating, except for a partial loaf of bread and some nearly out-of-date eggs. He could not stomach eggs again. However, he had to find something to eat.

Guess I'll have no choice but to go to the grocery. He went to the bathroom, grabbed his trusty bottle of aspirin, gobbling down four. Maybe that would help his headache. George then looked around for his wallet, finding it on the floor, partially hidden under the slightly sagging couch. Opening it, he carefully counted out his money, learning to his chagrin that he had only a twenty, a five and three one-dollar bills. *Where did my money go?* Then he remembered through his hangover, the down payment on his apartment, phone expense and a number of beers. Not only would his remaining cash not be enough to buy ample groceries, but also it would not even buy him a meal at a decent restaurant. Continuing with his newly forced frugal living, he was reluctant to use his car if not absolutely necessary. Gasoline would be an additional expense that he would need to minimize.

George grabbed his lightweight tan windbreaker from his closet, and ventured outside where he found that there was a moderate breeze. He would have enjoyed the wind whistling through the trees if he did not have such a headache. The walking and aspirin gradually helped clear up his physical aches. Now, with only his small amount of cash, George was beginning to panic. He was left with few options.

He knew what he would do. He would call Deborah and see if she would release some funds to him. He walked to where he had used the public telephone earlier, and called. No answer. Okay, he would sacrifice some gasoline, drive out to their old home, and see if he could find her. *Now let's see, today is Thursday,* he thought, *so she'll be at her hairdressers until about two o'clock this afternoon.* Yeah, he would meet her there at home when she got back.

Arriving at their former residence, he decided to go on in and wait for her. Then he recalled that he had left his house keys inside when he was there a few days ago, while picking up the remainder of his clothes and personal belongings. Damn! Sometimes lately, his brain simply was not functioning as it used to do. Nothing else to do but wait in his car and observe the condition of his neglected garden. He saw it gradually deteriorating, but did not really care. Obviously, Deborah was not tending to it either.

Deborah, upon returning from her hair appointment, spotted him and his car. She knew she did not want to speak to him. Therefore, she quickly stopped her car at the end of the street and turned around. After nearly two hours, George finally decided that she would not be arriving home soon. He disgustedly backed his car out of their drive and returned to his apartment. Things just were not going his way at all.

CHAPTER THIRTEEN

SITTING ON THE EDGE of his unmade bed, George realized that he simply had to have some money. What could he do? He was quickly becoming desperate. He had very little food left in the apartment and was now almost out of cash. *Okay*, he finally decided, *I'll accept humiliation and see if I can get a job at that local fast food down the street. He had seen the sign in the window stating that there were "exciting employment opportunities" awaiting him inside. Hell yes, he'd grill hamburgers for a few bucks. Maybe even get free meals out of it too.*

So, forty-six year old George Albert Sheldon, graduate and experienced mechanical engineer, began a new career of cooking and selling fast food. He was considerably older than the manager was, but quickly caught on to the standard operations. He found the work quite boring. He also felt that it was belittling, but no one around there knew him, so it was not quite so bad for his ego. Since his meals came with the job, at least that settled one of his problems.

Although George would be the last to grasp it, his appearance and mental focus were rapidly changing. His shaving had become irregular, he could not recall when he last had a haircut, and more frequently than not, he realized that his breath had become constantly fetid. He still tried to keep his clothes laundered; he had no access to an iron. Wrinkled clothing was rapidly becoming his standard dress. He disliked going home after his shift was over smelling like stale, greasy food. He realized that maybe it did not matter so much, since there was nobody there to complain. He hung his work clothes on hangers on the outside door to the deck of his apartment every evening, to give them a chance to air out somewhat. This particular restaurant did not pay laundry expenses, so he had no choice but to operate this way. What George did not realize was that since he was lax with cleaning his apartment, it frequently smelled worse than he did.

Ultimately, with at least a little income coming in on a regular basis and his food more or less provided at the restaurant, he finally began to accumulate a tiny amount of reserve. At last, he bought himself a cheap electric iron and washed his street clothes and uniforms in the laundry room of the apartment complex, where he would iron them as best he knew how. He was grateful that his manager never complained about his appearance. His responsibility at the restaurant was relatively easy, with only a small hourly wage, but at least it was subsistence. He did not need to drive his car to work, because it was only a few blocks away.

However, George's worries about the SUV never completely left him. After a while, he decided that maybe his moves away from his former home and employer might have actually relieved him of that burden. Perhaps it had "lost" him. He could not recall when the dreaded SUV last made an appearance to him, and did not care to remember. He was constantly relieved when each day passed and that peculiar ear sensation and unholy lingering taste did not return. His nightly indulging with alcohol might have dulled those particular senses, though.

Life gradually became somewhat more stable for him. He had a meager, but adequate income, had regular meals, and was accepting of his status. It was quite a step-down from his former life, but he felt as though he was adapting. Of course, his felt need for alcohol occasionally caused him to dip into his meager budget.

After working at the restaurant for several weeks, his young coworkers began to accept him and actually appeared to enjoy having somewhat of a father figure around them. Several of them came to him for various types of advice, ranging from temptations to try drugs, to pregnancies, gang activity and family difficulties. Although he was never certain that his advice was good, he tried to give them the best his life experiences could offer. He enjoyed the opportunity to try. Since he and Deborah had no children, he was grateful at last to act as a father, or perhaps an uncle.

As he became more settled into his new life, his desire to drink gradually began to become less of a need. His skin color and texture, as well as his general health, slowly began to improve, and he became almost happy again. A young lady at the restaurant volunteered to cut his hair for him on a regular basis. Although she asked for no money, he gave her two dollars each time.

There was an occasional letter from Deborah's lawyer, stating this or that, but George had just decided that he would just let her run with things in her own way. She could have the house, greenhouse, her car and everything else. That was a former life, and he simply did not have the will to argue. He had no serious money that they could get. He made a conscious decision not to hire an attorney to fight Deborah. Even if he never received his deserved half of their accumulated property, he simply no longer gave a damn. *The hell with it! Life goes on.* He was getting reasonably comfortable with his present situation, even putting a little money aside with which to pay the next months' rent on the apartment. He had become acquainted with a few of his neighbors, and was well liked and accepted by most of them. A divorcee about his age living in the complex was friendly toward him. He remained somewhat withdrawn from her, however, not certain about his future. His self-esteem continued to remind him that he was once again becoming a nice person and he did not want to encourage a relationship that might end in some kind of hurt for the other party. *Besides, what about Satan and his SUV?* Maybe, when he was a little more stable in his life, he would pursue a more intimate friendship either with her, or with someone else that might venture along into his world. But, who could see into the future?

One day the restaurant manager called him into her office. The young black woman was dressed in the standard restaurant uniform, and wearing a plastic apron. She had been making biscuits earlier and had flour on the apron as well as in her hair. He stood before her, expecting a chewing out and wondering what he might have done wrong.

"George," she said. "You've worked here for several months, and you're doing a fine job. I have found that you are steady, dependable, and never complain like so many of the young kids do. You have been a real good employee. I am sometimes a little upset when you walk in here smelling like a brewery. However, as far as I have been able to figure, you have always shown up sober. I'll say that much for you." She smiled, looked him directly in the eyes, and said, "Therefore, as of today, I'm promoting you to Assistant Manager."

George, surprised with this news, beamed, saying, "Hey, that's great! I sure do appreciate it, Lucille. Thanks, and I'll try not to let you down."

Lucille replied, "You already know how to do your new duties. I'll tell all the kids about your promotion."

Nodding happily, he went back out into the restaurant proper and began his standard routine. He thought *I'm really beginning to have my life come together again. Let's see, that'll mean a raise to nearly ten bucks an hour. That ought to help the old budget.*

CHAPTER FOURTEEN

For George, taking a day off from work became a real luxury. He had very little else to occupy his time—some TV now and then, and a touch of light reading. In addition, because he felt the continuing need to earn as much money as possible, he frequently accepted six and seven days straight of working at the busy restaurant. He occasionally did check the newspaper for advertisements for better employment, but had not located any possibilities that he sensed would enhance his life any better. He felt that he could stay just where he was quite comfortably, indefinitely. *Who needs to have the work pressures of a mechanical engineer, anyway? Maybe sometime I'll think differently, but not right now.* The promotion and subsequent raise would make things a little better for him. He was actually becoming reasonably happy for a change. Not much money, but very little pressure.

However, little did he suspect that a change was soon to come…

* * *

One bright Sunday morning George scheduled himself the day off, and he decided to take a leisurely drive out of town. He had seen a write-up and some advertising photos in the paper about a resort area only fifty or so miles from where he was living. So, for a change, he decided to get in his car and drive over there, just for a look-see. He harbored no illusions of purchasing one of the luxurious villas, but felt like it would be fun to visit.

It was a very pleasant and mild day, with numerous white fluffy clouds, drifting along like a flotilla of dogwood leaves meandering on a stream, so George decided to drive with his windows open. He knew he would enjoy the breeze and the smell of freshly mown grass along the wayside. He passed some ripe blackberry bushes, deciding to stop on his return trip, and pick a few. *Yeah,* he thought, *they'll be good on my breakfast cereal tomorrow.*

On the drive to his destination, he was running parallel to railroad tracks and recalled the pleasant times he experienced as a child, waving to the engineers on passing trains. Suddenly he became aware of some twitching sensations in the tips of his ears. He thought very little about it at first, assuming that it was the effect of the wind blowing into the car and across his face and head. However, as he continued to move along the highway, he closed the window, and the tingling continued—and was increasing. In addition, much to his dread, he became more and more aware of a bad taste in his mouth. He began to feel queasy.

Damn! He slammed his hand down upon the steering wheel, and nearly lost control of his car. *Damn it! So, it's happening again. Oh, why can't I get rid of this? That bastard devil is back. What did I ever do to deserve this horror?* Tears began to flow freely from his eyes, nearly clouding his vision. George slowed his car and pulled off onto the side of the road where he stopped. Then his remorse began to turn to anger. He opened the door, got out and, blinking rapidly to try to clear his vision, started looking around. He saw no light blue SUV. Drivers and passengers of several passing cars stared at him curiously. He felt slightly relieved as he got back into his car upon finding no SUV. He pulled back onto the highway and continued his trip. Yet, the ear stinging and foul taste continued to remind him that the SUV simply must be around. He just knew that a major tragedy was imminent. Somewhere nearby? His increasing fear began to nauseate him. He belched a taste of bile. *I've got to find some way to stop that evil son of a bitch. I can't let it go on.* He could feel his heart pounding—the muscles in his face tightening. *Oh, why do I have to be involved in all these terrible tragedies? I hoped it was gone from my life.*

Nevertheless, it was clearly signaling—alerting him. In effect, it was telling him to get ready for something big. What would happen? Where? When? Surely, he must find out what and when soon. He felt his nausea increasing. His anxiety was nearly overwhelming. *Should I stop the car and go back home?* However, he felt that he must go on. If he could locate Satan's intended victim, perhaps he could prevent the damage. Moreover, with any luck, he hoped to save some lives as he did at that mobile home park. He particularly wanted to eliminate any loss of life. *That damnable thing just keeps on killing and maiming.* George's bodily symptoms continued as he drove down the two-lane asphalt highway. His hands were sweating profusely, making it difficult to hold the steering wheel. He kept wiping his palms on his trousers. He felt the strong sting of his adrenaline flowing through his veins. He rubbed the tips of his ears vigorously, first one, then the other, almost to the point of blistering the tender skin on them. Yet, the tingling continued. He knew from his previous experiences that there was nothing that could relieve the bad taste. Not until the horror was finished. *Where is that damn blue SUV? Why, oh why, must this terrible thing be happening? These atrocious incidents don't kill me. They don't even injure me. Why is that devil teasing me this way? Maybe he just ought to kill me and be done with it. Is he testing me for some ungodly reason known only to him? I don't think I can stand much more of this. It has to be around here somewhere. Somehow, I have to put an end to this. Yet, there doesn't seem to be anything I can do.* Frustrated, George looked frantically from side to side as his car moved along. He agonizingly wondered just what to expect this time. He was clammy and not at all sure he would not lose his breakfast.

Still, with determination, he drove along at a reduced speed. Continuing to seek out some view of the dreaded SUV, he almost hoped beyond all hope that it would just be another unexplainable coincidence.

George prayed aloud, "Please God, don't let me spot it. Please don't put me through this again." He reached over, opened the glove compartment of his car and retrieved his camera. That thought helped bolster his resolve.

George, even at his reduced speed soon came up behind a slow-moving bus full of young children. It appeared to be a church group taking a field trip. He could see numerous youngsters, aged perhaps from six to maybe eleven years. They were all frolicking with each other as the bus moved steadily along. George found a spot where he could pass the bus and noted as he traveled beside it that it was from The First Baptist Church. He was concerned that Satan might choose this bus as his target. He could visualize the headlines: "Church Bus Crashes! Many Children Dead!" *Oh Lord, I hope not,* he reflected, as he again increased his speed. *Not those poor innocent children.*

There! Over there! Yes! Now I see it! I do! The damned vile thing. No doubt about it. The SUV was traveling at about George's same speed on an access road paralleling the one on which George was motoring. It was on the other side of the railroad tracks. George could not see the driver due to the higher level of the rails above the highway, but he knew who was driving. The devil! *That bastard! What should I do?* He wondered if it, indeed, was to be the bus of church kids. George's mind raced as he tried to make a reasonable guess as to what victim the SUV's wicked driver had in mind at this point. There was the blue sport utility vehicle and there was the church bus. Consequently, he judged, it just had to be after the bus.

Should I stop and flag the bus down? He would look very silly if he did and that was not the target. On the other hand, George could not spot any other potential targets for the type of disaster usually found when the SUV made its appearance. *Oh, I feel so sick and angry.* Fear and anxiety were overwhelming him. Yet, he could not just sit by and let a horrible incident occur.

George decided to sit tight for a while longer. He badly wanted to stop his car and take a picture, but then the SUV might have traveled further down its parallel road by that time. He was very uncertain as to how to handle this developing situation. He noticed that the bus's speed was constant, so he held the space between his car and the bus as close to the same as he could safely. He certainly did not want to cause a commotion or disturbance with the young people. He glanced over and saw that the SUV was also driving along on the adjacent road at about the same speed.

This was quickly becoming very unnerving to George. What was going to happen? And when? And where? Now George was becoming even more frantic. His hands ached from his continuous tight grip on his steering wheel. Just at that moment, as his car came over a slight rise, George spotted a huge factory complex about two miles ahead, just off the road to his left. *Maybe that's the bastard's target. Nothing's happened yet, though.* Nevertheless, in his heart he knew it would be some terrible tragedy. He could not see far enough ahead to determine if there were any shifts working on this Sunday morning or not. If so, there might be several hundred workers there to be involved in some tragic "accident." As he weighed the situation in his mind, George wondered if he should properly call the anticipated upcoming incident an "accident." *More likely,* he thought, *a planned murder of many innocents by that evil bastard in the SUV.* At least that was the way the other situations seemed to be to him. If only he could have been more aware of the involvement of the sport utility vehicle ahead of time, perhaps he could have saved even more people's lives than just those at the mobile homes.

Now George realized that he was in a serious dilemma. Would it be the church bus, and if so, how would it be involved? A wreck perhaps? Could he prevent it? Alternatively, would it somehow be the upcoming factory complex, and how would that occur? Moreover, how could he stop either thing from happening? Maybe it would be impossible to stop the catastrophe from coming to pass. He simply had no way of knowing.

George made his decision. He would attempt to control both, but was not at all sure that he could do it. First, he would stop the church bus. It might disturb the children's excitement and joyous anticipation, but it might also save their lives. Then, if he had sufficient time, he would dash over to the factory, and, as with the refinery, try to effect an evacuation. He kept glancing over the tracks for the top of the SUV as it continued down the parallel road. *Still there, that mean bastard.*

George turned on his emergency flashers, and sped up the road for a distance of about a hundred yards. Then he quickly brought his car to a halt on the roadside, got out and began flagging down the church bus. He waved furiously, but the driver showed no intention of stopping. As the bus moved past him, George thought *he must think I am trying to hijack them. Somehow, I've got to stop them. I've just got to. Time must be running out.* He got back in his car and speeding up, again passed the bus. In the process of the pass, George suddenly had to swerve onto the left shoulder of the highway. The oncoming auto missed his by mere inches. Once passed, he opened his window. Sticking his left arm out, he frantically motioned for the bus driver to pull over. Again, to no avail. *My gosh, what does a guy have to do?* Finally, in one last attempt to stop the bus, George again sped up, and then turned his car sideways across the road. *The bus driver will have to stop now.*

An oncoming pickup truck nearly hit George's car, but found just enough room on the shoulder to miss him. He passed by blowing his horn, swinging his fist at George and yelling a string of profanities.

This time the bus driver finally came to a halt. Relieved, George went to the bus door, and when it opened, the driver came rushing out, threatening George with his closed fist.

"What in the hell do you think you're doing, you damned idiot? You SOB!" screamed the enraged driver. His profanity quickly convinced George that the driver was, indeed, not the minister. George backed away slightly, but began to explain to the enraged driver that there was extreme danger ahead and that the driver should either return to town or at least make a major detour. He told him that at all costs the bus should not continue on its present path. The driver was unconvinced, still angry at being stopped—especially in such a reckless manner.

George said, in as sincere and calm a voice as he could muster, "Look. All I ask is that you at least detour from the road you were taking to wherever it is that you're going. I have no concern about your destination with all these young people, but you surely don't want to endanger any of them. Now, do you? What difference will a few extra minutes make?"

George's obvious anxiety and reasonable suggestions seemed to make an impression. The driver had calmed down somewhat by this time. He agreed to turn off at the next road to the left and make his way to the youth camp that way. He said it would take him an extra twenty-five minutes, but guessed that would not hurt the yammering bunch on the bus much. The driver stared at George with some disdain, but reentered the bus to renew his trip.

Very relieved, George got into his car again, about to head for the complex, now only a mile down the road. Maybe he would be in time, maybe not. All he could do now was hope. He glanced over across the railroad tracks and saw that the SUV was still there. It had apparently stopped while he tended to the church bus.

Now! Before starting his car engine again, George grabbed his camera and dashed up the rise of the railroad tracks. He snapped four quick shots of the resting SUV and its driver, the devil.

Angrily returning to his own car, George muttered, at least now I will have some photographs of the damned thing. Now he could get people to believe him. *Yes, that ought to do it,* he thought excitedly. *Damn 'em all. Now that I'll have proof that there really is a light blue SUV, and the frigging devil, everybody'll quit thinking I'm crazy.* He started his car again, and then hesitated. *No! Not yet!*

He pulled a lever and opened the car trunk. Lifting the flexible floor, he removed the tire iron. *This time, I'm gonna get that son-of-a-bitch devil to come out. Then, I'll beat the crap out of him with this tool. I've got to stop him.*

Once again, George ran to the top of the rise. *Still there.* Sliding down the gravel grade, he took his heavy tool and began to beat against the glass of the SUV. The devil continued to sit inside, unmoving. Now, however, his hands were on the steering wheel. George continued his beating—one blow after another. No damage. He tried banging against the metal hood. Still no damage. Tears of his anger and frustration flowed. *There must be some* way *I can get in there to him.* George ceased his banging and tried to wedge the flat part of his tool into the vehicle's door. He struggled, but could gain no purchase. The devil continued to sit unmoving inside and stared at him. *I can't do it! He's too much for me!* Exhausted, and in terrible torment, George dropped to his knees, crying out loudly. *Oh, God! Can somebody somewhere not help me?* The devil sat there staring down at him.

Realizing that he could not do anything here, George rose and ran back to his car. *By God, at least maybe I can get that factory evacuated. If I can't stop him, maybe I can still save some lives.*

Starting his car again, he sped toward the industrial complex. His ears were bothering him as much as ever and his bad taste had not decreased one iota. It was awful...nasty...absolutely unearthly...and getting worse by the minute. He wondered just how much longer it would last. He knew with certainty that it would not dissipate until after the "incident" was past. Although now speeding quite dangerously, he peered over toward the railroad tracks to see if he could spot the SUV. He could only see its roof, but he could tell that it was continuing to travel at almost his exact same speed.

Shortly he drove onto the plant's access road, where a closed gate confronted him. There was a guard in the small brown frame building, and George quickly exited his car. He entered the shack before the guard could even rise from his chair.

George said rapidly, "How many people are in the plant today?"

"Well sir," replied the scrawny, heavily tattooed guard, whom George quickly determined to be in his middle fifties. "Just who the hell are you and what business is it of yours?"

"I've got to speak to the plant manager. Quickly! It's a matter of life and death."

The guard raised his thick bushy graying eyebrows, casually picked up his thermos, poured himself a refill of coffee, and then looked defiantly back up at George.

"You still haven't told me your name."

"Look you," replied George, glancing at his watch anxiously. He was so frightened about how much more time he had left. "My name is George Sheldon, and the manager won't know me, but I've got to talk to him immediately. I said it might well be a matter of life or death. Now get him on the phone for me. Now! I'll talk to him from right here." George again looked toward the railroad tracks in an effort to spot the SUV, but he could not see it from his position.

The guard finally turned from George with a quizzical look in his dull green eyes and picked up the phone. He pushed a button. George breathed a silent moment of relief. "Mr. Jacobson. This here is Willie down at the front gate. There's a guy here, says he needs to talk to you. Matter of life or death, he says." He peered at George. "Yeah, I know, but he insists."

George's patience ran out so he reached over the startled guard and grabbed the phone. "Jacobson!" he screamed into the phone. "I've got information that your plant may be blown up at any minute. You must believe me. You've got to shut down and evacuate the entire plant immediately. I don't know how much time you've got, but you need to do it right now!"

Robert Jacobson was sitting at his desk this quiet Sunday morning, reading a newspaper. He loved these lazy Sunday shifts because they gave him an opportunity for some relief from the hectic workdays during the week. He also enjoyed getting away from those two spoiled teenage brats that came with his third wife. They were at his home with her on weekends, so he was glad to get away from them.

However, he was taken aback with this phone call from the front gate. He hesitated for a moment, flabbergasted, dumbfounded, however, his mind suddenly jolted into alert. He then spoke into the phone to George, "Hold on just a minute, buddy." He thought, *now, just who was this nut at the gate and what in the hell was he talking about? Shut down? That's preposterous!* "That is a heck of a statement you're making. It might not be all that simple. Let me think about this for a second."

He grabbed his outside telephone and called 911.

"Emergency. How may I help you?"

"Connect me to the sheriff's office, quickly!" Jacobson broke out into a sweat.

"Hello, Sheriff's office."

He spoke rapidly. "This is Mr. Robert Jacobson out at the Enterprise Industries plant. We are twenty-six miles west of town on Route 57. I have some sort of nut at my gate threatening my plant and me. Can you rush somebody right out and take care of this for me?"

"Yes sir. We will get someone right on it. In fact, we have a cruiser out that way right now. Is the individual there with you right now?"

"Well, no. He's out at my front gate. The guard will not let him in, but the fellow says the plant will blow up at any minute. Please hurry. I don't know if he's a crank or just what."

During Jacobson's phone call to the Sheriff, George was quickly looking around in the guard shack for some sort of switch that he could throw in order to open the chain link fence. Nothing. He grabbed the guard by the front of his uniform shirt, yanked him up out of his chair and, with his face not two inches from that of the guard's, yelled, "Open the damn gate!"

As a frustrated and anxious George was so forcibly hoisting him up, the guard reached down and quickly pulled his pistol out of his holster. He pointed it at George's stomach. George immediately let the man go and stepped back. He was breathing hard.

The guard said in a squeaky voice, "Back off mister. You're going to sit down in this here chair and we'll just wait and see what Mr. Jacobson wants to do with you." The guard nudged George around, put his bony hand against George's chest and pushed him into the chair. "Now just you sit there mister. You hear me?"

George saw no alternatives, so he did as the guard ordered, but continued to look around for a button or switch that he might use to open the gate. He was frantic, but suddenly felt helpless. He was sweating profusely, with his hair matted from the moisture. What else could he do now?

"Please let me talk to Jacobson again," he pleaded. "It's real important, believe me."

"Just you shut your mouth and sit there."

The guard continued to point his revolver at George. George noticed the hand holding the weapon was shaking and hoped the guard was conscientious enough not to pull the trigger. "I'm gonna call Mr. Jacobson again," he said.

"Hello, Mr. Jacobson? This is Willie down at the entrance again. Sorry to bother you, but I had to pull my pistol on this here guy. He tried to get rough with me. Now what do you want me to do with him?"

Jacobson spoke softly into the phone, "I've called the Sheriff's department. They said there'd be an officer here in a few minutes. Hold him there and we'll let them decide what to do with him. Are you hurt?"

"Naw, he didn't hurt me a bit," he said proudly. "I just caught him flatfooted with my trusty .38. I'll keep him quiet until the law arrives."

Hearing this conversation, George said to himself, *Oh damn. Here we go again.* He could just imagine going through another tiring, fruitless interrogation—maybe even being jailed for assault. *What in the hell can I do?*

Suddenly, there was the ear shattering thunder of a tremendous explosion. It occurred about three miles further down the road from the manufacturing plant. Almost immediately, a shock wave and a second huge boom shook the guardhouse. Both Willie and George turned their heads and saw a bright arrow of flame reaching skyward, piercing clouds like a welder's torch to a piece of cotton. Immense columns of thick black smoke were mushrooming upward. Willie lowered his gun and rushed outside the guardhouse, inadvertently allowing George to follow. They both stood there in astonishment, watching the ever-increasing flames.

George cried out despondently, "Oh my God! I was wrong!" He gawked at the distant developing catastrophe. *I was trying to go to the wrong things.*

He cried out in anguish once again, "I guessed wrong." *But, how could I have known? Here I am, in trouble, with the law on its way and I guessed wrong. I don't know what's happened up there ahead, but I clearly didn't help save anybody's life this time.* He was saddened, angry, almost to the point of hysteria. Tears formed in his eyes and flooded his flushed face unashamedly. "I couldn't stop that frigging Satan."

The guard, engrossed in the calamity, said nothing.

Soon George heard the siren of a deputy's car nearing the plant and guard-house. He presumed that he would be taken in for questioning again. However, to his sudden relief, the car sped by, obviously on its way to where the explosion had occurred.

George decided that now he could easily walk away from Willie and the guardhouse. He noticed that Willie was just standing there dumbfounded, peer-ing distantly toward the enormous tower of flaming yellows, oranges and reds. His hand was holding the pistol loosely at his side. George casually walked over to his car, started it and slowly drove away. He felt the necessity to seek out the all-too-familiar blue SUV, so headed toward the fire. Looking in his rearview mirror, he noticed that the guard had re-holstered his gun and was continuing to stand there, still observing the distant inferno. As he drove down the road, three more emergency vehicles sped up behind him with their blue, as well as red lights flashing. He pulled his car over onto the shoulder, allowing them to pass easily. There was no oncoming traffic. Since the explosion occurred about three miles from the industrial plant, George quickly arrived on the scene. He got out of his car when he found a police car shifted sideways as a roadblock. He hastily walked down the otherwise empty road beyond the blocking automobile and observed the horror.

George closed his eyes tightly, hoping against all hope that the tragic scene would go away. He badly wanted to awaken from this nightmare. However, he knew it was not a dream.

He saw that a freight train had somehow careened off the tracks at a moder-ately high speed. It had tumbled down the embankment, where at least four of the dozen or so tank cars had exploded into flame. Several kinds of highly flam-mable liquids had splashed like cascading ocean surf further down the slope, across the parallel road, and into a nursing home. The roar of the terrible inferno was nearly deafening, and he could feel the heat even from this distance. He wit-nessed another explosion occurring that blew a fierce wave of hot wind over him. It almost knocked him off balance. He could see that not only was the nursing home almost totally engulfed in flames, so were the thick woods beyond it. He spotted no people running from the building. He heard no screams.

George quickly surveyed the scene for the SUV as a deputy sheriff ran over toward him, shouting, "For God's sake, mister, get the hell away from this place. Some more of those tank cars might blow at any time." Before he left, however, George quickly scanned again for the SUV, but could not locate it.

George realized he could do nothing, so sadly, very distressed and sickened, got into his car and returned toward his home. He realized that he was also extremely angry. *Damn, I screwed up,* he thought. *If I'd had my head on straight, maybe I could have figured out something. Why was Satan staying along side me on that other road? And, why can't I get him out of his damn SUV?*

On his way home, numerous additional sheriff, police, highway patrol cars, as well as fire trucks and assorted emergency vehicles whizzed past. Glancing upward through the front window of his car, he noticed a helicopter flying rapidly toward the disaster. He saw the heavy smoke plume continuing to rise.

This heartrending incident shook George to the bone. He could barely hold his hands steady enough to keep the steering wheel under control. Twice he forced himself to stop his car in order to pull in several deep breaths and simply try to regain his composure. Torrents of tears continued to flow freely down his cheeks. He became nauseous and, jerking his car to a rapid halt, threw open his door and retched onto the pavement. His remorse at his inability to prevent the disasters was becoming overwhelming. He was livid. He decided that he needed a drink, and so he stopped by a package store before arriving back home. When he arrived at his apartment, he went in and promptly drank himself into oblivion. He wanted no more thoughts about the SUV and the revulsion he had witnessed. He had forgotten about the blackberries.

The tragedy had killed one hundred thirty residents of the large nursing home, with six bodies never recovered. The officials decided that their remains were cremated during the blazing inferno. Three of the four members of the train crew perished, as did one brave firefighter.

CHAPTER FIFTEEN

*K*NOCK! KNOCK!

George, lying on his crumpled couch, stirred. Slowly opening his eyes, he saw that sunshine was beaming through the half-closed blinds. Was it still Sunday? Or Monday? He had a momentary thought that he should do something, but could not quite get his brain to decide what.

Knock! Knock! Knock! This time the sounds were much louder and more insistent. George finally realized that someone was knocking on his front door.

"Ugh, Ju-just a minute," he yelled out, and then grabbed both sides of his head with his hands. He felt as though his head was being split like a log of firewood by an ax. His yell made him feel excruciating pain in his temples as if his head were the clapper of a ringing cathedral bell. He slowly pulled himself off the couch, accidentally kicking an empty whiskey bottle across the floor as he made his way toward the door. Oh, how he ached!

"Yeah," he whispered to the visitor as he opened the unlocked door.

"Sir, I'm with the county sheriff's department. Are you Mr. George Sheldon?"

George blinked twice and viewed a young man. He was wearing a beige turtleneck shirt, brown pants and well-worn tan deck shoes. The man flashed a sheriff's badge at him, and he immediately suspected what the man wanted. George knew he was to be questioned about the explosion that took place—was it yesterday?

"Come on in, while I make myself a cup of coffee." George uttered, in resignation, holding one hand against his temple. "I had a little private party last night, and you just woke me up."

The young deputy, issuing a half-smile, could easily sense that George had indeed had himself a party. There was the almost overwhelming smell of spilled alcohol in the room. The sight of the empty bottle lying against the wall helped confirm it. The living room was in disarray, with couch pillows scattered across the floor. Sheldon's jacket and shirt were strewn sloppily over the back of an easy chair.

He smiled and casually said, "Mr. Sheldon, may I ask if you had someone with you here last night?"

George meandered slowly into the kitchen, opened a cabinet door and removed a jar of instant coffee.

He quietly uttered, "Oh-h...Ah, no." He forced a small smile. "I just felt like having a few drinks and must have gotten a little bit carried away." He slowly and carefully turned his throbbing head toward the deputy. He said just above a strained whisper, "Want some coffee?"

"No thank you, sir. But, you go right ahead. It looks like you need that coffee pretty bad."

As George retrieved a saucepan from under the kitchen counter, he again held his head. The clatter of the pans sounded like hail on a tin roof. Standing up slowly, he half-filled it with water and placed it on the stove, turning on the gas burner.

"Excuse me," he whispered, holding his throbbing head. "I've go to go to the toilet and get me some aspirin. Be back in a moment."

The deputy glanced around the apartment and decided that George would not try to escape. He sat down in the easy chair; first moving George's abandoned clothes over to the couch. He was not enjoying the potent apartment odors. He waited patiently as he heard George run some water in his bathroom, then, after a moment, flush his toilet. George returned to the kitchen wearing a faded green bathrobe. He took some of the boiling water and poured it into the cup where he had scooped the coffee. He raised the cup with shaking hands to his mouth and took a tentative sip.

George began to slowly blow his breath over the top of the cup, gradually cooling it to a usable temperature. Maybe the coffee aroma would help clear his head.

The deputy finally said, "Mr. Sheldon, I have to ask you where you were yesterday morning."

George decided it would be pointless to make any excuses. After all, he knew he was completely innocent of any wrongdoing. Walking slowly into the living room, he took another sip of coffee, still holding the cup with both hands.

"Yeah," he whispered. "I know about the train wreck. I was out there. What about it?"

The young deputy was somewhat surprised because of George's spontaneous admission.

He stood and said, "Sir. I have orders to bring you down to the sheriff's department for some questioning. Will you please come with me now, sir?"

"Sure," George said with an expression of resignation on his face. "Do I need to call a lawyer?"

"I don't expect so, sir," responded the deputy. "As I understand it, they just have some questions to ask you. It's all quite informal, I think."

While the officer was speaking, George gulped down the remainder of his coffee, stood, took off his robe, and grabbed his badly soiled and wrinkled shirt and his jacket from the couch.

Expelling a big sigh, he uttered slowly, "Okay. Let's go."

Driving on toward the Sheriff's office, they happened to pass by a fast-food establishment.

Noticing this, George, feeling slightly nauseous and hearing his empty stomach rumble, said, "Hey deputy. How about stopping here so I can get some food. I've had no breakfast and am really hungry." George was still quite hung over, but his head was finally beginning to clear somewhat.

"Well," replied the young deputy. "Since you're actually not under arrest and have come along voluntarily, I suppose it'll be all right."

It was nearly ten o'clock when the patrol car pulled into a parking place at the restaurant. George and the deputy emerged from the car. As they walked toward the entrance, George glanced at a newspaper box, and read the headlines: "Major Tragedy. Freight Train Derails Over Bridge. Explosion and Fire Destroy Nursing Home. 135 Dead."

"Oh my God," stammered George, as he showed the deputy the newspaper's headlines. George then pulled two quarters from the pocket of his heavily wrinkled trousers, and bought a copy of the paper. The two men walked into the restaurant, where George bought a sausage biscuit and cup of coffee. He offered to pay for the deputy's breakfast, but was politely declined.

"Rules, you know," the deputy responded, as he ordered himself a soda.

After receiving their orders, the two men found an empty booth, where George quickly spread out the front page of the paper. Scanning it rapidly, as the deputy sought out the sports section; George learned that at press time there was still a lingering forest fire around and beyond the destroyed nursing home. The story mentioned that the freight train derailed over an old wooden trestle, and several cars tumbled across the access road and down the ravine toward the nursing home. Because these cars were filled with flammable as well as caustic liquids, there had been an almost instant explosion. The blazing inferno had flowed down the slight slope, across the road, and into the two-story frame facility. There were additional explosions as two separate tanks of propane were almost immediately overheated and ruptured, causing even more damage. There were no survivors. One attendant, who had been outside the residence on a smoke break was badly burned from one of the propane explosions and died within minutes of the arrival of the emergency crews. George was terribly shaken with the tragedy, remembering again that he had been unable to prevent it from happening.

As George learned later, the conflagration, being fed by the highly flammable materials, destroyed the building within thirty minutes. It had mercilessly killed all the home's inhabitants within that brief time. The heat from the fire, plus some remaining liquids still flowing from the tank cars, spread around the smoldering remains of the home, extending the holocaust to the adjacent thick woods. There had been no appreciable rain in the vicinity for over two weeks, and the result was that there was a great deal of dry tender available for ignition. The firefighters found it impossible for them to try to put out the fire in the home. Therefore, they directed most of their efforts at trying to control the rapidly spreading forest fire. Seeing that it had become out of control, they quickly found it necessary to call for assistance from the Forestry Service and other nearby fire departments. As the day went on, the winds became more of a problem, and fire-dousing airplanes were finally called upon to help quench the raging woods fire.

The deputy showed no serious interest in the news story that George was reading, and sipped his soda nonchalantly. George, however, was astounded and aghast at the holocaust. He realized instantly that he had totally missed it. He had seen the SUV, tried his best to stop it from triggering some form of calamity. Yet, he knew that some sort of disaster was pending. He could have only guessed at what kind it would be. He had been wrong on two counts—the church bus and the industrial plant.

Was there any way that he could have anticipated things better? How could he have saved some lives? What in hell was wrong that he could not even break into that devil's SUV? Moreover, George recalled, the bastard just sat there grinning at him. What could he possibly do the next time the depraved devil made its appearance? He felt extremely angry and disillusioned. He reviewed his responses of the previous day. However, he still could not determine a method of how he could have done anything else to eliminate or at least reduce the horrible carnage. At any rate, George's head was hurting too much to care at this moment.

Putting down his empty soda cup, the deputy said, "Okay, it's time for us to go along now. I guess the Sheriff'll begin to wonder why I've not brought you in. I ain't been with the force all that long, so I don't want to screw things up."

George pulled a last sip from his coffee cup. "Yeah, sure. I guess we do need to move on."

He was confident that he knew what would be forthcoming when they arrived at the Sheriff's office. Like before, he was ushered into a standard interrogation room. They had all begun to look more or less alike. Except, this one was constructed of concrete block and was painted a bright yellow with beige trim. *Unusual,* thought George. *I thought they were all institutional green.*

There were the same old questions that he had heard before from the other authorities. Was he involved in some sort of conspiracy? Who were his accomplices? If his plan was to derail the train, why did George stop at the industrial plant first?

"Oh yes," commented his questioner, a slender middle-aged man with a pasty face, "A church bus driver reported the crazy way that you stopped him and made him alter his direction. You must have realized that the church bus would have been driving right near the train when it derailed. Right? Did your conscience start bothering you? C'mon now, admit it. Confess it all to us and it'll go much easier for you."

George said, "Maybe I ought to call a lawyer."

The main questioner removed his black-rimmed glasses and laid them on the table. He then responded, "Well, you certainly have that right. However, we only have a few more questions. Calling in your lawyer would mean you would have to stay here for a lot longer time. Shall I continue?"

George intentionally ignored the investigators for a moment. He relaxed a little bit in his hard chair and pondered his situation with the devil. *Maybe I did save some lives. Perhaps the church bus would have been nearly adjacent to the train when it derailed. And maybe, just maybe, my actions had prevented some devastation and more deaths.* He felt a slight stir of satisfaction when he thought about that. He still could not decide what else he could have done to warn people of the impending doom by the blue vehicle. Since nobody else could see it, he could understand why he could not convince anybody about that damn thing. What on earth could he do to stop the evil? *Oh, hey yeah,* he suddenly remembered. *The camera! I took pictures of the stinking thing. That'll show 'em.*

He then told the police that he had taken several photographs of the SUV before the incident. He said that they could look in his car, get his camera and develop the film. Finally, maybe, people would understand his unfortunate situation and leave him alone. He was extremely tired of all the folderol. He badly needed to be relieved of the entire mess. He wanted to get back to a reasonably normal life again.

George knew all too well that his story generally did not sound plausible, but what else could he say? The truth of the matter was that things happened exactly as he told them. He was not involved with anybody else. There was no conspiracy. No accomplices. In fact, he did not even have much warning or premonition about most of the disasters. They could check with the Institute of Parapsychology for proof that he was neither psychic, nor a liar.

Unfortunately, however, these officials, as had the previous ones, chose not to believe his standard, but true, story. It simply made no sense to them. George realized that it did not even make any sense to him either. An invisible sport utility vehicle—with the devil himself inside. He knew it was a bunch of unbelievable bunk. The grilling continued for hours without letup. George grew more and more weary, his bottom becoming numb from sitting on the hard chair. His eyes were granular and very tired from his squinting. He badly wanted a break—just any kind of short respite from the constant hammering away at him. But except for brief and accompanied toilet breaks, there were none offered. He soon learned that the Sheriff's Department had more than one shift of detectives to come in and interview him.

The long day became a series of:

"Hey man. I'm Sergeant…"

"Hello Mr. Sheldon. I'm detective…"

"Mr. Sheldon, I am Lieutenant…"

He acknowledged that they were nice enough and extremely polite, but all the same, he, as well as they, knew that it was beginning to wear him down. Sooner or later, they determined, he would break. At that point, he would confess and tell them all about the scheme. However, the detectives could not ascertain any reason or advantage for such an involved plot. What would be gained? There had been no demand for anything. No call for money. No demand for any prisoner release. Not even any command for some revocation of county or city ordinances. Nothing. Not even any hint at terrorism. All they knew was that this guy was involved one way or another when a major disaster or a catastrophe had hit their area. There seemed to be no rhyme or reason about it. No one in the department could come up with any explanation.

Nevertheless, eventually, this Sheldon guy'd break. They knew it beyond any shadow of a doubt. Yeah, he would break, and then they would get their answers. In fact, among the deputies there in the station house, a friendly pool was started, as to how long it would take him to tell all. These men and women officers knew that previous questioning had taken place at other police stations, and the Sheriff's Department now had all of George's records, transcripts of his conversations with them as well as the police psychiatrist's report. Maybe that was it...he was simply a raving lunatic who got his kicks by destroying things.

However, George did not "break" for them. He told his interrogators all the answers he had to give. They kept repeating the same questions over and over, with slight variations, and he simply answered as before—truthfully. George had long ago decided that to try to evade the issue of the blue SUV would be fruitless; that one misstep or a lie would only lead to another. His big problem was that nobody believed him, period. It had never been seen by anybody, either at the scene of the tragedies or later. A search of newspaper photographs never showed it. The police had even gone to the local television stations and diligently searched their tapes of the catastrophes. No sign of any big SUV, blue or otherwise. Therefore, the net result was that nobody believed George Sheldon. However, they could not get him to change his story and admit to being criminally involved.

For several hours, the officials discussed among themselves why no letters, notes or even misdirected phone calls had ever appeared. Surely, the law enforcement felt, there must be some weird plot behind all these horrors. There just had to be. There always was.

All of the involved law enforcement agencies contacted each other. They mutually decided to hold George in the county jail for twenty-four hours. Meanwhile, a forensic psychiatrist from San Francisco was flown to North Carolina to interview George. He specialized in bizarre cases.

The officials told George why he was being held. In fact, by this time, he had spent so much time in such situations, that he almost felt comfortable...Not quite, though.

His primary concern was that he was not privy to what was going to happen to him next. That in itself was unsettling. Of course, the law enforcement people dealt with so many outright criminals on a daily basis, that they had no cares whatsoever about his feelings. In fact, they had found that this attitude helped create much more malleable crooks. Then, these people would be much more likely to answer pointed questions. Law enforcement people had long ago determined this fact.

"Mr. Sheldon, do you want to call your attorney? You're entitled to one phone call, you know."

George decided against calling an attorney. He thought, *Why even bother? What could an attorney do anyway? I'll just endure this mess and save myself a bundle of money.* "No," responded a plaintive George. "I've been interrogated by you guys so much and am telling the truth, so why bother?"

A police officer placed George in a holding cell where he would spend the next twenty hours. He did not like it and supposed that he could have requested an attorney and arranged for a release. However, in his now chronic depressed state, he simply accepted his incarceration.

George spent an uncomfortable, nearly sleepless night in the jail. There he was, with nearly a dozen serious criminal suspects in a large holding cell with just enough bunks to hold all of the group, and only a light blanket available. He found no pillow, so he rolled up his already-wrinkled jacket as an inadequate substitute. He felt lucky that none of the other prisoners paid any attention to him. They were all much younger, and several were obviously Hispanic, speaking quietly in Spanish, a language that George did not understand.

Shortly before dawn the next morning, George felt a hand on his shoulder, shaking him into consciousness. He lifted his head slightly, feeling a sudden sharp crick in his neck. He immediately presumed that once he finally fell asleep during the night, he apparently had not moved from a single awkward position.

"Sheldon," he heard a deep gruff voice exclaim. "Get your ass up, and come with me."

As he opened his eyes, George saw a dark hulk standing over him. It was that of a man, perhaps six feet, eight inches tall and no doubt weighing nearly four hundred pounds. George immediately noticed the giant's stale body odor permeating the entire area. He slowly rose from his hard bunk, grabbed his jacket, and obediently followed the man out of the cell. He was glad to hear the iron-barred door clank shut behind him. He was expecting release within a few minutes.

Walking past the detective's bureau, George caught a whiff of coffee. Glancing across the huge room, he spotted several men and two women devouring a box of doughnuts. He was quite hungry. The "smelly giant" had only allowed him to detour by the rest room, which, George quickly noticed, also smelled foul. He thought, *don't these people ever have their damn toilets cleaned?* His rumbling stomach continued to remind him of his need for nourishment. Surely, he would be provided sustenance of some sort. Even half a doughnut would be helpful.

He asked the giant, "Hey buddy. Where can I get some breakfast?"

Sneering at him with dark brown eyes, the jailer retorted, "Ain't part of my job description."

They walked on in silence until arriving at the familiar interrogation room. By this time, George could have found his way alone. Entering it, he found it just like he left it yesterday—or was it last night? While imprisoned, time had a way of passing by with immeasurably slow hours. The room was empty, cold, and smelled of stale coffee. He voluntarily seated himself in the familiar hard straight back chair. He was hungry. In addition, he was now hurting from that gnawing crick in his neck.

With nothing else to do for the moment, George crossed his arms, tilted the chair back on its rear legs slightly, and began nonchalantly studying the room. A single one hundred and fifty watt light bulb was attached to the ceiling. George realized that most of the other interrogation rooms like this these days contained at least one fixture of fluorescent bulbs. But not this one. And of course, the light fixture was enclosed in a heavy wire mesh. Since the ceiling was perhaps twelve feet high, he mused that no one, even by placing a chair on the table, could reach it. No, there was not any way a sole, overwrought prisoner could reach the light fixture, and hang himself. Nope, no attempted suicides in *this* room. (George, even in his most distraught, drunken and depressed moments, never contemplated suicide.) Besides, there was the omnipresent two-way mirror. One never really knew if the officers were observing him surreptitiously. Therefore, he sat there, variously twisting his head and neck in a swivel motion, trying in vain to ease the cramp.

Suddenly he saw a small movement along the floor near one wall. A roach! Should he let it live? *No!* George thought, *if I am going to be forced to be unhappy around here, the least I can do is relieve something of its misery.* George moved his chair back, walked over and messily crushed the roach with his shoe. Sitting back down, he again listened to his stomach growl. He belched loudly. After a while, he simply sat there rubbing his neck.

CHAPTER SIXTEEN

A FTER AN INTERMINABLE WAIT, the lone door beside the mirror opened, and in walked a man that George had never seen before. He was short, perhaps no more than five feet, two inches. He exhibited piercing dark blue eyes, and a balding pate partially covered with a few lingering dark brown hairs. He had a heavy, walrus mustache and a pointed goatee. The stranger walked quite bowlegged, with a near waddle. This reminded George of the eccentric character, *The Penguin*, from the old television series, *Batman*.

Funny, George thought when he observed the man's head. *Most men brush their lingering hair from left to right, whereas this guy does his scarce few from right to left. I wonder if that means he's a southpaw.* During one of his more introspective days before all this damned SUV mess started, George would occasionally wonder curiously why some men continued to sweep their very few remaining hairs over their increasingly expansive bald spot. Maybe it was from long-established habit, or perhaps it was for ego, attempting foolishly to disguise the obvious. He was also curious about those that were going bald having a tendency to grow various types of beards. *Grow it where you can*, thought George with a chuckle. These idle thoughts created a millisecond of remembrance of his own hair loss.

This new fellow certainly appears to be a real doozy. I wonder where the cops found him. I'm sure he'll ask me the same questions as everybody else, and I'll give him the same old unbelievable, but true responses. What else can I do?

For a brief moment George wished Deborah were there with him. She'd be comforting. Damn, he missed her, in spite of her distressing bad habits, and not believing in him. He wished that somehow he could have prevented her throwing him out and filing divorce proceedings against him. *Life just is not the same anymore without her.* He had had a few doubts about really loving her before she forced him out, but all the same, she was generally a real nice comfort to him. He had grown accustomed to her being there when he needed her. Now though, he was totally on his own. In fact, he realized that he had not even heard from either her or that divorce lawyer of hers in some time.

At any rate, this little man came bustling in, no jacket, only a sweat-stained pale blue Hawaiian-style shirt, jeans and dirty sneakers. He was carrying a grossly oversized and stuffed briefcase.

"Hello, Mr. Sheldon," said the little man in a high-pitched, squeaky voice. "I'm Dr. Gordon Royalle, from San Francisco." He held out his hand to shake with George. Finding the newcomer's hand clammy, George discreetly wiped his wet palm off on his trousers.

"Please keep your seat. I've been called here by the local Sheriff's department to have a little chat with you."

"Sure," responded George with a resigned tone.

Yeah, George knew what was coming up next. He had no doubts about that. First, he would start with the friendly, buddy-buddy approach, and get George's usual story. George had no doubt that the police had adequately prepped this little man in advance with George's story. Certainly, they had. Then, after hearing it, and supposedly not believing it, he would start on his mind-altering techniques, trying to trap old Georgie Boy into making some type of mistake. Just like all the rest. Same old, same old.

George happened to glance upward and spotted a moth fluttering around the light bulb. *Now how did he get in this place? Poor thing.* George felt sorry for this near helpless little insect. He presumed that the moth would only follow his inbred instincts to continue to flutter toward certain death once its body struck the ever-attracting light. Why couldn't it somehow anticipate that the burning heat from the bulb would cause it to perish? Yet, on it flew, fluttering its frail wings and approaching death closer each time.

Maybe that was about the same with me, George mused sadly. He was in a predicament that he seemed to realize could cause him irreparable damage, perhaps even death. Yet he felt powerless to stop or even seriously control it. It was controlling his life, altering it, ruining it. These thoughts almost threw George into a deep pit of melancholy. He felt so sad. He was all alone. He needed someone friendly at his side. Yet, he had no one. It would feel so good to "spill his guts" to someone nice that he could trust.

"Mr. Sheldon."

"Mr. Sheldon!" Dr. Royalle, raising his squeaky high-pitched voice, said, "Mr. Sheldon, please turn your attention to me. Please, sir."

George was suddenly pulled from of his dark cave of deep inner thoughts to the present situation. This little "Dr. Somebody" was trying to get—no, demanding—his attention.

"Oh yes," George replied as he brought his gaze down upon the psychiatrist. "I'm very sorry, *sir*, I am so hungry that I was searching for some flying bugs to eat." He grinned. "Say, doctor, you don't happen to have anything in that bag of yours to eat, do you?" George correctly assumed that the doctor did not, and had already had an ample breakfast, but he maliciously wanted to bug the guy a little. Besides, if he did happen to have something in there to nibble on, George assured himself that he would not turn it down.

"Have you not had any breakfast, Mr. Sheldon? I assumed that you'd been fed here."

George said, "I haven't had anything solid to eat since…yesterday before noon. They dragged me in here just before lunch then and all I've had since is a cup of coffee." George put on his hungriest expression to hopefully gather a little bit of sympathy from this person.

"Well, I'll tell you what," uttered the surprised doctor. "You sit right here. *(Now where in the hell can old George go?)* And, I'll scoot out and see about getting them to rustle you up some breakfast. We have a bit of talking to do, and I know you'll feel better on a full stomach. I see no need for them to starve a prisoner in here."

"Thanks," was George's tepid response. *"A bit of talking,"* he says. Yeah. *I'll bet*, thought George, somewhat annoyed. Dr. Royalle pushed back his chair and exited through the solid metal door. George heard a second door close outside somewhere. Being left alone once again (except for perhaps whoever was behind that mirror), George's thoughts traveled to his past. He wondered how Deb was getting along as a single woman. Would she date men again? Maybe she was already going with some guy. A fleeting thought hit him: Was she having an affair before their separation, and she used his situation as an excuse? A tinge of jealousy touched him somewhere in the back of his mind. George did not like the thought of that. She was still attractive, in George's viewpoint, and could offer a reasonably pleasant personality when she wanted. Frankly, he hoped that she was not going out with anybody else. George pondered if, after all this was over, he would go out with somebody. *Would it ever be over?* It had been so long. He was not at all sure that he would have the nerve to ask anybody for a date. What would he say? Who would he find? There was that nice woman that he had met down at the apartment complex laundry room, but she had only just smiled and said a few brief hellos. Should he consider that a come-on? He had no idea.

He remembered several fairly pretty faces that had come into the restaurant from time to time, sometimes as a couple and sometimes singularly. If a couple of potential dates came in together, could he break into their conversation and ask one of them out? Nope, he just would not be able to do that. He would have to wait for one of them to come in alone. However, that might never happen. *Oh well, enough of this mess. I am so damn hungry.* George's stomach suddenly hit him with a loud grumble and mild ache. Another loud belch exploded from his mouth, this one more like a small clap of thunder. He forced a smile. *That ought to shake up those bastards on the other side of the mirror.* He hoped that doctor would hurry back with some food. Those people eating the doughnuts in the big room outside could easily have spared him at least one. However, the smelly jailer kept nudging George in the back with his knuckle, so that George had no opportunity to resist and seek out some bit of food.

After a short while, the doctor returned, and as he once again sat down across the table facing George, said, "I spoke to one of the officers outside and they'll be bringing you some food in a few minutes. I think they're running down the street to a diner for some scrambled eggs, bacon and toast. And coffee, of course. I hope that will be okay."

"Fine. That'll be just fine. Thanks," said George pleasantly. He tilted back on the rear legs of his chair and rubbed the back of his hurting neck again.

"Well, until then, let's get started. The Sheriff called me in on this case because of the story that you keep insisting on giving him. Now George…May I call you George?" The doctor did not wait for any response, but continued to speak.

"Suppose you tell me in your own words, just exactly what happened. I've already read the police information about this latest calamity. There were also some reports concerning your presumed involvement with several other local tragedies."

So, once again, George ran through his version of the event. He emphasized that he was aware of the incredulousness of the happenings, but also pointed out that every word was true. He even went so far as to discuss his involvement with the other incidents.

"Now George, even though you think that you saw this big, oversized light blue sport utility vehicle with its weird-looking driver, you are obviously smart enough to realize that it was probably just an apparition, or figment of your imagination. You do have a vivid imagination, don't you? I mean, over the years, you have figured out that you are pretty good at fantasizing, haven't you?

Denying this aspect of his personality, George shoved his chair back a little, leaned over and scratched his itching left shin. He wondered if, by some chance, he had accumulated a flea infestation from the filthy jail cell. As he shifted forward again, he was sharply reminded of the soreness in his neck.

He did not answer the psychiatrist's question.

At last, the door opened and a uniformed deputy entered with a flat Styrofoam box and a small paper bag. Breakfast! The deputy said nothing as he placed the packages on the desk in front of George, nodded at the psychiatrist, and then left the room. The aroma emanating from the box stimulated another loud growl from George's midsection. He rapidly opened the box and sack.

George said, "You don't mind if I eat while you question me, do you?" Determined to ignore any of Royalle's potential protests, he pulled a plastic fork and cup of coffee from the sack, opened the flat container and dove rapaciously into the barely warm scrambled eggs. The two narrow bacon strips were just short of burned, so crisp that they broke into a myriad of pieces when George's fork pushed against them. Still, George knew he would eat every morsel, and quickly learned that he could more easily consume them by pushing the bacon bits into the eggs. This rendered them easier to pick up. He found that the lukewarm coffee tasted as though it had been brewed the day before, but after adding three packets of sugar, he could wash his bacon/egg mixture down more readily.

As this was happening, the psychiatrist said nothing, simply watching and studying the way George ingested his breakfast. George wondered if this was some kind of shrink's trick. *Set up a hungry inmate with cold, barely edible food, and lousy tepid coffee, and then see how he responds,* George mused.

Since no napkins had accompanied the meal, he wiped his mouth on the wrinkled sleeve of his shirt, sipped down the last of the coffee, and then spoke to the doctor.

"Okay. Thanks for the food. Now let's get on with it, Doctor Royalle. I can call you Dr. Royalle, can't I?" George felt very smug about his response, throwing Royalle's stuff right back at him. *Well, take that and chew on it, buster!*

Royalle slid his chair up close to the table, opened his case, and took out a yellow legal pad and a pen. When George saw the ballpoint pen in the psychiatrist's hand, he immediately had a flashback to the detective *(Now what was his name?)* that kept popping his pen in and out. Maybe this was a patented trick recorded in Chapter Four of the "How To Be A Detective" manual.

He said to George, "All right, sir. Now, if you don't mind, we'll again run through your story about how you knew something disastrous was going to happen."

So, George, one more time, went through all the details of his entire Sunday morning. No changes. By this time, George remembered each part of the event as it happened in more explicit detail. He had run through it with perhaps four or five other investigators during the past twenty-some hours and almost had his story memorized. He noted the shrink making numerous notes, and going back from time to time, underlining certain sentences that he had written. George was mildly curious as to what the little shrink was writing, but could not read his jottings from across the table.

This interview lasted over three hours. Finally, Dr. Royalle looked up at George, closed his yellow pad, placed it and his pen into his briefcase, and snapped it forcibly shut with a loud declaration of finality.

"All right, Mr. Sheldon. Those are all the questions I have for you. Now if you will just continue to sit here, I'll excuse myself. Thank you for your time." *As if I had any choices offered me, you jerk,* thought George angrily. The little psychiatrist stood abruptly, turned and left the room without bothering to shake George's hand.

Just as Dr. Royalle was leaving the room, he turned back to George and said, "Oh by the way Mr. Sheldon. Those snapshots that you said you took of the blue SUV showed no vehicle—of any color. They showed only a few bland scenes of a train track, woods and casual terrain. I thought you might want to know that."

George drew in his breath, devastated at that news. He had snapped the camera directly at the SUV. How could it be that it did not show up on the film? Surely, the police would not lie about a thing like that. Would they?

He looked at the Styrofoam box and cup. He could smell the dregs even though the box was closed and he had replaced the lid on the cup. However, by this time, the odor coming from the box and cup were becoming definitely unwelcome.

Angrily sweeping the box and cup to the floor with his hand, he loudly exclaimed, "But it was there. It should be in the pictures I took."

The room was suddenly feeling very oppressive. George felt as though the walls and ceiling were closing in on him. He was terribly deflated. *I sure could use a good stiff drink about now.*

Peering down at the table once again, George spotted the dust-like wings that were the final remains of the poor moth. It apparently flew into the light bulb. It must have happened while the shrink was pestering George with some impertinent and asinine questions. *Would this be his final determination?* The inquisition angered George, but he realized that he was in no position to do anything about it.

Needing to visit the toilet, George stood, walked over to the mirror and tapped on the glass. He said to his own image, "I've got to visit the toilet."

Moving away from the mirror, he sat back down on the hard chair. Presently, the door opened and a uniformed officer, saying nothing, motioned for George to follow him out. He ushered him into the toilet. The deputy remained in the nasty environment as George relieved himself, and then washed his hands in a rust-stained sink. There was no hot water. After George rinsed his face, the deputy handed him two paper towels for drying. *Well, how nice of him!* Then he had George move back into the interrogation room.

CHAPTER SEVENTEEN

AFTER A VERY LONG wait in the dank room, two uniformed officers entered. George had never seen either of them. They looked sullen, so he wondered, *what now?*

The larger one of the two, a man of about fifty, with a heavily acne-scarred face, and a shaved head, said to George in a brusque, gravelly voice, "Okay Sheldon, stand up and turn around."

George did stand up, but being rather surprised, asked, "Why? What's going on now?"

The other deputy, a barrel-chested man in his mid twenties, an obvious body builder, with sharp features and dark brown, penetrating eyes walked to the side of George opposite the first man.

"He said, 'turn around'," declared the second deputy rather forcibly.

Still without turning, George looked directly at the older man and asked again, "Will you please tell me what's going on? I have been here all night. I'm tired, and have been interrogated by everybody and his cousin. Are you going to take back to my apartment now?"

The first deputy responded by saying, "Okay, Sheldon, I asked you once to turn around." He added more emphasis to his booming, cigarette-smoke scratched voice.

Seeing no evidence of movement by George, he repeated loudly, "I told you to turn around. Now!" His face suddenly reddened, and both he and the second officer stepped closer to George.

George was puzzled and angered at the same time. This had never happened before. *What in the hell are these jerks trying to do to me?* He had been arrested, interrogated at length, thrown in jail overnight, but now these two idiots were acting as if he was a dangerous criminal of some sort. He backed away from the approaching men. The younger deputy reached out and grabbed George's left wrist. His grip was like a vise and immediately his hand began to go numb from the pressure. He jerked away and moved back against the blank wall behind him. At that moment, both deputies grabbed George's arms and violently wrestled him to the floor.

They were yelling loudly, "Turn over! Turn over! On your stomach! Now! Do it!"

George was trying to resist and fight back against this unexpected assault, but was nearly powerless. After a few uncomfortable moments, he gave in and allowed himself to be turned over. The older deputy promptly handcuffed George's hands behind him. As this was being done, the other officer grabbed George's legs and wrapped a large plastic tie around his ankles, in effect, hog-tying him. While they held his head to the floor, he noticed the remains of the squashed roach just inches from his face. George felt a pain in his right shoulder where the older of the deputies had banged him to the hard floor. He wanted to rub and soothe it, but found it impossible. He felt a slight wetness there and correctly surmised that his skin was scraped. He was furious at the insult rendered upon him. He'd never intentionally hurt anybody in his life, and yet these two bullies had practically beaten him up. He felt his anger building within him. He had never before been manhandled in such a manner.

Grabbing him by the upper arms, the two officers roughly lifted George to his feet. With his ankles tied together, George found it difficult to maintain a standing position.

Seeing this, the younger deputy said, "Mister, tell you what." He did not let go of George's arm. "I'll undo your ankles if you don't try anything funny with us. Otherwise, we'll tie you up so hard that you'll wish you were dead. Got that, *sir?*" He had put a special emphasis on the word "sir," as if to show his disrespect for his prisoner.

It took no thinking time for George Sheldon to answer with a meek, "Yes." Then, as an afterthought, he added, "Sir."

As the older man supported George, the younger one released his hold on George's arm and bent down in front of their prisoner to loosen the plastic ties around his ankles. As soon as his ankles were free, and before the deputy could rise from his crouched position, George drew his foot back and kicked the deputy in the stomach as hard as he could. He was watching the man sprawl back across the floor, a surprised and painful grimace on his face, as blackness suddenly overwhelmed George.

*   *   *

When he gradually opened his eyes, his head was pounding. He found himself on a hard cot in some unknown place. As his awareness came back to him, George realized that he was not in a jail cell. He found that he was no longer handcuffed so he sat up on his elbows and slowly looked around his surroundings. He felt there was something odd about this small enclosure. He noted that it was gray painted metal. He looked up at the ceiling and saw a translucent panel, which allowed only a modicum of light to enter. There seemed to be a lot of rumbling and shaking, and he could hear the loud rustling of wind outside.

A van! At first, he had a terrifying thought that he might be inside the evil blue SUV. *Has the devil caught me? Am I going to die a horrible death? Oh God, don't let it be so!* However, as his mental clarity began to come back to him, he realized that this was certainly not the inside of any kind of sport utility vehicle. He breathed a sigh of relief. George suddenly realized through the heavy fog of his aches that he heard traffic sounds, and was obviously in a van being driven somewhere. But where? Where were they taking him? Who were they? And why? He wanted some answers, and wanted them now.

There had been no explanations by the deputies arresting him. None at all. The psychiatrist had left the room, and then the deputies had arrived. *Why?* George lay back down gingerly. It was much easier on his head as well as his shoulder that way. He happily realized that the crick in his neck was now gone— or was it simply that he was being overpowered with other, more pressing hurts? With his hand, he felt his shoulder cautiously and realized that he had only a small scrape. His now-filthy shirt was slightly ripped and he could feel a small amount of crusty blood around the edges. After a few minutes waiting for the cobwebs in his head to clear, he finally decided to sit up on the edge of the cot. However, as he attempted to swing his legs over toward the floor of the van, he realized that one leg—the one toward the center of the truck—was handcuffed to the cot. The cot, in turn, was welded to the floor of the vehicle. So much for that. He sat up as much as possible and tried to get some idea of what was happening to him. Where were they taking him? And still, that persistent question in his mind: *Why?*

allowed into the common room where we have a television and various games and activities available. Any questions?" Observing his new patient shake his head, the orderly pulled the door shut and locked it.

George sat down on his bunk and looked around his stark new surroundings. George thought, still angry and frustrated, *maybe it won't be so bad here after all. Three months! Damn it all to hell! That goddam devil has really screwed up my life.*

He stood and walked over to the plain wooden desk. He pulled out the single drawer and saw that it was empty. Nothing to write on or with. *I'll have to get somebody to notify my boss at the restaurant and the people at the apartment complex that I'll not be back for a while.*

The next morning at breakfast George gave an attendant some money and asked him to inform his apartment manager and restaurant manager that he'd be gone for awhile.

CHAPTER EIGHTEEN

T HE THREE MONTHS AT the institution went by fast for George Albert Sheldon. There were, at first, four sessions weekly with Dr. Villines, during which they discussed the same old stuff. They reviewed George's life before the first appearance of the sport utility vehicle, and how his marriage had been up until the end. He and Doctor Villines also discussed his youth in exquisite detail. George found a great deal of this quite interesting, as he had forgotten many of the points that were uncovered. He thus remembered how his family had been under a harsh paternal rule, with his father making nearly all the major decisions for the family.

One day in a session with George, Dr. Villines inquired, "George, tell me about your siblings. Any brothers or sisters?"

"Yeah, I've got a sister. Well, sort of."

"What do you mean, 'sort of?'" responded the psychiatrist.

George hesitated for a moment, glancing across the dimly lit room where he looked at a seashore painting. This picture was placed on the wall directly across the room from his comfortable overstuffed chair.

"She was three years younger than me," he said somewhat somberly.

"Was? You mean she died?"

George looked directly into Dr. Villines' large brown eyes. "Well, I really don't know. Maybe, maybe not."

"I think you need to tell me more. Don't you?"

"She left college after her sophomore year and eloped with a guy named Geoffrey something. She'd only known him for three or four months," he said flatly.

"Remarkably, that marriage lasted for six years. No kids, thank goodness." George glanced at the painting once again, then continued. "My sister's divorce distressed my parents almost as much as her elopement. Didn't particularly bother me, though. We never heard from her again. So what I meant was that I have no knowledge of her whereabouts."

"How do you feel about that, George?"

"Well, I'm somewhat curious about what happened to her, but otherwise, I'm unconcerned. She and I were never very close."

Dr. Villines said, "That seems to make you sad, doesn't it?"

"Yeah. I guess. A little."

George mentioned remembering that his mother doted on his father, showing that she absolutely adored him. She seemed, to George, to be quite happy to accept his dad's every command. In fact, George could remember only a single argument between the two of them, a seemingly innocent one where they had a loud "discussion" as to whether or not to attend a meeting of some sort. He assumed that, perhaps, they had other disagreements from time to time, but certainly not in front of George and his sister.

George grew into manhood with rarely a serious misstep. He had done well in high school, He ignored sports, and joined the debating club, history club, and he was in the honor society. Scholastically, he finished in the top five percent of his class.

Off to college, George had continued his academic excellence in engineering school. He had several brief flings while there, losing his virginity one steaming night in the back seat of a borrowed automobile. The girl never dated him again, leaving George with an unfulfilled void. He felt as though they had something "special" between the two of them. However, unknown to George, the young woman had gone out with him on a lark, at the urging of some of his fraternity friends, with the sole idea of allowing herself to be "seduced" by George. On the contrary, George himself was seduced.

Dr. Villines interrupted George's reminiscences at this point. "Oh? And how did that make you feel?"

George blushed. "First I was happy that my buddies thought enough about me to help me lose my virginity."

"And…?"

"Then I got real mad. No, maybe more embarrassed about it. I guess they thought they'd be helpful." He hesitated in brief thought, and repositioned himself in his chair. "Maybe helpful's not the right word…" His voice trailed off. "Anyway, looking back on it, they could have gotten me in real serious trouble."

Dr. Villines glanced at a beautiful male Cardinal that had landed on the sill outside her window. She looked back at George, saying, "How?"

"I learned later that she was two months pregnant by somebody else. I'd bet if it were today, I'd probably be slapped with a paternity suit. I don't know whatever happened to her, or, for that matter, who the father was." He sighed deeply.

Dr. Villines said with deep seriousness, "George, what are your present feelings about all that?"

"Too long ago to worry about now. Those days are gone forever." He looked at the clock on her desk and said, "Looks like my time is up for today." He rose from his chair without saying anything else and left the room.

The psychiatrist made some additional notes on her pad.

During his last summer before graduation, George's father arranged for him to work as an "intern" at the Williams Company, and thus, George eventually became a mainstay at that business...at least until his firing last year.

Dr. Villines helped George uncover many hidden subconscious feelings of various kinds. These had inevitably affected his life, and to bring some of them out into the open filled George with serious doubts about where his life had taken him. The two of them discussed how his father had made most of George's major decisions for him and this left him lacking in responsibility taking until long after his father had died. Fortunately, as long as no major difficulties appeared before him, George's life had run reasonably quietly and smoothly. Until the first SUV incident.

Dr. Villines pushed George into the SUV happenings, and yet could never uncover any reason why he would create such an absurd fantasy. No matter how deeply the two of them delved into his subconscious, nothing came out that would explain it. Nothing.

The psychiatrist reiterated to George that he had been incarcerated because the police were absolutely convinced that he was involved in some sort of conspiracy with others. Certainly, they surmised, he had to have had some accomplices for such an elaborate undertaking. Yet, there had never been any proof of any. In fact, not a single law enforcement department had been able to tie anyone else into the disasters. Following his interview with George, Dr. Royalle had convinced the sheriff's department that George had some obscured psychoses that needed to be exposed. Royalle felt as though George was, in fact, creating these disasters himself as a way of "getting even" for some hidden and deeply repressed anger. This, in Dr. Royalle's professional opinion, made George dangerous to society. He recommended that he be confined to an institution for an undetermined amount of time for intensive psychotherapy. The Sheriff, upon discussing the situation with Dr. Royalle, determined that George would certainly not go willingly into such an institution. Therefore, he had obtained a warrant from a judge for George's arrest. His fight with the deputies, though brief, reinforced the Sheriff's opinion that George could be considered somewhat dangerous. Local law enforcement agencies familiar with George reinforced their own opinions because since his incarceration, there had been no further disasters.

After many intensive and often emotionally painful sessions with the hospital psychiatrist, George finally decided that he could see through the direction her questioning was going. *If I'm ever going to be released,* he realized, *I have to give her the kinds of answers that she wants.* Therefore, he finally "admitted" to her that the devil figure and his SUV must indeed, have been figments of his imagination. However, she could never bring him to any admission of triggering any of the disasters. *Just a curious series of coincidences,* she thought.

Interestingly enough, every time he had described the bald and shiny round-headed red-skinned man, he noticed that Dr. Villines had subtly raised an eyebrow. In fact, each time, she brought him to delve into his sexual fantasies—to no obvious avail. At least not to George.

The many hours spent at the institution also gave George time to ponder about his future. He thought, *if that guy really is the devil, why did he choose me to pick on? What in hell did I ever do to deserve his wrath?*

George frequently spent his vacant time lying on his bed staring at the white stippled ceiling. He felt it was better for him than wandering around in the big game room. He had to figure this whole matter out—alone.

I don't feel as though I'm really crazy like everybody says. Sure, with what I have to tell them, I guess it must sound nutty. However, I know in my heart that I'm okay. I wonder if Satan decided to play some sort of evil game; and used me as his gambit. If I'm declared incurably insane, and face a lifetime of being institutionalized, what would that mean? Would that mean he won his devious game? Would he turn himself loose on the whole world? However, if I can get hold of myself and get myself released—and maybe keep alcohol from controlling me—will I win? Somehow, I've got to get out of this place and get back on my feet. If I can do that, I'm certain that I can work myself back into some kind of normalcy. I've simply got to. I'm not going to let the devil win. He will not defeat me!

Nevertheless, he knew he did not imagine the continued incidents with the devil and SUV. They were too real. He saw the thing clearly, as well as the round-headed red-faced man—the devil—every time. However, he could not prove it. His hopes via the photos he took of the SUV had been dashed. In order to get himself cleared and out of this place, he realized that he would have to change his story. He was very convincing.

In her final report concerning George Albert Sheldon, Dr. Villines stated that she could uncover no reasons for his SUV declaration other than his previously unrecognized need for self-induced excitement and importance. He had led a quiet, unassuming life, whereas his father had been a strong, forceful man. George harbored a powerful resentment for this fact. Therefore, she declared, George Sheldon had been forced—through her excellent psychiatric guidance— to recognize his faults and so, was now truly repentant. She pointed out that he was otherwise reasonably well adjusted, and with a caring concern for his fellow man. She did not consider George Sheldon dangerous, and was hereby releasing him from her custody.

CHAPTER NINETEEN

ARRIVING BACK AT HIS apartment complex, George was astounded to learn that, having not heard from him, and having been paid no rent for three months, his lease had been canceled. The complex had rented his unit to some-one else. His clothing and personal effects had been placed into a large black plastic trash bag, and casually tossed into the back of a utility shed behind the agent's office. His automobile had been taken off to some impoundment station. The secretary at the rental office could not remember the name of the wrecker service that had hauled George's car away.

"Sorry," she said nonchalantly. The woman was somewhat taken aback at George's anger when learning about the disposition of his property. After all, he had had ample time to notify her and did not, so there! He could "just get his stuff and leave," or else she'd call the police. Maybe he could learn from the police department where his car was.

The orderly at the hospital had duped George when he asked him to notify the apartment complex and restaurant that he would not be back for a while, and to keep everything and his job intact. *Apparently, the son of a bitch took the twenty dollars I gave him as a tip and spent it without even calling anybody for me.*

Oh my God! Now what the hell else is going to happen to me? George was almost beside himself. He had been through three months of torment and interesting but sometimes unpleasant introspection, and now learned that he had been thrown out of his apartment. Would it never end? He realized that he still carried a lot of bottled-up anger.

After retrieving the black garbage bag with his belongings, George walked out onto the front stoop of the apartment office, took out his wallet and checked on his funds. He had only seventy-three dollars in bills, plus some change. He surmised that this cash on hand would not "buy" his car out of its impoundment. In addition, it probably would not even cover his expenses for a cab to a cheap motel and a couple of meals. He had no credit card, no job, and minimum funds. He had no friends or relatives that he could call. He had learned from the last letter from her attorney several months ago that Deb had sold the house and moved away, and now George did not even know where she was. He did not much care at this point. However, he was now feeling desperate. What could he do?

George opened the bag widely and rummaged through it in the vain hope that perhaps he could find a few dollars. Nothing. Well, two quarters, one dime and three pennies, but that was all. That would not even buy him a hamburger.

Hamburger! Yes, that might be something I could do. He picked up the bag, slung it over his shoulder and started walking toward the old fast-food restaurant where he worked before his arrest. After all, he had been assistant manager there and surely, they would spot him a meal. Probably give him his job back, too, just for old time's sake.

As he began walking the several blocks toward the fast-food restaurant, he was feeling somewhat more upbeat at the prospect of seeing old friends, and presumably receiving some food. However, as he turned the final corner, he saw to his dismay that it was closed and locked up tight. "Out of Business," read the sign on the front door. He peered through the dirty glass door, and determined that it must have quit doing business shortly after he left. He could not help but wonder what had happened. It had been a thriving business when he was arrested.

Frustrated, George turned around and looked up and down the street. He spotted two cars parked at the far end of the parking lot. The loud beat of "heavy metal" music was blaring from the open doors. Among the cars were several young people, some in the cars, some out. *Just what do they call it? Rapping? Oh, to be a teenager again, with minimum responsibility.* He remembered the term from listening to the kids that worked with him at the old fast-food restaurant. Hit on old Dad for a few bucks, and spend your free time listening to music and chatting with friends. George did not recognize any, so he decided not to bother them.

Maybe there was another fast-food place nearby. He did not remember one, but then, his usual walking route to work did not take him onto many of the alternate streets. George had had no food since breakfast, and here it was, approaching seven o'clock in the evening. The growling from his stomach was telling him that it was long past time to be fed. In addition, he was feeling increasingly weak. Where to go? He just had to find some food somewhere.

He walked over to a phone booth and turned up the heavily enclosed phone directory. Well used, he noticed, with a multitude of soiled, wrinkled edges. He would check the yellow pages for a nearby place to eat.

"The Yellow Top Eatery—Good Home Cooked Food!" He noted that it was only a few blocks from his present location, so he started walking toward that spot. *Oh boy, am I hungry? Never heard of the place, but I hope it'll be okay.*

Arriving at the restaurant, he found that not only was it located in a rather unsavory area of town, but also that it was an old-fashioned train car renovated as a diner between two abandoned brick tenement buildings. He noted that its original yellow top was now a very faded beige. There was a large amount of graffiti painted all over the bricks adjacent to the establishment. Yet, the fluorescent lights coming from inside made it look inviting enough and the windows were relatively clean. Besides, at this point, George felt as though he would have eaten just about anywhere. He was worn-out, angry, depressed and famished. He did not see that he had any other choices at this point. He had to get himself some nourishment. He was also very tired of walking and his legs and feet were demanding some relief.

Entering, and seating himself at a booth, he placed his bag on the floor beside his feet. There was a lone waitress—a young Hispanic lady wearing a short black faux leather skirt, and off-white short-sleeve blouse. She casually rose from the squeaking counter stool where she had been sitting and walked over to his booth. He noticed that she had several small splotches of food spotting her blouse, and several tattoos on her arms and calves. She looked him over with a "Who in the hell are you and how'd you wind up in this place?" attitude, then offhandedly tossed a menu down onto the Formica tabletop. She said in a slothful manner, "Yeah, what you have?"

Mentally noting yet otherwise ignoring her attitude, George quickly scanned the listings, and, remembering his meager funds, ordered from the breakfast menu: one scrambled egg, well-cooked, fried potatoes, toast, and coffee. Remembering Deborah's cautious admonitions, he felt that he should stay away from "over-easy" in this particular establishment. He had noticed the sign behind the diner's counter, "Free Coffee Refills." *Well, thank goodness for that,* he mused.

When the waitress returned with his coffee, he looked up at her, smiled, and asked her if she knew of somewhere nearby where he could get a night's sleep. He noticed her raised eyebrows and sudden show of indignity. He quickly pointed out that he was not trying some sort of come-on to her, but truly needed a cheap place to lay his head. He told her that he was new in town and had very little money.

"Nope," was her curt response as she turned and returned to her counter stool. She called to the back of the restaurant, "Hey, Tomas. This guy wants a place to spend the night. Got any ideas?"

George saw a face appearing from behind the kitchen. "Nope."

Disappointed, but having completed his fairly satisfying meal, George left the diner. He left no tip. As he stepped onto the trash-cluttered sidewalk, he thought, *where do I go?* He saw with much chagrin that it was beginning to rain. *Now what?* He had very little money—certainly not enough for a motel room—and no idea at all of where he could spend the night. He wandered aimlessly up one street, and then another as the rain increased. He tried in vain to shelter himself with his plastic bag, searching desperately for a place to rest his head. Even so, he was soon completely soaked. His shoes squished in rebellion with each step.

George passed by numerous modest apartments and private residences, wishing that he had some shelter such as he was seeing through their lit windows. He was quickly becoming despondent in his plight.

An alleyway! Maybe there's some shelter down here. Even though the downpour drastically dimmed the streetlights, George could just make out a type of shed at the end of the passage. Excited by his find, he literally ran into the shadowed alley to the shelter.

Its construction consisted of two-by-fours, roughly six feet high in the front, perhaps set ten feet apart and sloping upward to a tall wooden fence in the rear. The roof appeared to be made of several sheets of plywood of random thickness nailed together. He thought it was probably a "fort" or clubhouse constructed by some local youths, and appeared very fragile. But, at least it would serve as a cover from the storm.

However, upon reaching the shelter he heard a loud viscous snarl and a wet-haired skinny mongrel dog bared its teeth at him. George jumped back, but in his wet misery said to himself, *No way am I going to let this damn dog keep me out from under that shelter.* Stepping back a few steps and searching the cluttered alley, he found a broken wooden chair. Quickly grabbing the chair by one of the remaining legs, he stepped toward the dog and viscously struck the poor animal. Stunned, the dog let out a loud yelp and abandoned the shed.

George suffered two immediate emotions. He felt distressed that he had to hurt the poor animal, but at the same time was determined to find himself some shelter.

Consequently, the lean-to was his for the night. He shoved some debris away and sat down on the hard alleyway surface. He used his black bag as a pillow, stretched out and, though soaking wet, quickly drifted off for a welcome night of sleep.

*   *   *

For the next three days, the rain continued, and George was so upset that he teared up each day. He was despondent, cold, soaked and very angry. He was also hungry, but determined to allow a small bit of hunger, so as to retain what little cash he had remaining. He walked the same streets once more during the days. He would dart under porch overhangs when the downpour became too heavy. All too often, however, the owners would chase him away. His unshaven and drawn face spoke of his dilemma to everyone passing by. To them he was just another bum walking the city streets. His every breath seemed to be a cursing of the devil that put him into such a horrid predicament in the first place. Once, he passed a small group of men standing under a park overpass. They appeared to be eating some kind of food. His evolving hunger directed him to speak to them. He hoped perhaps to gain a morsel or two. Unfortunately, however, they threatened him and literally chased him away. *What can I do?* He only had seven damp dollars left in his pocket. Finally, just as it was turning dark on the third day, his increasing hunger got the best of him. So, he ventured once more into the Yellow Top Diner. Once again, he dined on one scrambled egg, toast and coffee. And, still, neither the waitress nor the cook had any help for him.

Leaving the eatery, he went directly to the lean-to shelter where he had spent the previous nights. His clothes were now beginning to smell from the continual wetness from the rain. He no longer cared. He was too tired, angry and nearly stupefied from his worries. *Surely, there must be some way out of this damned morass.* When he arrived at the lean-to, George was happy not to have to contend with an angry dog. Once again, he placed his black bag on the damp pavement. He stretched out for what he hoped would be a decent night's sleep. Perhaps tomorrow will be better.

*   *   *

George opened his eyes slowly, seeing the sun rising above the tenements across the street. No more rain, thank goodness! However, something was wrong.

There was a body lying closely beside him. Where did it come from? Moreover, when? Was it dead? Alive?

George placed his hand on the figure's shoulders and gently shook it. There was no response. He shook it again, this time more vigorously. A low groan emanated from the figure. At least it was alive.

"Hey," George said. "Hey fellow, wake up."

"Ugh-h. What you want? Leave me alone," groaned the man. He went into spasms of wheezy coughing.

Not to be put off by this intruder into his newly acquired shelter, George said angrily, "Who the hell are you and what are you doing here?"

The stranger slowly rose onto his elbows and looked over at George. His eyes were resting in red caverns, and the skin of his unshaven cheeks appeared stretched to its limit. He had the appearance of a cadaver. When he opened his mouth to speak, his breath was so fetid that George involuntarily turned his head away.

The man said, somewhat angrily himself, "What's wit you, man? I's been staying here near 'bouts ever night fer over two years. You think you owns it?"

This took George aback. He did not know what to say. He had no idea that his newly found shelter "belonged" to anyone else at night. He simply did not know what to say under such circumstances.

George hesitated, and then finally uttered, "Sorry, but it's been raining so much, and I was so tired and wet. This was the only place I could find."

"You be's new 'round here, ain't ya?"

"Yeah. And, I'm stuck with what I've got in my bag here and, frankly, not enough money for much food. I don't even have a regular place to stay."

The man hesitated, turned over, felt under his coat for a moment. He then brought out and thrust a nearly empty bottle toward George.

"Hey man, here's my bottle. I'm almost out of wine, but you can have a swig if'n you wanna."

"Well, that's real nice of you, but no thanks. I don't think it would help much. I really need something solid," responded George gently pushing the bottle away. He thought, *I sure could use a drink right now, but no matter how lousy I feel, I'm sure as hell not drinking after this bum.*

"Hey man, that's okay. If'n it's food you want, come on wit me," said the bum. He turned it up and swiftly drained the bottle of its remaining contents. He roughly wiped the dribble from his mouth with his still-wet jacket sleeve, and tossed the empty into a shadowed corner with a crash.

"Where to? What do you have in mind?" George asked suspiciously.

"Come on and we'll git on down the street to the soup kitchen. I'll show you. We'n git you a bunch o' food there."

George said warily, not really trusting this half-drunk stranger, "How far is it? Which way?"

"Only a coupla blocks down this here way. C'mon."

So, the two set out—the bum and George, who by now looked much like a bum and ne'er-do-well himself.

After a walk of thirteen blocks, the two arrived at an ancient building, "The Mission."

"Well my man, I's leaving you here. I gots to go find myself another bottle of wine."

George, not offering to shake the man's hand, replied, "You've been most helpful, and I appreciate it. Good luck to you."

Walking up the eight heavily worn sandstone steps, he entered through a squeaking wooden door that contained a large section of beautiful stained glass. The oval panel contained a kaleidoscope of bright colors. George immediately recognized that this building had obviously been a refined residence in its former life. A young man in cleric's garb came up to him.

"Good morning, my friend. May God shine his blessings on you. Can I be of service?"

George, grateful to find a friendly individual, said, "I know I look like a bum, but was told that I could find something to eat here. I'm new in town and have lost most of my money."

"Sir, I think we can help you. Just come with me. May I ask your name?"

"George."

"George. Certainly, sir. Just follow me" Relieved with this answer, George glanced around and could not help but note the fine ornamental architectural trim of the building. His university studies had pictured and talked about such elaborate decorations, and George was able to quickly place the era of the house's construction at around the beginning of the twentieth century. Former elegance abounded throughout the building. There was a huge six-tiered chandelier hanging in the center of the large entrance hall. At least half a dozen of its bulbs were missing, however. Now there was shredding red-flocked ornate wallpaper, chipping paint, and squeaking, heavily worn floors.

He followed the young cleric into a large room filled with long paper-covered tables. There was an upright reciprocating fan in one corner. An assortment of men—young as well as old—occupied most of the well-worn folding chairs. The priest directed George to a jury-rigged cafeteria line where his plastic tray was loaded with scrambled eggs, one piece of link sausage and two pieces of dry white toast. At the end of the line was a large coffee urn.

George found a vacant seat and dove into the delicious breakfast. There was no conversation with any of his neighbors.

After downing a second cup of coffee, he sought out the attendant again.

He said, "I've had a run of real bad luck lately, and have run out of money. Do you know of any place where I can stay for a day or so?"

Smiling gently, the priest replied, "Well, my friend, we do have a limited number of cots available upstairs, first come, first served. I do not think there are any open spots now, but if you come back around dinnertime, I will try to keep one available for you. I cannot promise you anything, understand, but you appear to be severely down on your luck, and do not speak like the average poor souls we serve here. Show up about six. Okay?"

Thanking the young man, George picked up the black trash bag containing his meager belongings and walked out the front door.

What now? Where can I go? What can I do? Why, oh why did that damned SUV pick me? It's ruined my life. I'm not going to let it continue like this. I'm just not. I've just got to do something to pull myself up out of this cesspool of horror that I'm forced to live in. I have to find myself some kind of work. Gotta get some money and get back on my feet.

George stood on the sidewalk in front of the mission. He was unkempt, hair unruly, a four-day growth of beard, and large bags under his bloodshot eyes. He was wearing a wrinkled shirt, filthy pants, and mud-splattered shoes. He knew that he smelled foul. George began walking aimlessly along the sidewalk. He noticed that the few people passing him stared ominously at him and gave him a wide clearance. *Gotta find a job somewhere. Where?* In his depressed state, he decided that one direction was as good as another. *Maybe I'll find a burger joint along here somewhere.*

Finally! A family-style restaurant. I'll apply here. However, the manager, after looking at this dirty, grungy man standing before him, said an emphatic "Nothing here for you."

Disappointed but not really surprised, George walked on…and on…and on, with one rejection after another. He realized that his appearance was not at all appropriate, but he could do little about it save for using his hand to smooth down his hair somewhat. By late morning he had tried a total of eight businesses—from fast food places to bars, yet not any would give him any consideration, not even as a dishwasher.

The noon hour came and went, and by now, George was getting quite hungry, and very tired. Finally, he decided that his nearly aimless walking was getting him nowhere.

I've got to get something in my stomach. Maybe that will boost my spirits. Guess I'll find a paper and look in its "help wanted" section. Spotting a convenience store up on the next corner, he saw a newspaper box beside it.

He started to insert two of his remaining precious coins into the box, when he glanced up and spotted a sign on the glass door of the store. "Applications Accepted. Inquire Within."

Hey now! I may as well try here for a job. Got nothing to lose. He used the plate glass window as a mirror and tidied himself up as best he could. *I'll pick myself up a pack of Nabs and maybe a soda while I'm here. I'm starved. Maybe that'll solve one of my concerns,* George said to himself.

Entering the small store, he went up to the counter and asked about the job. The clerk, obviously, to George, the store's owner looked him over and said, "Can you read and write?"

George, somewhat chagrined at being asked such a question, replied simply, "Yes."

Not saying a further word, the man shrugged his shoulders, reached under the counter, and pulled out an application for George to fill out.

When George completed the brief form, the owner looked it over with raised eyebrows. "When can you start?"

"First thing tomorrow morning, but I can hang around for a little while right now," said George smiling. "I'm new in town and need this job real bad."

"Come on around to this side of the counter right now and I'll show you all about the place here. It's really not too hard. By the way, do you have a razor and another set of clothes?"

George said, "Well yes. I know I look like a bum right now, but I'll be in much better shape tomorrow." He looked across the small counter and over the store, immediately beginning to familiarize himself with the place.

"You just sort of follow me around today. Once I know you can handle the ropes, I'll try you out alone. Okay?" said the store's manager.

George added, "Sure, but first, I want to buy these Nabs and a soda. I haven't had much to eat lately."

Following about an hour's instructions, during which several customers came in, George quickly felt as if he could handle the job with no difficulty.

"Just call me Henry. And oh yes, payday is on Friday."

"Fine," George said. "Oh, by the way, Henry, I'm okay for tonight, but I've got to find myself a permanent place to stay. Any ideas?"

"Hmm. Lemme think about that for a little bit…Yep, maybe. My brother's got a room not too far from here that he rents out from time to time. I'll call him in a few minutes."

A gas customer walked in and Henry said to George, "Okay now. Let's see you handle that."

It was a simple cash payment, so George pushed the button indicating the amount of gasoline purchased, and the amount owed, and gave the young lady back her correct change. No problem at all. *Pretty young thing. Looks too young to own a sporty car like that; wonder who it belongs to. Her boy friend? Her daddy? Oh, what the hell. It doesn't really matter.*

After about half an hour, Henry picked up the store's phone and punched in some numbers. In a couple of minutes, Henry came over to where George was restocking some shelves with packages of pretzels.

He said, "My brother'll let you have that room for twenty-five bucks a week if you want it. It's got a separate entrance, private bath and everything. No kitchen privileges, though. Want it?"

George asked, "Maybe. Where is it?"

"Oh, it's not too far from here. Just about a mile down that cross street out there."

Realizing that his options were severely limited, and that his meager funds were nearly gone, he was tempted to take it sight unseen. However, he really did want to at least make sure it was not bedbug infested.

He said, "Hey. Do you mind if I go over there right now and take a look at it?"

"Sure, George. But, your pay here doesn't start until tomorrow. Got it?"

"Yeah, I understand. How do I find the place? What's your brother's name?"

Happily, George found the room immaculate, and very much to his liking. Clean linens, a nice firm easy chair, desk and straight back chair, clean bathroom. No television but a small ancient radio, though. He took it, agreeing to pay twenty-five dollars for one week's rent when he received his pay.

George walked back by the store, and informed Henry that he had taken the room and would return in the morning. Then he left the store and walked the thirty blocks back to the mission. Nearly exhausted, he arrived about an hour before the evening serving. After having ample amounts of beef stew and several slices of white bread followed by two glasses of iced tea, he endured some boring conversation with fellow "guests." Then following a semi-obligatory religious service, he spoke to the priest. George mentioned his need for a bed for the night.

"Certainly brother. Just follow me upstairs."

At the top of the worn and squeaky stairs, the priest directed George to a large room, obviously formed by tearing down several walls. The room was filled with cots, many of which were already taken with sleeping and snoring men. Foul body odor cast a pall over the room.

"The bathroom is through that door over there," the priest said. "You may have any vacant bed."

George pushed his black bag under his chosen cot, and then visited the often-used and foul smelling bathroom. He looked forward to being able to wash up—at last.

Upon returning to his bed, he found that his bag of personal items was missing. *Oh no! Well dammit to hell! And, just that quick, too.* Although the overhead lights in the big room were not on, there was some illumination from streetlights shining through the several dirty windows. There was also some from the hallway and toilet area. He quickly looked around the room in his attempt to locate his missing bag. He bent down on the dusty floor and peered under the multitude of cots. He could not spot it. He looked to see if anyone seemed to be awake that he could question.

He put his hands on the shoulder of the young man in the cot next to his, and shook him. The man angrily glanced up at George, mumbled some unintelligible sounds, turned over and went back to sleep without saying anything that George could understand.

George went out into the hallway, then downstairs and located the young priest.

After hearing from George about his loss, he said, "I'm truly sorry. I saw no one coming down the stairs, but I was busy in the back. If you've lost something, I'm afraid you'll just have to endure it." The priest turned his palms upward in despair, saying, "I can't help you."

George returned to his cot, upset, disappointed, disgruntled. Life was not treating him fairly. In fact, life had not been the same for a long time. His "perfect" pre-SUV life had deteriorated into a jungle—a maze—of discouragement and discomfiture and intense anger. Somehow, he must find a way to turn it around. Well, he would sleep on it. Tomorrow was another day. His body and mind could carry him no more this night.

The next morning, following a brief religious service, George and his fellow lodgers had a breakfast of stale doughnuts, watery orange juice, and strong coffee.

George thanked the day-shift priest, and told him that he'd had his bag stolen last night, just in case the mission's night manager had not told him.

George left and walked back to the convenience store worried about his appearance. As he entered the store, he said to Henry, "Sorry, but I had my bag of personal items and other clothing stolen from me last night. Otherwise, I'd present a much better appearance."

Henry shrugged with disappointment and said, "Oh well. Grab yourself a pack of razors and some shaving cream from that counter over there and at least shave. I can't let you work here with such a grubby looking beard. Get yourself a toothbrush, paste and a comb too.

So, after a few minutes in the rest room, George emerged looking and feeling considerably better.

"Hey Henry. Will it be okay with you if I walk down the street to that Goodwill store? I passed it on the way back here. Maybe I can pick me up some better clothes." He had decided to invest his last few dollars in a nice used polo shirt and even a pair of trousers. *I'll wash out my underwear and socks tonight at my new room.* When George returned, he went into the men's toilet and changed.

When he emerged, Henry smiled and said, "Hey now, George, that's a bunch neater. Now I feel better about having you work for me."

So, finally, George's life began to get back on track to a reasonably decent and level plane once again. True, he was working long hours at minimum wage. And, had only a tiny "apartment," but at least he had what he hoped would prove to be steady employment. Maybe he could soon accumulate enough extra money with which to "buy" his car out of hock. He was pleased that the police readily informed him where it had been taken during his incarceration in the mental institution.

After one week, Henry found George to be a capable and apparently honest employee. He turned the store completely over to him, even giving him the keys to the place. George, of course, knew that he would make him a good worker. No matter how bad things had gone for him, George Albert Sheldon maintained his honor and dignity.

CHAPTER TWENTY

LIFE FOR GEORGE GRADUALLY began to settle down into a reasonably satisfactory and acceptable mode. He was working on a regular basis and was even being known by a large number of customers—the "regulars."

One day he was tending to standard business in the store when an attractive lady about George's age entered the store with a distressed look on her face. She was slender, just slightly shorter than George, with deep auburn hair, high cheekbones, sparking green eyes, full lips and a complexion that many movie stars would happily kill for. She was immaculately dressed in a dark blue plaid skirt and light blue sweater, and was wearing matching pearl earrings and necklace.

"Hi. What can I do for you?" asked George cheerfully.

"I'm embarrassed to tell you," she said in a hushed voice. "I need some gas, and I don't know how to work that self-service pump. Is it possible that you can show me how?"

George was astounded. *How, in this day and time, can any car driver not know how to put in their own gas?* Nevertheless, having no other customers in the store at the time, George thought, *Why not?* Besides, she was a very lovely person. Before he had even peered outside the store, he thought to himself, *if it's an SUV, I don't think I'll do it for her. Damn, I hate SUV's!* He locked up the cash register and followed the lady out to her car, a foreign luxury vehicle—a spotlessly clean black four-door high-dollar Mercedes-Benz.

He said casually, "Now that's a real fine car."

She responded with a simple, "Thank you."

The two of them walked around to the pump, and as George started to open the lid exposing the gas tank cap, he realized that it was on the opposite side from the pump. This naive lady didn't even know on which side of the pump she should have parked.

"Ma'am, the hose won't reach from this side. If you'll let me have your key, I'll move the car to where I can put the gas in."

Without hesitation, she handed him her keys, and then walked over to the front of the store to wait.

After moving the car, George smiled, got out and called to her, "If you'll just walk back over here for a moment, I'll show you how this whole system works."

She walked around the automobile and said, "I feel so foolish. You see, my husband and I just recently divorced and he always did this type of thing for me."

George returned her keys to her. "I'm divorced myself." He nonchalantly said to her, as he set the automatic cutoff lever on the nozzle and showed her what he had done. He moved back from the side of the car a little, and said, "You live around here? I don't see many nice cars like this in this neighborhood." He chuckled lightly. George checked on the pump nozzle, glanced up at the flow meter on the pump, and then facing her again, said, "Except for the pimps and crooks, that is." He grinned broadly, and then said, "You're not one of those, are you?"

"Silly," she said smiling. "Of course not. But you really didn't think so, did you?"

At that moment the nozzle snapped, indicating a full gasoline tank. George reached down and, carefully pulling the nozzle out, replaced it in the pump. Finally, he screwed the gas tank lid back on and gently closed the car's outer gas cap cover.

"There. That's all there is to it. And, you see, I didn't even get my hands dirty. However, I must warn you, that sometimes you may get some gasoline on your hands, so you have to be careful. If you get even one drop of gas on your hands, you'll smell like a garage mechanic the rest of the day." He looked at her closely, being impressed with her bearing and statuesque beauty. She noticed his observations, and smiled demurely.

He continued, "To be blunt about it, a lot of stations won't put your gas in for you like I've done. But, if you ever plan to pump your own gas, I've got a couple of suggestions for you to consider. One would be to carry an oversize pair of plastic gloves that you can wear when filling your tank. The other would be to carry a roll of paper towels, and tear off a couple to hold the gas nozzle with."

He stopped speaking a moment. "No!" he said grinning. "I mean, *with which* to hold the nozzle." She burst out laughing. She could certainly appreciate his humor and grammar correction. He started walking back into the store, as she followed.

"How do you want to pay for the gas? Cash or plastic?"

She entered the store's confines and stood at the counter while George unlocked the cash register. She frowned slightly and stared at her purse.

"Oh dear me, I really don't know. What do most people do? Does it matter?"

George said, "Well, not to me. It's thirty dollars and sixteen cents. Do you want to pay me with your credit card?"

"Oh I suppose so. I'm so used to my 'ex' doing all this for me, I never really paid much attention to how he paid. The divorce was a terribly messy thing and he just finally moved out last week. Our marriage was actually over a long time before that. We had one argument after another about who would stay in the house. He was living in one end, and I was in the other. Thanks to my lawyer, I finally won." She stopped speaking, breathed deeply and exhaled forcibly. "Oh my goodness. Why am I telling you all this? You must think me a terrible bore." Opening her purse, she asked George, "Seriously, does it really matter if I pay cash or use a credit card. I can do either."

"I don't have a credit card now, but when I did, it helped me keep track of how much I was paying for gas and such things."

"Well, I'll just do it your way then," she said. She fumbled in her purse for a moment, then withdrew a wallet, and slipped out a "titanium" credit card. George had never before seen one of those.

He looked at it for a moment and said, "So your name is Mildred, huh?"

"Well, most of my friends call me Millie. And your name is…"

George held out his hand formally, and said, "I'm George Sheldon, and most of my friends call me George." He grinned at his own humor.

Millie laughed as she extended her own hand and joined in the polite shake.

"I like your humor," she said. "And I also appreciate the fact that you didn't make fun at my not knowing how to gas up my own car. That ex-husband of mine teased me unmercifully about it. He nagged me on and on." Millie glanced around the store. "I think I'll get myself a soda while I'm here." She walked toward the huge wall of coolers, and hesitated for a moment while she searched for her favorite. George's eyes traced her every step. Then she opened the glass door and slid out a can of decaffeinated diet soda. Arriving back at the counter, she asked, "How much is this?"

George said, "Tell you what. Let's just say that this one is on the house." Again, he grinned broadly, as he rang up a "No Charge." "Just because I think you are the nicest person that I've seen around these parts in weeks." Grinning broadly, he added, "Why, they jest ain't no folks 'round here wit much class a'tall." He built in a momentary pause, then added, "Ceptins fer me, o'course."

"Why, George," she said, smiling in pleasant surprise, "You're so funny. You didn't have to give me the soda, but thank you. And, after putting in my gas, too. You're awfully nice." She took a dainty sip from her soda. "If I can be perfectly honest, you don't seem to be the kind of fellow that I would have expected to run into working in a place like this."

"Well, thanks," said George chuckling. "As a matter of fact, I'm trained as a mechanical engineer. However, there are several reasons why I'm not doing that kind of work right now. Maybe I'll tell you about them sometime." Just at that moment, a customer walked in, picked up several snacks, and a six-pack of beer, and approached George at the counter to pay. Millie stood aside, continuing to sip on her soda. She casually glanced at the rack of tabloid newspapers, noting no new extraordinary gossip of interest.

"You have a degree?" asked George of Millie after the customer left.

"Yes. I have a Masters in Nursing Administration from Duke University." Taking a final drink of her soda, she turned and tossed the empty can into a trash bin. "But I haven't worked at nursing since I got married. As a matter of fact, as fast as medicine is moving these days, I doubt if I could even fit in anymore."

George nodded in agreement, saying, "Probably the same with me in engineering, but I doubt if the basics have changed too much."

Millie shrugged her shoulders, reached in her bag for her car keys, and said, "Well, let me say, this stop for gas has been a very pleasant surprise. I have enjoyed our conversation. I think I will just have to come this way again sometime. Are these your regular hours?"

"Yes, Millie, I've enjoyed our brief visit also. It made a boring day much more interesting for me. As you might imagine, it's really a lousy job, but one that I have to have right now. I hope you will indeed come back. I'm here most days, and some evenings and a few nights. The big boss sets my schedule, so I never really know. When he says work, I work."

As Millie left the doorway, she smiled broadly at George and said, "I'll just have to drive my car a lot and run out all the gas so I can come back and visit with you again. Bye-bye for now, George."

As she drove away, George smiled and thought, *Wow! What a nice refined lady. I wonder if she really will ever come back here. Somehow, I doubt it because of this terrible neighborhood. But, it'd sure be nice if she would.*

CHAPTER TWENTY-ONE

Y ET ANOTHER BORING WEEK went by for George. It was get up, go get breakfast, work, eat supper somewhere, go home, read, and go to bed. Repeat the same day after day. What a drag—very monotonous—but at least it was making him some money.

He had finally retrieved his car. Now, just maybe, he might well get on with what he now called "normal" (though meager) living. He slowly improved his wardrobe with new (cheap) clothes, and even began to accumulate a small, but steady amount in his new bank account. He had put a great deal of effort into it, but he decided never to become a drunk again. He felt quite proud of himself at his regaining of self-importance.

But, one thing continued to give George pause. *What about the devil's SUV?* He had not seen it for a long time now. It had been "away" longer this time than ever since its first appearance. He hoped that in all of his travails during the past several months, plus changing his locations, it had "lost" him. *Could it be so?* What a pleasant thought for George. *However, how had it found me in the first place? If it could find me then, it just might find me again.* George hoped it would never locate him again and ruin his life more. He mused about what it had already done to him: caused him to lose his wife, home, and reputation. He had lost his excellent job and very good salary. He had been jailed, as well as forced to endure the humiliation of three months in a mental institution. He admitted to himself that he had nearly turned into a lowly drunk—a slovenly bum. What a hell of a thing to happen to someone. And, why him? What had he ever done to deserve such mental and emotional trauma? *I still don't understand why I was picked to absorb all this horrible turmoil.*

*   *   *

One sunny afternoon Millie drove in again. The warning bell rang as usual when a vehicle ran over the cable, notifying him that someone had stopped for gasoline. He glanced out the window and saw who was there. He smiled broadly to himself. *Oh boy! She's returned.* He immediately realized that the sight of her excited him. Although he was busy with several customers, he waved at her and received a return smile and wave of her hand. He noticed that this time she had positioned her car correctly beside the available pump.

Millie got out of her car and went to the pump, correctly retrieving and inserting the nozzle. He noticed that she was holding the pump handle with a paper towel. She looked up and grinned at George, who was just finishing with his last customer. He locked up his cash register and strolled out to where her pump was running.

"Hey there!" George said exuberantly. "Glad to see you ran out of gas again." He grinned, walked around to the nozzle, waited a few seconds, and then, hearing it kick off, replaced it on the pump for her.

"George, you are so sweet," Millie replied. "Would you believe that I've gone five miles out of my way to buy my gas here?" Her coy grin made George feel wonderful. He had not had anyone show such an appreciation for him since long before his divorce.

"Ah ha! I knew you would appreciate our service here," said George as he ushered her into the store. "We try harder, you know."

"George, I'll have to admit that I was delighted and impressed last week. You certainly made me feel good about being here, even for those few minutes. I'd been through several months of hell."

He walked over to the wall of coolers and picked out a soda. Handing it to her, still smiling broadly, said, "I'll admit that I hoped you'd stop back by. Our conversation was quite pleasant, wasn't it?"

Millie was smiling also, but stopped talking and began sipping on her diet soda as a young teenage couple came in. After buying themselves some snacks and sodas, the young man paid for his ten dollars worth of gas. He tried to purchase a package of cigarettes, but when George demanded to see his proof of age, he growled angrily, and left the store abruptly.

Millie, having already handed George her credit card, restarted her conversation. "As a matter of fact George, that's one of the reasons I returned. I hope you do not find me too forward in saying this, but honestly, I have found you very easy to talk to. I have realized that many of my former friends have more or less forsaken me since my divorce from old whatsizname. I suppose they were afraid to take sides. I have been rather lonely, to say the least."

Again, their conversation was halted, as several customers entered the store. A school bus had stopped in front of the building. As it released its hostages, eight youngsters paraded into the store. Their excited jabbering was happy and incessant, and Millie stood aside finishing her soda and observed their actions with interest as they filed by George, making their payments, some in numerous coins. Their pockets would now be considerably lighter in weight. She noted with some regret that most of the children were buying candies and processed sugar treats of various types.

At last, the store emptied, and quiet reigned, but only for a brief moment as George and Millie's conversation was interrupted by two gasoline customers. George truly wanted to have some quiet there in the store so that he and Millie could continue their conversation. He wanted to get to know her better. He had often wished that the convenience store owner would install some of the new pumps where customers could pay with their credit or debit cards at the pump. But, it was not to be, and he was happy for that fact at the moment.

George said, "Look, Millie. I'd really like for us to have a chance to talk more and get better acquainted." An older woman asking for directions to a nearby branch library interrupted him. After instructing her, he continued, "How about we go out for dinner this coming Saturday?"

Millie smiled, thought for a moment, then said, "Why, I think that would be very nice. One thing is for sure; my calendar is certainly not filled for Saturday night. About sevenish?"

"Seven it is. Oh by the way, Millie. I have no idea where you live."

As she gave George her address, he realized that it was in an exclusive section of the city. In fact, he correctly presumed that it must be a gated community near the one where his former employer, Williams, lived.

He said, "Now, I don't have as nice a car as yours, so you'll have to rough it a little bit." He grinned again. Darn, this was exciting. A date with a lovely lady. And so refined, too.

The following Saturday evening, George drove his freshly washed and vacuumed, six-year-old Japanese sedan over toward the upscale section of the city where Millie lived. George stopped at the closed ornamental wrought-iron gate and gave the attendant his name. After checking his list of names to be admitted to the community, the attendant gave George a modified hand salute, turned and opened the gate, waving George on through.

He said, "It's the fifth house on your right, sir."

Driving through the gate reminded George of the horrors that he saw when passing though other gates.

As he arrived at the address, he could scarcely believe what a nice home she lived in. Admittedly, he had some preconceived ideas about her residence, from the address, as well as the type of expensive automobile she drove. He also remembered that she carried a titanium credit card—the only one he had ever seen. This place was something to behold indeed. The house itself was a large two-story brick Colonial, obviously architecturally designed. There was a vast opulent lawn, immaculately landscaped with a multitude of well-pruned shrubs and with background lighting over all. Off to one side was a charming flower garden that surrounded a sizable re-circulating bronze fountain. Its figure of a woman carrying a vase on her shoulder centered a twenty-foot pool. George had a momentary flashback to the pleasures he had with his gardening hobby in his former life. Although it was too far away to see closely, George would have bet money that the pool was home to numerous large goldfish. He slowly drove up the laid brick circular drive, stopping in front of the door to her house.

Walking up the three brick steps, he pushed the button and heard a chime from deep within the house. After a moment, Millie opened the door exhibiting her charming smile.

"Well," she said cheerfully, "talk about promptness. I just this moment heard the seven chimes from my grandfather clock in the hallway. Come right in, George. I'm almost ready." She ushered him through the marble-floored foyer and into the elegant living room with a wave of her hand, and said, "Have a seat while I finish getting ready. I'll just be a minute."

George seated himself on a velvet-covered love seat, and, crossing his legs, relaxed. He looked around the room, admiring the several oil paintings on the walls. Each had an accent light above it. Since the weather was mild, the gas logs in the huge elaborate marble-faced fireplace were not lit, and the decorative glass doors were closed. He noted with interest the ornate hand carving around the brown-stained wooden mantle. The comfortable furniture exhibited themes from an Italian villa, and reminded him of spectacular photos from *Architectural Digest Magazine*.

After about five minutes, Millie entered the room, dressed in a lovely dark green medium length dress, made, George presumed, of silk. It complemented the shade of her hair. The silken pleats flowed as smoothly as waves on a quiet ocean as she walked. George immediately stood, feeling an aura of excitement about this beautiful woman now standing before him.

She reached out and took both his hands in hers, saying, "Shall we go?"

The two of them left her house, and pleasant conversation took over as George drove through the darkening evening toward the restaurant he had chosen for them. *Track's End* was a restored brick building where, decades earlier, train engines had been repaired and rebuilt. They entered and followed the maitre d' over the highly polished old oaken floors to a table covered with a white linen tablecloth. It was centered with a vase of fresh red carnations, baby's breath and fern. Bone china plates and sterling silverware graced the settings. In a corner of the large room, George and Millie noted a trio of formally-dressed young ladies performing on piano, harp and violin. The music was from European composers of years ago, some of which George did not recognize.

As the dinner of mixed green salad "prepared table-side with special house dressing," thick filet mignon (medium-rare, for George, medium for Millie), twice-baked potatoes, and pickled crab apple slices progressed, both George and Millie found the restaurant deserved its reputation for fine, elegant dining. Millie, correctly anticipating George's limited budget, insisted on buying the wine. Her choice was *Chateau Margaux, 1979,* and George felt that it was the finest wine ever to cross his lips. Sipping sparingly, however, he reminded himself to be wary of overindulging.

Their conversation moved along steadily as each elaborated on their past life's experiences and their personal attitudes about various subjects. Still, George held back about the SUV difficulties. He admitted to Millie that he had a somewhat checkered past—nothing illegal, he reassured her—and promised her that he would indeed tell her about it sometime in the future. For now, however, he asked for her indulgence and patience. Following the delivery of some perfectly cooked cherry tarts, covered with mountains of pure white whipped cream, they enjoyed cappuccinos while the trio continued to play in the background.

"George," said Millie. "This evening is just what I needed. I am having a grand time. Are you enjoying this as much as I?"

"Absolutely, Millie." George took another sip of his coffee, wiped his mouth with the white linen napkin and continued, "Millie, I'd have been at home with a fast-food burger and a dull novel. This is just marvelous. No, fantastic!" He sipped again, and, continuing, said, "Millie, it looks to me like you and I have a lot in common. I will be honest with you. I like you and your company—a lot.

You're the best thing that has happened to me for a long time." He grinned at her broadly, reached over and laid his hand on hers.

"George, I have to admit that I feel the same way. I guess I must have determined that first day that you and I just might share many of the same interests. That's why I came back a second time."

"I'm awfully glad you did," replied George.

She smiled coyly at him, sipped at her own cappuccino and then said, "Me too."

The two finally decided that the hour was getting late, and left the restaurant to travel back to Millie's home.

"George would you like to come in for a while?" she said, squeezing his hand slightly.

"Damn, I'd certainly like to, but unfortunately, I have to get up before six in the morning and work at the store." He held both her hands, and gazed into her eyes. They reminded him of a quiet clear spring he once discovered in a deep lush green forest.

"May I take a rain check on that offer?"

"Certainly," she spoke in a quiet near-whisper. "When can we have another evening like this?"

George said, "Actually, I have to check on my schedule, but I'm sure I'll have an evening shift off again in a few days." He let go of her hands, and reached into his jacket pocket. "Millie, I don't even have your phone number. Will you tell me what it is? Then, I'll call you in a day or so."

She told him, adding, "It's unlisted, so please don't tell anybody about it." She hesitated in a moment's thought. "I certainly don't want my ex to learn it." She added, "But, and no offense meant, I don't suppose you'll see anyone at your store that might know him." Millie stood up on her tiptoes and gave George a firm kiss on the lips. "Goodnight, George. I'll be looking forward to your call." She then turned, unlocked her door and went into her house.

On his drive back to his room, George was totally elated; floating, like a kid who had received his most wished-for toy for Christmas. He had a wide smile glued to his face as he recalled various parts of the evening's conversation. In fact, he found himself humming in joy along with the popular music emanating from his car radio. He was indeed a happy man! Oh, how happy! Finally, some real joy in his wretched life.

Several weeks passed and George and Millie quickly became fast friends. George felt wonderful about his developing relationship with her, and she had already felt the early stirrings of what she thought might be love. She found

George to be intelligent, thoughtful, caring, and a great deal of fun. She had yet to learn much about his earlier days, and was increasingly curious, but refrained from pushing the issue. She was reasonably confident that his past would not prove to be a detriment to their expanding relationship, and that he would tell her when he felt the time was right.

The couple began to take in numerous musicals and shows. However, much to George's chagrin, these things quickly exceeded his earning power. He spoke frankly about it to Millie, and explained his difficulty. She was very understanding and immediately offered to "share" the expenses. To George this meant, halving the cost to wherever they chose to go. But to Millie, it meant that she would pick up the tab most of the time.

George and Millie had their first mild—a simple disagreement, really—argument over such an arrangement. George had been raised in the old traditional school that the man pays the bills. Millie, he learned, was quite wealthy in her own right and more than willing to cover her chosen amount. It took much persuasion to convince him that it would be just fine this way. Although George badly wanted to preserve his self-imposed proud image, he eventually surrendered. This was so that the two of them indeed, could go to nice places as often as Millie desired.

In her effort to mollify George's ego, she suggested a few other outings. They began to visit art museums, and take long walks together in a local park, stopping occasionally to feed the squirrels and pigeons along the way.

One evening George said to Millie, "Honey, I've got an idea. How does this sound? Since I'm off work tomorrow, if you will fix us a picnic lunch, we'll go out to the city lake and rent a canoe. Then, we can spend the day out there, just lazing around. How does that sound to you?"

Millie cuddled up closer to George on her couch and said, "Oh, sweetie, that sounds just great. I'll fix us a special lunch. Just you wait and see."

George picked Millie up at nine o'clock the next morning and drove the ten miles out to the lake. Renting a canoe, George began rowing, with Millie seated in the front, facing him.

After a while, George grinned and said with a flourish, "Okay Mildred. I've rowed us this far, and now it's your turn."

He handed her the paddle and slid down into the bottom of the canoe, while she playfully stuck her lower lip out in a friendly pout. She rose to her proper seat, turned and began rowing in earnest.

"Hey," said an astonished George. "Where'd you learn to row like that?"

"Girl Scouts, honey. I guess I didn't tell you about all my great skills, did I?"

"Whoo-ee! What a woman!"

After a short distance across the waters, the two nudged the canoe up against the far shore and got out. George pulled the canoe up high enough on the shore to prevent its floating away while Millie playfully ran up the grassy hill carrying their picnic basket.

She spread out a large red-checkered cloth beside a large willow, and the two lay upon it. Their view could not have been more idyllic. From there could be seen the wide expanse of the big lake, surrounded by numerous trees in full leaf. Several other people in canoes and a few rowboats were moving across the waters. They saw some children cavorting in the adjacent sanded playground.

The lunch that Millie had prepared consisted of her special recipe of Southern fried chicken, fresh potato salad, homemade biscuits that were as light as a feather, and sweetened iced tea. She also brought thick wedges of a German chocolate cake she had made the night before.

For both of them, there was a special hue to the sky that day, with a multitude of white clouds floating leisurely by. The temperature was mild, creating a perfect day for a picnic. After the luncheon, the two lay on their backs, observing and describing the shapes of the clouds.

George turned to Millie and said, "Millie, I could just stay here with you forever. This is marvelous. No, our word, fantastic!"

Millie said nothing in reply, but cuddled up to George more closely. She leaned over and kissed him tenderly. George quickly returned her kiss. "I love you so much," George said, holding her affectionately.

Millie looked deep within his eyes and reminded him of her love.

George thought, *if only the damn devil doesn't come around again…*

George and Millie had begun making love some weeks prior. In their "pillow talk" following their lovemaking, they had expressed their mutual feelings for each other. To George this was a somewhat awkward and scary situation, due to his position as a lowly clerk in a convenience store. This mattered little to Millie, and she told him so, but it did not seem to pacify George very much. He was now earning only slightly above minimum wage, and continued to keep his personal living expenses at a minimum. However, he badly wanted to give Millie "things" to help demonstrate his affection for her. He found this impossible, but she said, truthfully, that she did not mind. After all, she had nearly everything she desired.

One evening Millie brought up the subject of marriage. This nearly floored George because of the vast difference in their wealth.

"Honey," George said, "I love you very much, but you know how little money I have. I can't even consider marriage now." He took her hands in his. "Maybe someday I can find a way to get back on my feet. Maybe even begin my own engineering company. But not now." *And, what about the damned SUV? Where is it? Will it return to change my life again? Oh God, please don't let it bother me again,* he prayed. *Maybe my life is coming back together. Please! Please, let me be able to live a good, reasonable life once again.*

In the back of his mind, he had already considered forming his own engineering company, based on his past training and experience. Yet, something of that nature and size would require a great deal more cash than he had available, or could even grasp in the foreseeable future. However, he felt that this idea would be his only opportunity to improve on his present standing. He had already decided not to ever again work for any business like the Williams Company. He would be his own boss and either make it or break it on his personal initiative.

One evening he sat down in his apartment and listed all he would need to start such a company. He also jotted down all his past personal contacts in the industry. He had lightly chatted about this with Millie. He was aware that, although he had been fired—with due cause, he had to admit—from Williams Company, he still had numerous friends that he felt would help him if asked. And, in addition, he was totally confident of his abilities, these having been proven repeatedly at his former employer. He confidently felt that he would have only a minimum of "catch-up" studying to do.

However, the money obstacle stopped him cold every time. George would not discuss this with Millie because he suspected that she would quickly offer to bankroll his company, or at least arrange for him to get needed financing through her own contacts. His ego simply was not ready for that.

Someday, maybe. And providing the damned devil did not make another appearance in his life…

CHAPTER TWENTY-TWO

PERIODICALLY GEORGE HAD REQUESTED that he not be required to work evening and night shifts, but his boss had remained adamant.

"It just wouldn't be fair to the other people here," Henry responded. "It just might show discrimination, you understand. And you and I both know how that is these days. Sorry, George, but you have to continue with evening- and all-night hours. Besides, frankly, you ought to realize that I already treat you better than my other people, especially on the evening and night shifts. You don't get 'em as often as the other employees. You know that."

No amount of pleading would break his employer's resolve. George even considered offering to work extra day shifts for other employees, but Henry would not even allow this.

"Gotta be fair. Now that's the last time we'll have this discussion." He smiled, placing his hand on George's shoulder. "You're a good man, George, but don't ask me again."

So, unhappily, George was forced to continue with his rotating shifts. At least he felt fortunate that the night shift only came by every ten days or so. Millie had suggested that George should be thankful for that, and he had to agree.

Even so, he was never comfortable working the midnight to six a.m. shift. The store had some difficulties with petty thieves from time to time, especially in the early evenings. These were usually managed satisfactorily, but during these hours, there was a reasonable amount of foot- and auto traffic at the store. Therefore, if anybody came in and tried to make off with a six-pack of beer, or some snacks,

George could usually get to them in time to prevent the potential thieves from escaping.

In spite of his past unpleasant encounters with them, George tried to remain friendly with the local police. After all, he had to call them in at least every week or so for various confrontations with customers.

In fact, there was an obvious running prank among a certain group of teenagers, to see what they could swipe. One or two of them would try to distract George while the rest of the group would attempt to make off with some goods. It took only a couple of times with this *modus operandi* until George caught on. The faces might be different, but he was on to their plans and immediately kept his eyes peeled widely at the "wanderers" in the store while the leaders were making some token payment.

Henry had provided a shortened baseball bat under the counter to use as "persuasion."

During the midnight shift, George was happy to know the police were usually not too far away. He was not all that sure about his personal safety in the late night. He knew that frequently drug sales went down just across the street from the store. There was also a great deal of prostitution in this particular neighborhood. As a result, he was constantly on his guard against thieves in the store. There was a sign on each gasoline pump declaring that payment had to be made inside the store before he would turn it on. This eliminated most of the gasoline thefts, but even then, some was occasionally stolen. George would try to get the license number of the automobile, but this frequently led nowhere, because of switched license plates and stolen cars.

One evening, when business in the store was relatively placid, George heard a ruckus outside at the street. Peering out the front window, he saw that about twenty youths, apparently from two opposing gangs, had begun fighting. He could see several participants with clubs and knives. He spotted one kid with a length of chain. George immediately called the police. Soon, hearing sirens coming from the distance, the entire group quickly broke up and scattered.

They left one youth lying beside the curb, bleeding profusely from her head. Locking up the store, George hurried out and began to tend to the injured young woman. He was surprised when learning that there had been mixed sexes in the apparent turf warfare. George helped her up and half-carried her into the store. There he got a wet paper towel and began to gently wipe the blood from her scalp and face. She was groggy, and said little. He was happy to note that her wound was only superficial, not as severe as the amount of blood would have had him believe. The arriving paramedics entered the store and tended to her as George once again retreated to his spot behind the counter. He sat on his high stool, sipped on his coffee and watched.

"Thank you, Mister Sheldon," she said groggily as she slowly left the store. He was surprised that she even knew his name.

Later, telling Millie about the incident, she praised George for his goodheartedness in helping the young person. She quietly said, "George honey, I know you are such a concerned person." Her reassurance was comforting to him. He too felt good about his actions.

About two weeks later, about three o'clock in the morning, business in the store was essentially nonexistent, so George was performing his customary restocking of some shelves. He was interrupted as two nervous and jittery looking young men in their mid-twenties entered the store. One wore a tight black stocking cap, the other dreadlocks. Both wore loose clothing and baggy trousers. George immediately sensed something bad was about to happen. For one thing, he had never before seen either of them. Most of the store's evening customers were regular, so he recognized many of them, even though he might not know their names. These guys kept looking all around as if afraid to be seen by any authorities.

"Good evening fellows," he said to them casually as he returned to his position behind the counter. He surreptitiously glanced down at the bat.

The young man wearing the cap mumbled "Yeah."

George waited somewhat anxiously while the men rambled casually through the small store, presumably inspecting various and sundry goods. As he observed the disreputable looking young men, he could clearly see that they were quite nervous, looking this way and that as they ambled around the confines. George was concerned, and suspected trouble.

Just at the moment when he thought he spotted one of the men casually sneak a package of chips from a shelf and slip it into his jacket, something else got George's attention. His ears! The tips were beginning to tingle. *Oh no! It just can't be starting again. Not the devil again? No! Damn it all! Not now. I need to be alert for these punks here in the store. Oh, crap! I can't believe he's found me again.*

He rubbed his tongue around his mouth and began to detect the foul taste that he remembered from before. *I can't allow that to distract me now. Concentrate, George Sheldon, concentrate! Dammit, watch those two thugs.* He reached under the counter and reassured himself that the shortened baseball bat was readily convenient if needed.

After several minutes, the men walked up to George's counter, in an appearance of paying him for the two six-packs of beer they now carried. One man, slightly larger than the other, sat his beer on the counter and suddenly reached under his jacket and pulled out a pistol. This took George aback! He gasped! He had not expected a gun. His eyes centered on the dark hole on the end of the gun barrel. He instantly became fearful for his life. *Surely, these guys won't shoot me just for a couple six-packs of beer. And now, with the SUV symptoms apparently happening on top of this attempted robbery!* He wondered about what type of catastrophe the devil and his SUV were going for this time. There was nothing valuable in this neighborhood. However, George's anger at these two thieves was commanding his attention.

"Okay you white bastard," said the second man. "Open up that frigging cash register and give us all the money."

George cautiously reached under the counter, at the same time that he was pushing the key to the cash register. *That gun's probably not even loaded.* He grasped the hidden shortened baseball bat and started to raise it in a threatening motion at the punk standing before him. Not expecting any resistance, the thief suddenly jumped back, and pointed his weapon directly at George. *He is going to shoot me!* Terrified, George grasped the counter and started to duck. He heard only a loud click. There was no explosion. The gun had misfired! George was still alive!

"Goddam, Reggie," yelled the second robber in his nervous excitement. "Let's get the hell outta here!" Now having lost their nerve, the two young men grabbed their stolen beer and rushed out the door.

George, sweating profusely, his hands shaking violently, was feeling very relieved that his life was still with him. He shuddered and suddenly felt a rush of extreme anger. How dare those young thugs try to shoot him! Inexplicably, he grabbed the baseball bat from the floor behind the counter where he had dropped it, and began chasing after the two robbers out toward the street. His ear and taste symptoms were increasing, but his anger at the two hooligans overwhelmed him.

He was yelling at the top of his voice, "Stop! Stop, damn you!"

Later, he was to wonder why he had chased after them. After all, they carried a gun. Remarkably, he was gaining on them. He saw in the orange glow of the streetlights that they had suddenly stopped in the middle of the street and turned. The thief with the gun once again aimed it at George. In a rapid flash of thought, he said to himself, *uh-oh. I've had it for real this time. That gun's sure to get me.* He stopped running abruptly. Should he turn and run away? To the right? To the left? Crouch?

At that very moment, George caught a fleeting glimpse of light blue out of the corner of his left eye. There was the dreaded SUV. Before he could move, it hit and ran completely over the surprised hoodlums, killing them both on the spot. George could almost feel the thump of the second body as it bounced like a discarded rag doll from under the blue wheels of his familiar nemesis.

What in hell? George, bat in hand, stood there thunderstruck, stupefied, as he looked first at the bloody bodies, then at the SUV as it sped up the street away from him.

At that same instant, George heard a siren in the distance, coming closer all the time. He saw flashing blue lights reflecting off the surrounding buildings and a police car arrived with tires screeching. He continued to be frozen to the concrete sidewalk. The two officers rapidly exited their car, guns drawn on George.

"Drop that bat and put your hands in the air, sir," yelled the female cop. "Now!"

George came alive again. He dropped the bat and raised both hands as directed. The officers came from around their vehicle, glanced at the two bloody bodies, and then approached him cautiously. George noticed the bat roll into a congealing pool of blood from one of the dead youths. Both officers made an incorrect assumption that George had pummeled the two youths to death with his bat.

"Keep him covered," said the male cop. He donned a set of rubber gloves and carefully picked up the bloody bat and the robber's pistol. He placed them into a large plastic bag and into the trunk of his cruiser.

Oh my God, thought George agitatedly. *They probably think I clobbered those two jerks.* Now he realized, with all that blood on the bat, *how am I going to prove my innocence?* He knew that although the bat was clean prior to his being forced to drop it, his evidence that he had not bloodied the bat on the two youths was now gone.

There seemed to be nothing for him to say. A mere accident had now gotten him in more trouble with these officers. *Oh my God, what now?* Turning his head, he noticed that the SUV had stopped several blocks up the street. *Now that's strange!*

"Now just stay calm, sir, and tell us what has gone down here," she said.

"Those two punks robbed me and I was chasing them," said George, trembling with anguish as the female officer listened intently. "Then an SUV ran 'em down." He could not imagine that the officers would be able to see the SUV.

She had George bring his arms down slowly behind his back and he was unceremoniously handcuffed. He was then led over to the police car and placed into the rear seat.

"Why are you arresting me?" he asked. "I told you what happened. I've done nothing wrong here."

"You just stay put there in the back seat while my partner and I study the situation."

"Well at least, let me go up and close the store. There's nobody else here."

"Umm. Okay," replied the arresting cop as she looked over at the store. "I'll just walk over there with you."

She turned and called to her partner, "Hey Bill. I'm letting this guy close up his store."

After George turned off the lights and locked up the store, he was once again handcuffed and moved back and placed into the rear of the police car.

She asked him, "Was it you that called in the report of a robbery? We had word that somebody reported this mess. Was it you?"

He replied, "No ma'am."

Who did? (Subsequent investigation identified the call as having been from a cellular phone apparently from a moving vehicle in the general vicinity of the convenience store.) George pondered, *but who knew enough to call?* He was aware that there had been no vehicular traffic around that night.

Except for the big blue SUV...

She said to her partner who was kneeling down over one of the victims, "Harry, you finding anything?"

"Yeah. A bloody bat and a pistol, but it looks to me like these two people have been squashed flat by some kind of truck. What's that guy say?" Although he didn't care much for the coppery smell of blood, he continued to kneel over the mangled bodies. He fought off his slight tendency to gag and gingerly picked through the pockets of the victims.

She leaned partially into the open car door and inquired of George, "Sir, can you tell me more about what you saw happen here? You say you saw a vehicle run over these people. You didn't happen to get the make or its license number, did you?"

George just peered up at her, saying nothing. He was angry at having been cuffed and placed into an uncomfortable position in the patrol car. He thought with resignation, *there's no point in mentioning the SUV up there. They won't see it anyway.*

At that moment, another police car and an ambulance arrived, almost simulta-neously. The driver of the second cruiser, a sergeant, exited his car and stared at the bloody victims.

He spoke to the male officer, "Okay. What's gone down here? That guy in your car the perp? Got his story yet?"

"Sarah's talking to our witness now. Maybe he saw something and will tell us." The officer stood and backed away slightly as the medics from the ambulance came up to tend to the two bodies.

"You guys don't need to spend a lot time trying to find a pulse on either of these guys. That truck really did them in," said Harry. He rose and stepped gin-gerly away from a pool of congealing blood. With disgust, he brusquely kicked the flattened six-pack of beer off to the side of the street. He then walked over beside the sergeant at the cruiser where George was confined.

"I've pretty well gotten his story," said the woman officer to the sergeant. "Says his name is George Sheldon. He tells me that these two guys robbed him over there in his store and even tried to fire a pistol at him. Luckily for him, the punk's gun misfired and the guys ran away with the beer you saw over there on the street. For some stupid reason," she turned and glared at George, "George here says he chased after them…all for stealing just a couple of six-packs. He says that the two guys stopped in the middle of the street and turned to shoot at him again. He told me that just at that moment a big blue SUV of some sort came out of nowhere and ran right over them. Left them like you see."

George knew in his heart that he would have been killed if the kid's gun had not misfired in the store. He could not possibly have survived in such an instance. Not a chance! *Why had he even grabbed for the bat?* And, then there was his insane move to chase the two hoods. *What kind of idiocy was that? The worry about those SUV symptoms must have thoroughly muddled my brain. Symptoms? They…they're gone!*

The sergeant asked Sarah, "Where's that SUV now?" He glanced back over at the two mangled bodies, as she said, "Gone, I guess."

As additional police vehicles arrived, a more thorough investigation at the scene of the crime began. One officer located two late-night passersby that hap-pened to have witnessed the events.

"I saw it all," declared an anxious young woman. "We were just walking home from a party when these dudes came running 'cross the street."

The police officer was jotting down his notes of her conversation. "Then what did you see?"

"You saw it too, didn't you, Antwan? One of them dudes pointed his gun right at that white fellow over there. Then, this big blue van or something swooped down the street and rolled right over those guys."

She turned her face toward her friend. "Ain't that right, Antwan?"

"Clobbered 'em real good," her friend replied.

"Ain't never seen a dead guy before," she said.

"I seen one last year," said Antwan. "A cousin of mine. His name was Reggie. Got shot in his head. Bled all over tha floor over to the projects."

The officer stopped his writing, looked at the male witness for a moment, and then back to the young woman.

He asked, "And what happened next? Are you the party that called it in?"

"Naw. We ain't got no cell phone. Anyhow, it just drove away."

Antwan looked up the street and pointing, said, "Hey man, there's that blue truck up yonder right now. Looks like it's kind of waiting for you guys. You see that man standing there beside it? Maybe he wants to 'fess up to you officers."

The officer turned his head, and noting the large blue vehicle about three blocks away, suddenly called to one of his companions, "Hey Sam. Go check out that blue van up the street there. Looks like I see some guy standing beside it. Be careful. These people say he's the one that ran over these two guys."

Inside the rear of the police car, George heard the policeman call out to his friend. *What the hell? They can actually see it? Really?* He stuck his head over beside the side window, trying in vain to see if it actually was "his" light blue SUV.

"Let me out! Please! I need to see if that's the thing that ran over these two guys. Come on…Please!"

George was allowed to get out of the police car, still handcuffed. He anxiously looked up the street to where the SUV remained. He could see the devil standing beside it.

They can see it! They really can! I can't believe it. It's finally shown itself to other people!

Just at that moment there was a intense flash lasting several seconds, nearly blinding those watching. It was as if daylight had suddenly arrived. When the flash subsided, the SUV had strangely disappeared. Yet, nobody felt any heat and there was no shock wave. No sound had emanated from the area.

Moreover, curiously, the bright light did not even produce any shadows!

"My God!" exclaimed the nearest cop, blinking his eyes vigorously. "Did you guys see that? That damn thing just evaporated!"

Sam, the officer, rapidly drove his vehicle up to where the SUV had been standing. He exited his car and looked around. He found no remains of a body, no torn sheet metal, no burning rubber. No smell of an explosion. Nothing. He could see no collateral damage to any of the nearby trees or buildings. He moved his car's spotlight all around the area and still found nothing awry.

Radioing back to the other patrol cars, Sam said, "Hey guys. It's crazy. There's absolutely nothing up here to show that there's been any kind of explosion. I don't know what the hell we saw but there's nothing here now. The street's not even marked."

"What'd'ya mean 'no explosion?' We all saw it!"

"Nope," said an incredulous Sam. "I don't know what in hell happened, but there's nothing up here at all. I'm coming back down to where you are."

*   *   *

After the hubbub began to settle down, the medical examiner's office removed the two dead young men, now enclosed in black body bags.

After watching the ambulance drive away, the sergeant said, "Sorry, Mr. Sheldon, but I've got to take you in. I know it probably looks strange to you under the circumstances, but this case is bizarre."

Again, George queried if he needed to contact an attorney.

"Probably not. I don't think it'll take more than a couple of hours. Possibly just a few more questions."

George was taken to the police station and placed into a single holding cell. Jails were becoming an all-too-familiar place for him. He knew he was innocent of battering the two young thugs to death, yet he was required to remain in custody until (he hoped) the autopsies would prove his innocence.

*   *   *

The quiet night in jail gave George an ample opportunity to ponder about his life once more. He was reasonably confident that he would be released soon. His primary thoughts went inevitably to the devil and his light blue SUV that had been so devastatingly prominent, and how it had affected him during the past few years. *What did it all mean? How or why was he picked for all this mess? Better yet, who had chosen him? That red-skinned driver—was it actually the devil himself? Was he testing him for some evil reason? Was the devil playing some kind of game? A game to see how well George would stand up under pressure and torment?*

Nevertheless, George reflected, the macabre SUV, or rather, the red-skinned driver, if it truly was the devil, had saved *his* life. It had not murdered any innocents this time. *Why not?* All these past many months, it had caused him what seemed like a full lifetime of agony and exasperation. It had disrupted his entire existence. He had lost everything and disintegrated into a drunken street bum. *Why did the devil do such a monstrous thing?* Since it had been several months since its last appearance, George had hoped that that segment of his life was behind him. However, perhaps luckily for him this time, the SUV had made one more appearance.

*   *   *

George was released from jail the next afternoon. "The two deaths were clearly caused by being run down by a vehicle," reported the medical examiner. The man they were holding was innocent, and there was no sign of the bat having been struck against either victim.

The Chief of Police and the Sheriff came to see George personally. They each apologized for all the difficulties that their and other law enforcement agencies had put George through. They hoped that he understood, because until last night, no one else had actually seen the light blue sport utility vehicle that he kept talking about.

"So, naturally," the Sheriff pointed out, "no one believed your story. Why should they? Anyway," the Chief said, "you're now cleared of all past charges and your record will be expunged." Soothed, his confidence somewhat restored by the officials' declarations, George left the police headquarters. He hailed a taxi and returned to his room. From there he called the annoyed and perplexed store-owner and explained the happenings of the night. George decided that no matter what else might happen, he simply would not go through such a terrifying time again. He wanted no more confrontations where weapons of any kind were likely to be pointed at him. He told Henry that he was quitting immediately.

He then called Millie and told her that he was coming out to her home. He decided that when there he would confess all his background to her. He hoped that she would understand and accept all he would tell her. *No more withholding from Millie. I just don't know if I can take anymore of this,* George thought. *I've had it! No more of this crazy living I've been forced to do. There must be a job out there somewhere that would suit me better.* He recalled his previous job at the fast food restaurant. *Maybe flipping burgers wasn't too bad, even if the pay was lousy. However,* he sadly reminded himself, *doing that would mean I could no longer afford to keep seeing Millie. She deserves more than I can offer now. I wish I could find a way to start my own firm.*

As Millie opened her door for him, she gave him a tender kiss and then said, "George honey, you look terrible. Are you all right? I thought you had to work today."

As the two of them walked into her living room, George replied that he had spent several hours at the jail. "They just released me an hour or so ago."

Her voice trembled slightly with apprehension, as she hugged him tightly. "Oh good Lord. You poor thing. Do you want some coffee? Something stronger?"

As the two sat down on her living room couch, George said, "Not right at the moment. Millie, I've got to have a serious talk with you."

She frowned. "Oh certainly. I have something to tell you also. But you first."

So, George began to tell Millie about his ordeal, and the past terrible connections with the devil, the SUV, and how it had begun mysteriously without any warning. He added how it disappeared after finally being seen by other people.

"Honey," he said remorsefully, "I don't understand any of it. I don't know why I was picked to endure the horrible mess. As you might imagine, it's been absolutely awful for me. Scores of deaths and horrible injuries occurred because of that damn SUV, or at least its driver. I began to realize that whenever I got those symptoms, something ghastly was going to happen. I never knew what it would be and I could not seem to do anything about it. None of it has ever made any sense to me. Those things were happening all around me, but yet, I was never directly involved. I just had to watch—to see all the horror, blood, and gore. It was sickening. I never could adjust myself to the devastation. I wished several times that I had been the one killed." He breathed a deep sigh. "I don't understand how medics and EMT's can handle it."

George admitted to Millie that the anxiety and worry had caused him to become a serious alcoholic, and that he lost his job and wife on the same day. By this time, tears were flooding down his face as he spoke quietly to her. Millie held his hands gently. He finished his admissions with the fact that he had quit his job at the convenience store.

Millie's brow creased with her concern for him and tears formed in her own eyes. She perceived the emotional pain George was going through as he solemnly spoke to her. She remained silent.

The hall clock chimed, but distracted neither of them.

He squeezed her hands and reluctantly said, "Frankly I don't have enough money to keep seeing you. I'll try to find another position right away, of course, but minimum wage at a fast food place won't pay enough. I will not go back to any convenience store. In the meantime, I simply don't have sufficient savings to manage for long. I don't know when or where I can locate a reasonable job at this point." He took a deep breath and sighed once more. Then he added, "I guess I'll have to give up my apartment at the end of the month, too."

He continued tearfully, "You know that I truly love you. Sweetheart, I really don't want our relationship to end this way, but, I want to be completely honest with you. I know that although I haven't had much to offer you before, now I have nothing. So I guess this will be my good-bye."

Millie smiled reassuringly as she placed a hand over his lips. She said, "George, dear. I believe it's time I showed you something. Come with me in my car." She headed for the door to her garage.

Surprised, George rose and followed her. "Where are we going? What's happening?"

Smiling, Millie turned her face toward him and said, "Patience honey. I have a big surprise for you. Just hang on a little longer."

After a drive of twenty minutes, Millie turned into the parking garage of a large building. The structure was twenty-four stories high and visually striking with its exposure of chrome and green tinted glass.

"What now?" queried a perplexed George, after he walked around and opened Millie's car door for her.

"Hang on just a bit more, honey," she said as the two entered the elevator.

Exiting on the eighteenth floor, George obediently followed her around a hallway corner.

Millie stopped at a glass office door. "Here, my dearest one!" Millie beamed with excitement as George peered at the door.

Painted on the glass in gold with black background was "George A. Sheldon Engineering."

"What?" George was thunderstruck. He had gained no sense whatsoever of his love's intent. He remained speechless for several moments. Regaining his composure, he turned toward Millie and embraced her lovingly.

"Dearest," she said. "I've sensed that you badly wanted to get back into engineering. This is my way of proving my faith in you."

"I don't know what to say. This is such a surprise. I had no idea you were doing this."

She removed a key from her purse and, grinning broadly, handed it to George. "Mr. Sheldon, shall we go into your new office? Now, I have to tell you, it's not a large suite, but it'll get you started."

Inside, standing on the plush beige carpet, she said, "Honey, I've been planning this for several weeks. You mentioned to me that you'd need adequate funding to get started, so I've arranged with my bank for a substantial line of credit. I sensed you'd not want any funding from me directly."

George glanced around the small anteroom, and then walked down a short hallway aligned by several offices. He opened each paneled door in turn, noting that every room was fully furnished, including new full-size desk computers. Smiling, he walked into the largest room at the end of the hallway. There was a floor-to-ceiling window overlooking the city. The sun's rays bouncing off the various tall buildings made the office colors appear unusually bright and cheerful.

Millie, seeing how happy her idea seemed to be making him, said, "I called your friend Dan Patterson. You know, the one you told me that you read about in the paper; the fellow that was striking out on his own from the Williams Company."

"Yeah?"

"Guess what? He told me he'd love to join forces with you in a new company. He advised me on setting all this up for you. He said he has a lot of new contacts, and would welcome your input and help."

George's eyes lit up. "Really? He said that?"

"He sure did, George. All you have to do is call him when you get organized here."

He took her in his arms, holding her tightly against him. "Millie," he murmured quietly, "I love you. You know that. However, I just can't let you do this for me. It's too much."

Millie took George's hands and replied quietly, "It's what *I* want, because I'm sure you can be a success, dear. I know you well enough to be certain of that. Besides, Dan surely has a lot of admiration and confidence in your abilities. His reassurance made me more comfortable in continuing with this surprise."

George replied hesitantly, "I don't know." He scanned the suite again. "I think I can, but I might not be able to make it. I'll try hard to reestablish the good reputation I had before all that devil's mess began. Millie, I promise you I'll try, but it'll be a lot of work. Your confidence in me is overwhelming, so I'll do my very best to not let you down."

Just at that moment, there was a noise behind them. The large computer on his desk suddenly came to life, its keys rapidly moving as if by invisible fingers.

"What the hell?" George exclaimed, turning around. "There's no electricity in here yet, and that's not a portable."

"What's happening?" Millie asked, somewhat startled. "George? How can that computer be running?"

"I have no idea."

Moving over to the machine, George and Millie read the message that was typing itself across the screen. It said, "GEORGE ALBERT SHELDON, I HAVE PUT YOU THROUGH A SERIES OF TRAUMATIC OCCUR-RENCES. I DESIGNED THEM TO SEE IF I COULD MAKE A NORMAL MAN COLLAPSE. I STUDIED YOUR PERSONALITY AND THOUGHT YOU WOULD BREAKDOWN EASILY. YOU NEARLY DID. YET, YOU HAVE SHOWN A REMARKABLE SPIRIT OF DEEP RESOLVE, AND FOUGHT YOUR WAY BACK TO NORMALCY. I CONGRATULATE YOU. I SHALL NOT TRY THIS GAME AGAIN. YOU WON."

Shocked at what they had just read, they looked at one another. How could it be? And, from a non-powered machine.

After a moment of complete silence, Millie took one of his hands and held it tenderly, her other hand on his wrist.

George said quietly, "Well, I'll be damned. This message is obviously from the devil. It was really him after all. So, finally, that is it. It is done—over with. For all those months, I was never sure that I could make it. I still have trouble believing that it was the devil that was behind all that stuff. Who could have ever figured that the devil would choose me? I'm just an ordinary guy. In addition, why did he decide to involve me with all that revulsion and devastation? I don't understand the point of it all."

"A game." Millie declared. "George, I believe it was simply a scheming, evil game. The devil had an idea that he could turn the world upside down. He wanted to twist normal people around to where they would collapse. If his game had worked, soon, everybody would be so devastated that he would have no trouble at all spreading his evil ways around the world. That is what I think, honey. But, you persevered, didn't you? You showed that devil what humankind is like. You did it! You made the devil strike out."

He turned to face Millie. He sighed deeply. "I believe that you must be right. But, now it is over, honey, and you know what? I feel like I've been born again. Since that horror with the devil and his damned blue SUV is now behind me, I'm ready to start a new life…with you at my side."

He turned away from her, and peered down the empty hallway, continuing to hold her hand, "Now, let's see. First, I've got to hire me a…"

THE END

978-0-595-39210-0
0-595-39210-5